WIND AND FIRE

Cheryl Landmark

DEDICATION

With love to my husband Mike, who keeps me from
becoming too lost in my fantasy worlds.

ACKNOWLEDGMENTS

Thank you from the bottom of my heart to Sandra Dugas, owner of Asylett Press, for taking a chance on me back in 2009 and introducing "Wind and Fire" to the reading public. Her acceptance of this newbie author's manuscript showed me that my writing had merit and encouraged me to continue pursuing my lifelong ambition of being a published author. A big thank-you also goes to Rachel Baker, who once again lent her editing expertise to helping me polish this book into an improved second edition.

CHAPTER 1

Against a blood-red sky streaked with flashes of lightning stood a giant figure, silent and terrible, arms outstretched in a triumphant gesture towards the sky. Hot ashes, borne on a wailing wind, fell like sooty rain around the figure as hungry flames licked at its feet.

"Are you daydreaming again, girl? Get back to work! Those potatoes won't hoe themselves."

A hard hand cuffed the side of her head and Tenya stumbled. Instantly, the fire and the terrible, mysterious figure in its midst disappeared. She blinked uncertainly, wondering for a moment where she was.

The scowling face of her stepmother hovered into view, the woman's thin, tight features springing into clear focus.

"Useless, that's what you are!" Dianis snapped. "I've told your father that a hundred times. But, will he listen to me? No. It's a wonder he even has a functioning brain left, with as much time as he spends at Drogan's Tavern. When he bothers to think at all, he thinks his daughter can do no wrong."

Tenya ducked her head, concentrating on loosening the dusty hills of potatoes at her feet. She tried to block out her stepmother's shrill voice repeating the bitter, monotonous litany that she had heard countless times before.

The images of the great, roaring fire and the black, misshapen figure in the midst of it had shaken Tenya. It wasn't the first time she had experienced such a vision. They occurred often, coming at odd times when she least expected them, and leaving her with vague, troubled feelings. Sometimes, the daydreams appeared sharp and clear, like the fire had been--images of strange beasts and demonic riders; of trees splitting down the middle and flying through the air; of sickly purple skies glowering over a charred land. At other times, only formless, unfocused images of evil monstrosities hovered just at the edge of her vision.

She hoed automatically, her raven braids angling by her cheeks. Dianis was forgotten in the contemplation of this latest daydream.

What did all these visions mean? Why did she see such terrible images? For as long as she could remember, the dreams had come to her, but she had never told anyone about them. Certainly not Dianis, who would either accuse her of inventing stories for attention or as an excuse to get out of work; and certainly not her father, Bentar, who had become very distracted and melancholy of late. In fact, he did spend much of his time down at Drogan's Tavern, but Tenya knew his reasons for frequenting the tavern had more to do with escaping his wife's bitter, inexhaustible tongue than imbibing intoxicating ale.

Not for the first time did she feel an acute sense of loneliness wash over her, and she wished for the presence of her real mother. She'd been gone for sixteen years, and Tenya's memory of her was vague--a tall, slender woman with a soft smile and raven hair that smelled of wildflowers and sweetly scented breezes--but no matter how hazy that image was, it had remained in the back of Tenya's mind like a precious dream, sustaining her throughout the lonely years.

Her father had told her that her mother had gone away when she was three years old. But, he'd told her no more than that, and he never talked about her. Tenya suspected her mother's disappearance was responsible for her father's long moments of melancholy and depression.

She sighed wearily and gradually became aware that Dianis had at last left her in peace. She could hear her inside the hut, banging pots and pans around. Grateful to be left alone, Tenya continued with the hot, monotonous job of hoeing, slowly working her way down the rows of potatoes.

Despite the early hour of the day, the sun's rays were already strong. Tenya wiped her perspiring forehead. Strands of dark hair had escaped her braids and straggled across her hot cheeks. She had wanted to start the hoeing earlier in the morning, before the sun had risen above the eastern horizon, when a slight, cool breeze smelling faintly of the unseen

Tempest Sea to the north had wafted on the air. Instead, her stepmother had made her do chores inside the hut before sending her out to the garden. The hot summer sun had already climbed nearly halfway up the sky by then, and even if she'd thought it would do any good, Tenya could not appeal to her father for respite from Dianis' orders. Bentar had disappeared shortly after breakfast...no doubt to his usual table at Drogan's Tavern.

Dianis appeared in the small window facing the garden. "When you're done with that job, there is still the washing to hang out."

Tenya's frustration reached its snapping point. Instead of meekly bowing her head in resigned acceptance as she always did, and as Dianis expected, she threw down the hoe and glared up her stepmother.

"No, Dianis, I will *not* hang out the wash! In fact, I refuse to do anything else today."

Dianis' eyes narrowed. "Watch your mouth, miss!"

Strangely, Tenya didn't feel frightened or intimidated by her stepmother's rage. On the contrary, the sudden release of her pent-up frustration left her feeling as though a heavy burden had abruptly been lifted from her shoulders.

"I'm not a slave, Dianis," she said, firmly, "and it's not fair of you to treat me like one."

"I will treat you any way I please," Dianis snapped. Her dark eyes flashed with contempt. "You're a worthless, lazy girl who would rather spend her life daydreaming than doing honest work. You're as bad as your mother."

"Don't insult my mother!"

Dianis sneered. "She was a dreamer, too. Only, she didn't call them dreams, she called them visions. Visions! Hah! She could no more predict events or see omens than I could. But, she tried to convince everyone she was special and possessed a rare gift. Indeed! How special was she to run off and leave a husband and small child without any explanation whatsoever?"

"My mother had dreams?" Tenya asked, eagerly, ignoring the rest of Dianis' tirade.

Dianis' face twisted in contempt. "That's what she claimed. More likely than not, they were only the imaginings of a demented mind."

"My mother was not demented!" Tenya cried.

Folding her arms across her chest, her stepmother looked her up and down, a sardonic smile stretching her lips. "How would you know, girl? You were just a babe when she left. Oh, yes, your mother was crazy, all right. Some people accepted her claim of seeing visions because they were so blinded by her beauty they couldn't believe she was anything but perfect. But, others of us weren't fooled by her charm. We could see beyond it. She only invented those stories to gain attention, and when she didn't get enough, she ran away."

Tenya could only stare at Dianis, shocked by the venom in her voice. She'd guessed long ago that bitterness and hatred flowed through her stepmother's veins; she'd just never realized how strong those feelings were until this moment.

"Anyway, she's gone," Dianis continued. "And good riddance, I say! But, you, young lady–how dare you defy me. That washing had better be hung out on the line before noon, or you'll answer to me, I can promise you that!"

Tenya's cheeks burned, but not from the heat of the sun. "The washing can wait until the air has cooled. I need a rest out of this heat."

Dianis' face flushed angrily and she clenched her teeth. "*Now*, miss!"

Tenya stared back at her, refusing to move. She'd had enough of her stepmother's harsh orders, of being treated like a slave. For far too long, she'd submitted meekly to Dianis' abuse and had accepted her fate with resignation, but no longer. From this day on, Dianis could share in the backbreaking, monotonous chores.

"You will be sorry, my girl, if you continue to defy me!"

"If you so much as lay a finger on me again, you will regret it even more than I," Tenya warned in cold, measured tones.

Her stepmother stared at her in astonishment, her mouth slightly agape. That Tenya no longer feared her obviously came as quite a shock.

"Who has been filling your head with nonsense, girl?" Dianis demanded. "Your father? Though, heaven knows, he's never around long enough to bother with either one of us."

"Is it any wonder?" Tenya spoke boldly. "The tavern is the only place he can go for peace and quiet, away from your ceaseless nagging."

Her stepmother's mouth dropped open once more, her thin-featured face twisting and contorting in alarming movements. Then, with an audible snap, her mouth clamped shut and she turned abruptly away, out of sight of the window.

Tenya stood still for several moments, as stunned and surprised by her outburst as her stepmother had been. She wondered, somewhat shakily, if the hot sun beating down upon her head all morning long had addled her brain. On the other hand, perhaps the time had come to get matters out in the open; to let Dianis know in no uncertain terms that she no longer intended to be treated like a witless drudge.

Tenya sighed, feeling that acute stab of loneliness once again. She had no one she could turn to for comfort or sympathy. She believed that her father loved her, but he had become so distant lately, so anxious to escape the nagging, domineering presence of his wife that he rarely spent any time with his daughter. She doubted he had any idea how cruelly Dianis treated her.

Unconsciously, she straightened her tired shoulders and raised her chin a fraction. From now on, she would have to rely solely on herself in troubling times, and after her defiance of Dianis, there could be no doubt that trouble would arise. Her stepmother did not take such blatant disobedience lightly. In fact, it had been quite unlike her to leave Tenya's last bold remark unanswered. Why had she abruptly left the confrontation without meting out any form of punishment? What dark plan of abuse might she now be plotting? Surely, it would be something much worse than a mere slap across the face or being sent to bed without supper. Dianis was adept at finding the most difficult, unpleasant chores to give her.

Her stepmother didn't show herself for the rest of the afternoon, although Tenya uneasily kept an eye out for her. After finishing the hoeing, she walked down to the narrow, languid river that ran through the north end of the village and lazed in the cool shallows of the water. Some of the village children joined her and the time passed with frolicking and laughter. It had been a long time since she'd spent such a carefree afternoon. Rarely could she enjoy even a quick swim after supper before having to return to the chores that kept her occupied until bedtime. The sudden sense of freedom left her euphoric, to the point where she almost forgot her unpleasant encounter with Dianis.

All too soon, however, the freedom came to an end. She knew she couldn't stay away from home forever. She would have to go back and face Dianis sometime. Although the thought of the upcoming confrontation intimidated her a little, her newfound sense of resolution remained unshaken. She would make it perfectly clear to Dianis that their relationship had changed. No longer would she meekly submit to all of her stepmother's orders without question. Working hard didn't bother her, but she also needed some time to relax as she had done this afternoon. Dianis could not continue to drive her as hard and relentlessly as she had been doing for years.

Slipping her shoes back on, she trudged reluctantly home.

Dianis stood at the stove preparing supper and didn't even look up when Tenya walked through the door. Her father sat at the narrow table in the middle of the scrubbed, wooden-planked floor. He looked up as she entered and gave her a pensive smile.

Her father had been a handsome man once, with strong, rugged features and a shock of black, curly hair. Now, deep lines etched his face, gray liberally streaked the hair at his temples, and a look of weary sadness dulled his blue eyes.

Returning his smile, Tenya's heart ached for her once strong, handsome father. He'd been beaten down over the years into the sad wreck of a man sitting in front of her now.

Not for the first time, she wondered why he had married her stepmother. She could understand his need for a mother to help raise a child, but why had he chosen Dianis? From all the accounts she'd heard of her real mother, Dianis was the complete opposite. What could possibly have attracted Bentar to this hard, bitter woman who carried so much hatred and jealousy inside her? Why did he continue to live with a person who made his life–not to mention her own– so miserable?

Dianis still did not speak as Tenya set the table for supper. Once or twice, she glanced up to find her stepmother's speculative, unreadable gaze on her. For some reason, Dianis' silence unnerved her. The woman had always been ready with a verbal or physical retaliation whenever she thought Tenya was being lazy or forgetful or slow. Tenya wondered what this uncharacteristic reaction to her earlier outburst could mean.

During the meal, the silence continued. Dianis did not speak a word, though her cold, intent gaze flicked several times in Tenya's direction. Tenya pretended not to notice.

Her father didn't seem to sense the strained atmosphere, but he rarely lifted his gaze from his plate during mealtimes. This evening, as like any other, he reserved his attention for his food, slowly eating as though totally unaware of his surroundings.

Then, shortly after supper, he again disappeared in the direction of the tavern and for once, Dianis let him go without flinging shrill, heated words after his retreating back.

Tenya instinctively tensed. Now that Dianis had her alone, she would no doubt launch her attack. But, once more, her stepmother fooled her. With a final speculative glance her way, Dianis left the hut without a word.

Puzzled, Tenya stepped out into the warm summer evening and watched her stepmother disappear down the dusky street. She had no idea where the woman intended to go at this time of night. Dianis never went visiting after supper. In fact, she never went visiting at all, since few people in the village liked her.

Shrugging her shoulders, Tenya set about her evening chores, trying to ward off the unsettling foreboding that Dianis' strange actions could only mean trouble in the near future.

CHAPTER 2

Neither her stepmother nor her father had returned by the time Tenya retired to bed in the small, curtained-off alcove to one side of the hut's main room. She slipped into the worn cotton tunic and pants that served as her nightclothes and sank down on the narrow mattress filled with fresh river rushes. She lay awake for a long time, staring into the darkness, listening for Dianis' footsteps.

Her stepmother's mysterious and unusual behavior made Tenya wonder if perhaps the woman had finally realized just how cruel she'd been. Perhaps she'd decided to change her ways. But, just as quickly as the thought occurred, Tenya dismissed it. Dianis would never become contrite and remorseful in one short afternoon. A wood cat did not change its spots so readily.

Tenya had trouble quieting her thoughts and falling asleep, but sometime during the dark hours, she finally managed to doze off. Her dreams, however, were unsettling– creatures lurking in the shadows just out of sight, fires that blazed out of control, hideous faces leering at her...

A sound woke her.

Darkness pressed down on her and she felt groggy and confused, uncertain of the time or what had awakened her. Something huge and white hovered close to her face. For a moment, she thought she was still asleep and an even more dreadful nightmare had suddenly descended on her. Then, she realized she *was* awake and the ugly white object hanging over her was a face–an old, wrinkled face with glittering eyes and a toothless mouth.

The mouth opened wider to emit a low cackle and reeking breath.

Tenya lurched up in bed with her heart hammering in her chest. "W-who…?" A dirty, black-nailed hand clamped tightly over her mouth, cutting off her frightened voice.

The dreadful face leaned closer and Tenya shrank back in fear, staring into beady black eyes so close to her own. A scream tried to work its way up her tight throat.

"Now, now, my pretty, don't be frightened." The old woman crooned in a rasping voice. "Old Mordis won't hurt you. Oh, no! Mordis needs you strong and healthy. Zardonne wouldn't be pleased if we were to bruise his special prize."

Tenya struggled desperately, not understanding the low words but sensing that grave danger threatened her. She frantically searched the darkness beyond the leering face. Nothing could be seen beyond the tattered curtain hanging over the entrance to the tiny alcove.

Her only hope for rescue was her father, or Dianis. She had to make some kind of noise to rouse them from their sleep. She tried to twist away from the filthy hand covering her mouth so she could scream, but her attacker possessed a surprising strength. The old woman grasped Tenya's arm above the elbow with her free hand and gave it a painful squeeze. Tenya stopped struggling.

"Oh, no, my pretty, you can't get away from old Mordis. Zardonne wouldn't like that."

Tenya closed her eyes, feeling sick and faint. The stench of the old woman's filthy body in the close confines of the alcove almost overwhelmed her, as did the terror that coursed through her shivering body. She'd heard tales of young girls stolen from their beds in the dark of night, but never had she thought it might happen to her.

From out of nowhere, it seemed, the old woman produced a dark rag and tied it roughly around Tenya's mouth, bruising her lips and causing her to whimper involuntarily. Fresh panic gripped her spine as the old hag hauled her upright. She yanked Tenya's hands behind her back and tied them with a length of coarse rope that bit cruelly into the tender flesh of her wrists.

With Tenya trussed up to her satisfaction, Mordis stepped back and gazed down at her. She cackled with glee. "Well, now, ain't you just a pretty one. She was right about you, she was."

Her cackle sent a shiver of revulsion up Tenya's spine. She stared helplessly at the raving old woman, wondering what she intended to do with her. Why hadn't her father or Dianis woken by now? Surely, they must have heard *something*...

The hag suddenly reached for her and she tried to shrink away. But, the woman caught her firmly by the arm and dragged her off the narrow bed. Shoved roughly through the tattered curtain into the main room of the house, Tenya stumbled, but the old crone's gnarled hands bit painfully into her arms, keeping her upright.

Tenya could dimly make out the table in the middle of the floor with its three wooden chairs, the small square of paler darkness that was the window overlooking the garden, and the washstand in the corner with its stone basin. The hut was simple and rustic, but it was home. Would she ever see it again?

Mordis hissed behind her and roughly pushed her along, and Tenya stumbled toward the door. Suddenly, she caught movement out of the corner of her eye, near the ladder to the small loft where her father and stepmother slept.

She swung her head to look and her gaze widened when she realized a person stood beside the ladder…a tall, thin figure in a gown of white.

Dianis!

Tenya whimpered behind the tight rag binding her mouth, and lunged desperately toward her stepmother. The sudden movement startled the old woman, but only for a second. She yanked Tenya roughly back.

Her foul breath fanned over Tenya's cheek. "Oh, no, you don't, my pretty! You ain't gettin' away from old Mordis." The old woman jerked her head towards

Dianis. "And don't expect no help from that quarter, neither." She cackled again, her mirth so great she nearly choked on it.

Shoved towards the door, Tenya craned her neck to stare at Dianis and plead with her eyes, but Dianis didn't move.

A horrifying thought invaded Tenya's numbed mind.

Dianis had somehow engineered this late night abduction. Was it punishment for Tenya's earlier disobedience? Her stomach lurched at the realization. But, what exactly had Dianis done? Did she just intend for the old woman to terrorize Tenya, and then send her back home again, once more the meek, submissive slave?

Or, did this night attack have a more sinister purpose?

The old crone shoved Tenya out the door into the warm, quiet night. She lost her balance and fell sprawling in the dust, rolling awkwardly with her hands bound behind her back. Mordis cursed her for being clumsy and hauled her back onto her feet.

A small wooden cart stood near the house, a horse waiting patiently between the shafts. A dark figure slumped over the reins on the box seat and straightened when she and Mordis approached. She had no idea if the huge, hulking shape belonged to a man or a woman...or even a human, for that matter.

Her mind reeled with shock, unable to grasp the reality of her kidnapping. Surely, her stepmother could not be responsible for arranging such a horrendous act, and, yet, she had made no move to help her. If the old woman could be believed, Dianis was a willing accomplice to her abduction.

Tenya strained to look back at the dark house, desperately hoping that, even now, Dianis would come running to her rescue. Or that her father would suddenly charge out of the house to save her. She thought she saw a glimmer of white in the doorway but could not be certain. All remained silent and dark.

Mordis jerked her around and shoved her toward the waiting cart. "In you go, girlie. And, don't try to jump back out. I'll be watching you."

Tenya tumbled into the back of the cart, hitting her head on the high, wooden side. Black spots danced in front of her eyes as she struggled for consciousness. Dimly, she became aware of something warm and wet trickling down the side of her face into the corner of her mouth. Its metallic, salty taste told her it was blood. She fought not to moan.

"All right, Falgar, go!" Tenya heard Mordis hiss after she'd climbed into the cart and sat beside her.

The cart started off with a violent jerk that once more threw her against the side. She whimpered softly. The old woman made no move to help her sit comfortably so Tenya tensed, trying to keep from rolling from side to side.

The nightmare ride seemed to go on forever. After a long while, she lost track of time and her surroundings. Soon, she felt herself slipping into a deep, dark well of oblivion and willingly gave herself up to it.

When next Tenya became aware of her surroundings, she found herself lying on her back, gazing up into a sky no longer black and sprinkled with stars. Dark branches and leaves traced inky designs against the delicate hues of dawn.

Mordis' wrinkled face appeared above her and she shrank back in fear, but the woman didn't even glance at her, merely leaning forward to tap the driver on the shoulder. "Stop here, Falgar. We're far enough away that it should be safe."

Immediately, the cart stopped its jerking and swaying. A moment later, Tenya felt it lurch to the side as the driver got down off the seat. The old woman climbed out of the back, grunting and muttering as she did so. Tenya lay quiet and rigid as she wondered what was going to happen next.

Huge hands reached in and lifted her easily from the bed of the cart as though she weighed no more than a bird's feather, and she found herself looking up into a face so gruesome, she nearly fainted from sheer fright.

A deep, raw scar ran from the left temple of the man's huge head right down to his blunt chin, pulling down the left corner of his fat, wet lips. His left eye was puckered in a ghastly mass of flesh and scar tissue. His right eye, small and startlingly light in color, looked out of place on his wide, round face. Hair, the color and texture of brittle straw, stood out in tufts and spikes on his massive head.

Tenya struggled to get away, but his large hands held her firmly, with no apparent strain whatsoever. The man stood well over seven feet tall and weighed easily three hundred pounds. His grotesque face held a vacant expression.

The old woman cackled at Tenya's useless attempts to escape the monstrous creature holding her. "What's the matter, girlie? Don't you like Falgar? Why, he's just the most handsome, sweetest young man around, aren't you, Falgar?"

Mordis patted him on the side of his face where the deep scar hideously disfigured his skin. The giant man grinned foolishly.

Tenya closed her eyes against a tide of nausea. Her heart hammered so painfully she feared it would leap right out of her chest.

The man carried her over to a gnarled oak tree. Although he could easily have crushed her body with his huge hands, he set her down beneath the tree as though she was a fragile piece of pottery. Then he straightened and grinned vacantly down at her.

"Take off the gag," Mordis ordered. "She can scream all she wants to out here. No one's going to hear her."

The giant removed the dirty rag and Tenya sighed in relief, working her stiff jaw muscles to loosen them.

The old woman bustled about the cart. She returned with a sack from which she removed a blackened pot and wooden cup. The huge man named Falgar gathered wood for a fire. Mordis filled the pot with clear water from a small stream running nearby.

"Why are you doing this?" Tenya demanded.

The old woman glanced sidelong at her, her black eyes glittering. "I can see where she might have been jealous of you, girlie. You have all that thick, black hair and those big green eyes, and she's so skinny and pale."

"What are you talking about?"

The hag cackled like a noisy crow. "For the amount of money she was willing to pay, I'd say she was mighty eager to be rid of you."

Tenya frowned. "Dianis paid you money to kidnap me?"

Mordis shrugged. "She heard I was asking about you in the village and came to find me last night. 'Course, I didn't tell her what I wanted you for, but when she offered me money to take you, who was I to turn it down?" She grasped the side of her tattered, filthy skirt and shook it. A slight jingling sound could be heard. "Yes, indeed. Two lovely dracons she paid me. Not bad, eh, for a quick night's work? And, I ain't ashamed of taking her money, neither. Why shouldn't I prosper from this deal? Zardonne won't mind. Long as he gets you, that's all he's concerned about."

Tenya felt numb with shock. Dianis had *paid* this horrible woman two dracons to steal her away in the middle of the night? And, someone–this Zardonne person–apparently wanted her for some reason. But what reason and how did he know her? She had no idea who *he* was.

"What's going to happen to me?" she asked, fearfully.

Mordis set the blackened pot on the fire that Falgar had made. "Why, I'm taking you to Zardonne, of course," she answered in a surprised tone of voice. "Considering your identity, you're a great prize for him."

Tenya's throat constricted with dread. "Who is this Zardonne?"

Mordis turned abruptly to fix her with a stare. "You've never heard of Zardonne?" Tenya shook her head and Mordis clucked. "Well, I guess no one in that rat hole of a village of yours talks too much about him. Not that I can blame them, especially after what he did to *her*." She cackled as though at something very amusing before settling her gaze on Tenya again. "Zardonne is the Master of the Dark Rift, girlie. Soon, he will be Master of all of Tellaron and neither you nor she will be able to stop him!"

Tenya recoiled from the venom in her tone. "What are you talking about?"

Mordis glared at her. "Don't be acting so innocent with me! I know who you are and so does Zardonne. But, it won't do you no good. You ain't no match for him, and *she* can't help you, neither. The Master will be pleased when I bring you to him. Then, he can lock *you* away, too. Who knows? Maybe he'll even put you in the same prison as *her*."

The old woman might as well have been speaking another language for all the sense she made. Yet, something tickled at the edges of Tenya's mind, something that pricked her senses to attention. "Who is this *she* you keep talking about? And, what has she to do with me and Zardonne?"

Mordis glanced sharply at her. "Could it be you really don't know?" she muttered. "Or, are you just trying to be clever, thinking to fool old Mordis?" She shrugged. "Well, it ain't up to me to tell you what's what, girlie. Perhaps Zardonne will, before he destroys you, but that's up to him. I'm just his servant."

Tenya opened her mouth, wanting to coax the old woman into revealing more. Before she could ask another question, however, a breath of freezing wind came from nowhere and chilled her, even though the morning sun filtered warmly through the trees.

In the next instant, a tower of gleaming ice rose before her, spiraling into a sky suddenly filled with stinging snowflakes. Shards of iridescent light shot through the walls and the denuded trees surrounding the base were draped in shimmering icicles. A silent wind swept around Tenya, freezing her to the bone.

CHAPTER 3

As suddenly as it had appeared, the tower of ice vanished, and the warmth of the sun chased away the chill of the silent, winter wind. She blinked her eyes. The image was gone, replaced by Mordis staring curiously at her.

"What's the matter with you, girlie?"

Tenya looked away, trying to ignore the old woman and the ugly, disfigured giant by her side. What did the vision of the ice tower mean? Did it have something to do with the woman who, according to Mordis, had been imprisoned by Zardonne?

She willed the vision to reappear, wanting to see inside the tower of ice. Nothing happened. The small summer clearing remained bright around her, birds singing overhead in the treetops. A breeze sighing through the trees promised another hot, summer day.

Disappointment pricked her. She couldn't control the appearance of the vision. She'd never been able to consciously trigger the daydreams. They came of their own accord, without her being aware they would happen. But, now her senses hummed with suspicion, fueled by Mordis' veiled references and insinuations. "What is the name of the woman you keep talking about?" she asked.

Mordis set her lips in a thin, straight line. Turning away, she lifted the pot from the fire and poured some of the boiling water into the wooden cup. She rummaged in the sack and came up with a handful of dried leaves that she dropped into the cup of water.

She brought the cup over to Tenya and thrust it into her face. "Here, drink this," she commanded.

Bitter fumes wafted from the cup, nearly choking Tenya. She ignored them and the cup, and stared up at the old woman. "What is her name?" she insisted.

Mordis scowled. "Drink this."

"Is it Elea? Is that her name?"

The old woman refused to answer, but Tenya saw her black eyes flicker before her gaze slid away. "I ain't saying another word."

Tenya sank back against the tree, unmindful of the rough bark digging into her arms and back. Her mind reeled with the almost certain, incredible knowledge that *her mother*, Elea, was the woman Mordis referred to in her incoherent ramblings.

Had Elea been imprisoned in a tower of ice all these years, unable to escape her wintry bonds and return to her family in the Ardis Valley? If so, why had this Zardonne, of whom Mordis spoke with such venomous glee, taken Elea captive in the first place?

"Drink this!" the old woman growled, but Tenya ignored her, clamping her lips tightly shut. She turned her head away, stomach twisting at the vile smell.

"It's not poison," the old hag snapped with disgust. "It's taraweed. I told you, I want you to be strong and healthy for Zardonne. The taraweed will relax you and heal that bump you have on your head. You'll see. You'll feel happy and content and all your fears will be gone. Go on, now, drink it. You'll see."

The offer was tempting. The situation looked so hopeless that even a temporary release from it seemed appealing. But, she knew she must keep her wits about herself if she hoped to escape. Her mind must remain clear and sharp, not clouded by the euphoric effects of the taraweed drink.

She shook her head stubbornly, refusing to open her mouth. The old woman hissed in anger and tried to force the brew past her lips. Tenya lunged forward, knocking the cup from Mordis' hand. Mordis cried out in pain as the hot brew splashed her.

"You fool!" She drew back her hand, slapping Tenya hard across the cheek.

Tenya's head jerked back, cracking on the gnarled trunk of the tree behind her. For a moment, she almost blacked out. Dimly, she tasted blood where Mordis' hard blow had split her lip.

The old woman stood over her, glaring down for a moment, hands on her hips and chest heaving angrily. "You're a stubborn one, ain't you? Have it your way, girl. If you want to go to Zardonne full of fear and terror, then so be it. Don't say old Mordis didn't try to help you. You'll wish you had drunk the taraweed when you had the chance." The old crone turned abruptly and stalked off.

Tenya sat with her head hanging, waves of dizziness washing over her. Gradually, the wavering black spots in front of her eyes disappeared and the pain in her head dulled to a throb. Her thoughts returned to her mother and Zardonne and the fate that lay ahead of her.

Was her mother still alive? Or, had she succumbed long ago to the brutal cold and ice of her tower prison? What had she done to deserve such a cruel fate? Who was Zardonne, this so-called Master of the Dark Rift? And, why did he want Tenya abducted and, according to old Mordis, destroyed? What possible threat could she be to him? She had not even known he existed until now.

She did her best to keep her expression neutral, hiding her whirling, confused thoughts from the sharp eyes of the old woman. Mordis knew the location of Elea's prison, Tenya was certain. Somehow, she must wrest the information from her abductor–whether by force or trickery–and then escape so she could find and free her mother.

The absurdity that she could perform such a daunting task nearly caused her to laugh out loud. Even if she could learn from Mordis the location of the tower, how could she escape the old woman's watchful eye? Or, the simple-minded giant, Falgar, who could crush her with his bare hands, and would, no doubt, as remorselessly as he would a bug. Mordis intended to deliver her to her master, Zardonne, at all costs, and she would not let Tenya out of her sight until that task had been accomplished.

Even if she did manage to somehow escape, how would she find the tower of ice? She had never traveled far outside her village and had no idea what lay beyond the Ardis valley. For all she knew, beasts and monsters of unspeakable horror roamed the other lands of Tellaron.

I must take that chance, she decided, resolutely. *I dare not return to the village. Now that I know the extent of Dianis' hatred, there can be no doubt she will kill me if I return...or pay someone to do it.*

No, she must escape and somehow save her mother. Her fate decided, she gingerly leaned back against the rough bark of the tree, closed her eyes and allowed herself to drift off.

A steady jostling motion woke her from a troubled sleep. She found herself lying on her side once more in the back of the small cart. Through narrowed eyes, she saw Mordis' back, heard her muttering and cackling, and beyond her spied the huge bulk of Falgar hunched on the driver's seat.

Tenya guessed it to be late in the afternoon. The sun's subdued rays flashed through the leaves overhead. The pain in her head had been replaced by a dull, throbbing ache. With her hands tied behind her back, escape wouldn't happen now, so she closed her eyes, preferring more sleep to the horrid old woman's cackling.

They stopped again several hours later, this time in a narrow ravine with steep walls of purplish rock. Tangles of yellow vines crawled up the walls and into the crevices. Coarse golden sand covered the bottom of the ravine.

Tenya was surprised to see the ropes had been removed while she'd slept. She struggled to sit upright in the cart, rubbing her chafed wrists and stretching the cramped muscles in her arms. Mordis and Falgar had established a small camp. The old woman squatted by a fire, while the giant sat on a log nearby. Tenya awkwardly climbed from the cart and stumbled over to the fire, aware that the old woman kept a sharp eye on her every move.

Sunset was upon them, dusk rapidly approaching. Vivid streaks of orange followed the sinking sun beneath the western horizon. As Mordis prepared the evening meal, a huge black bird rose against the darkening sky. Tenya could hear the slow, ponderous beating of its enormous wings as it circled the treetops.

Mordis thrust a tin plate filled with some kind of stew into her hands. She had no idea what was in it, but ravenous hunger overcame her concern and she dug into it eagerly. She'd had nothing to eat since supper the evening before.

As she ate, she constantly watched the old woman and the vacant-faced giant for any signs of inattention on their part, prepared to flee into the darkening night at the slightest opportunity. But, old Mordis seemed to know the plot she was spinning, for she maintained a sharp vigil. Immediately after Tenya finished her stew, Mordis ordered Falgar to bind her hands again. The giant gently knotted the rough rope, making the bonds much looser than the old woman's had been, yet they still held fast.

"How much farther do we have to go?" Tenya asked.

Mordis' wrinkled features looked fiercer in the flickering light of the campfire. Her eyes glittered as she shoveled stew into her toothless maw in great, smacking gulps. Swiping away a dribble of meaty juice running down her chin, she stretched her gums in a wide, revolting grin. Tenya shuddered in disgust.

"Getting anxious to meet the Master, my pretty?" she crowed. "Don't go getting any ideas about using your powers on him, girlie. You ain't no match for him. The other one was older and more powerful than you, and look where she is now."

Tenya shook her head. "You've mistaken me for someone else. I have no powers."

"The Master don't make no mistakes," Mordis snapped. Then, apparently deciding it would do no harm to tell her where they were headed, she said, "The lands of Zardonne are many leagues from here, 'cross mountains and plains, and a wide, rapid river. To enter his domain, you must first survive the Plain of Naryn and pass through the Gate of Death. The fortress of the Master lies in the very center of the Plain, inaccessible to enemies, surrounded by quicksand and strangling vines and Guardians."

"What are Guardians?" Tenya asked nervously.

Mordis chuckled coarsely. "The Guardians are creatures that are half-bird and half-human. They stand seven feet tall with a wingspan of nearly ten feet. They can tear a man to pieces in seconds with their claws."

Tenya recoiled, and the old woman grinned, obviously enjoying her revulsion.

"They guard Zardonne's fortress, perched high on the walls on every side. None can get by them but by Zardonne's will. And, should any manage to slip past without being torn limb from limb, there is the Portal of Fire to contend with."

The old woman paused, gazing at her expectantly, and Tenya obliged her by asking, "What is the Portal of Fire?" She wanted to keep Mordis talking. The more information she could glean, the better her chances of surviving in this unknown land, and possibly finding the tower of ice.

"The only way into Zardonne's fortress is through the Portal of Fire. Its heat is so intense it can melt a man's eyeballs from a hundred feet away." Drool slithered from the side of Mordis' mouth, her beady eyes glowing at the graphic description.

Tenya tried to keep her face expressionless.

The old woman's joy faded to apparent disappointment but she continued, though in a grudging tone, "Only with the Master's permission can a person pass safely through the fiery door. I have seen–with my own eyes–Zardonne walk through the flames and emerge untouched by them. And, I have seen a man, who tried to pass unbidden into the fortress, ignite like a torch and die a horrible, screaming death, his flesh melting from his bones like candle wax."

This time, Tenya couldn't stop the shiver of revulsion at the horrible image. Mordis grinned wickedly, delighting in the effect of her gruesome storytelling.

"There are not many who have been foolish enough to challenge Zardonne's domain. Those who have tried have either died an agonizing death or were banished to a place where they can do no harm."

"Like the woman in the tower of ice?"

The old woman glanced sharply at Tenya, her eyes suspicious. "What do you know about the tower of ice, girlie?"

Tenya silently cursed her carelessness. She hadn't meant to reveal that she knew about the tower and wished she could take back the impulsive words.

"You-you mentioned it earlier," she said, hoping her voice carried conviction.

The old woman looked skeptical for a moment, and then shrugged, seeming to accept the explanation. "Once inside Zardonne's fortress, there is no escape, so, don't go getting any ideas, my pretty. Your powers are still too young for you to even think of challenging the Master."

Again, Tenya's frustration and curiosity welled. What powers? Even if her mother was the woman in the tower of ice and she possessed some kind of magical powers that she had tried to use against Zardonne, Tenya herself possessed no such magic. Certainly her ability to see strange images could not be considered a *power*. They were just that– unexplained visions that had plagued her all her life and appeared without any provocation on her part.

"I really don't know what you mean," she said to Mordis. "I have no powers and I have no intention of challenging Zardonne. I don't even know who he is. Truly, you must be mistaking me for someone else."

Mordis shook her head and clucked. "No. You're the one, all right."

Tenya slumped in helpless frustration, and then straightened as a sudden idea occurred to her. What if she could appeal to Mordis' enormous sense of greed?

"I'll pay you two more dracons if you let me go," she offered, eagerly.

Mordis' eyes lit up at the prospect and for a moment Tenya's hopes soared. Then, the hag cackled and demanded, "Let's see the money first."

"I-I don't have it with me," Tenya stammered. "But, if you take me back to my village, I can get it for you. And, I would say nothing of this to anyone."

"Hah! Like as not, the very moment we set foot in the square, you'd start screaming at the top of your lungs and bring the whole village down on my head. Besides, my girl, you are worth much more than four dracons, and old Mordis intends to see that she delivers you safe and sound to the Master."

"But, if I'm no threat to Zardonne, why not let me go? You said yourself I'm no match for him."

Mordis' wrinkled face held a sly expression. "Oh, you're not much of a threat right now, but you could be later, if you're anything like the other one. And, I've no doubt Zardonne would prefer to eliminate any possible danger now, not in the future when it's too late."

Tenya's heart sank at the old woman's words. Clearly, Mordis would do everything in her power to see that she did not escape before she could be turned over to Zardonne.

CHAPTER 4

Tenya sensed the presence of an invisible creature. Hot breath brushed the back of her neck, causing the fine hairs there to quiver. Panic seized her in an iron grip and she tried to run, but her legs felt like blocks of wood, refusing to do her bidding. She tensed, fear crawling up into her throat and building into a strangled scream.

She felt a light touch on her shoulder and her heart leapt, her scream trying to work its way out of her constricted throat. Before the sound could pass her lips, a hand clamped over her mouth. Tenya bolted awake, the nightmare still vivid in her mind.

"Sh-h, it's all right. Don't scream," a soft voice whispered close to her ear.

She started again, staring wildly about, her heart pounding hard. The moon had risen, bathing the narrow, rocky ravine in soft radiance. A few stars sparkled across the inky sky. Several feet away, she could see the dark, motionless humps of the old woman and the giant huddled by the dying fire. Snores issued from both of the sleeping figures-- Falgar's deep and sonorous and Mordis' noisy and stuttering.

Tenya moved her eyes, trying to see who or what pressed close against her left side.

"I'm a friend," the voice whispered again. "Will you promise not to scream if I take my hand away?"

She nodded, sensing that the person did not mean to harm her. Curiosity began to override her panic and fear. The hand eased away from her mouth and the person moved around in front of her.

At first, she thought he must be a young boy, very short and wiry, with dark eyes that regarded her mischievously. Then, she noticed lines in his small, pointed face and gray liberally streaking his dark, curly hair and beard.

Her *friend* proved to be a little, middle-aged man, and a very strange-looking one at that. He wore an outlandish, floppy hat on his small head and a short cape of multi-colored bird feathers. In his left hand, he held a short staff with what appeared to be a dark jewel on its tip. The stone caught rays of soft moonlight and threw out glittering sparks.

"Who are you?" she whispered, glancing nervously at her snoring captors. They appeared to be fast asleep and unaware of their prisoner's strange visitor.

The little man grinned. "A friend," he repeated. "We have no time to talk now. We must be off before daylight." As he whispered, he untied the rope binding Tenya's hands. She flexed her wrists in relief.

"Come," he urged, rising swiftly to his feet and beckoning.

She hesitated. How could she be certain he meant her no harm? Perhaps she would escape two dreadful captors only to fall into the hands of someone even more unscrupulous and evil.

The little man saw her hesitation and his bright eyes regarded her kindly. "I mean you no harm," he said, quietly, as though reading her thoughts. "The old woman will stop at nothing to deliver you to Zardonne. I can help you escape that fate."

Tenya stared at him, biting her lip. How did he know what Mordis intended to do with her, unless he had hidden somewhere nearby and overheard them talking earlier. She wanted desperately to believe him, for she knew he spoke the truth about Mordis, but…

Suddenly, she had no time to debate the issue any longer. Over by the fire, the old woman's snores checked abruptly and she suddenly sprang to her feet, surprisingly agile for her age.

"Oh, no, you don't!" she screeched, pointing a finger at Tenya and her rescuer. "You're not going to get away from old Mordis that easily."

Tenya froze, paralyzed by fear. The old woman looked terrible in the moonlight, her eyes glittering insanely in her wrinkled face. To Tenya's frightened senses, she seemed to grow bigger and more hideous by the second.

Terrified as she was, she'd almost forgotten the little man until he spoke in a calm voice, "Zardonne will not get this prize, old woman. This is one time you will fail in your quest."

WIND AND FIRE

"Mind your own business, you little toad!" Mordis shouted. "She's mine, mine and Zardonne's! And, you can't stop me."

The little man seemed undisturbed by her fury. In fact, he moved swiftly and surely until he stood in front of Tenya, shielding her from the shrieking old woman.

Despite Mordis' screeching, Falgar remained fast asleep on the ground, his deep snores unchecked.

"Wake up, you bumbling fool!" Mordis delivered a swift kick to his side.

Falgar snorted and jerked awake. He sat up slowly, blinking sleepily in the moonlight.

Mordis kicked him again, her face contorted with rage. "Get up, you mindless idiot!"

The man's vacant expression never changed. He clambered to his feet, looking around blankly, his long arms hanging loosely at his sides.

Tenya did not move a muscle, frozen with terror and hoping to blend into the shadows. The situation looked hopeless. What chance did she and the strange little man have against Mordis and the giant Falgar, whose huge hands could crush them like eggshells?

Mordis spun back to face them, hands on hips, glittering eyes narrowed and a smug smile on her face. "Don't meddle in this, little man," she warned. "Falgar, here, will break every bone in your scrawny little body."

"You underestimate me, old woman. I may not be as easy to break as you think."

"Hah!" she snorted derisively, her eyes raking him up and down. "Falgar, kill him!"

35

The blank-faced man obediently shambled forward, raising his huge hands. Tenya shrank back. She didn't have the strength to jump to her feet and run as Falgar advanced.

Suddenly, the narrow ravine lit up with a brilliant red light that streamed from the dark jewel on the little man's staff. A wall of glowing sparks sprang up before the advancing giant. Falgar slammed into the sparkling curtain and stumbled backward. He shook his head groggily and ambled forward again. The wall of sparks once more repelled him and drove him backward.

Behind him, Mordis shrieked in rage, shaking her fists. "Kill him, you oaf, you worthless imbecile, you wretched fool!"

The man obediently attempted to do her bidding, though the red wall of sparks drove him back time and time again.

The little man reached down to grasp Tenya's hand and pull her to her feet. "Come quickly!" he urged.

This time, she didn't hesitate. She stumbled along behind him, clinging to his feathered cape. The red glow continued to bathe the ravine, and she could hear Mordis screeching behind them.

"Don't let them get away, you fool!" Her voice rose higher. "You won't be able to hide from Zardonne's wrath, little man! Mark my words. You'll soon regret interfering with old Mordis!"

The little man paid no attention to Mordis' threats. He moved swiftly down the sandy bottom of the ravine, with Tenya close behind. At the far end of the ravine, he stopped abruptly and Tenya nearly collided with him. She started to speak, but he silenced her with a gesture and pushed her toward a dark clump of bushes to one side of the narrow opening. A large animal, tethered to a bush, whickered softly to the little man. He soothed it with a gentle hand.

At first, Tenya took it to be a horse, but it had a much longer neck that tapered down to broad shoulders and an even broader sloping back and hindquarters. Wide, tissue-thin ears kept up a constant motion on the sides of its head and its large eyes swirled with rainbow colors in the moonlight.

She had no time to wonder what kind of creature it was for the little man urgently beckoned her to climb up on its broad back. The sound of Mordis and Falgar scrambling down the ravine reached her ears, causing her heart to hammer even harder in her chest. Imagining them close behind in the darkness hastened her efforts. She scrambled up on the back of the beast without hesitation. The little man quickly untied the animal from the bush and vaulted up in front of her.

Unmistakable sounds of Mordis and Falgar's pursuit reached her ears, punctuated by Mordis' curses and shrieks. The little man nudged the animal with his heels and the creature started forward with a leap. Tenya nearly toppled backwards down the sloping hindquarters, but the little man reached back and grasped her arm, holding her fast behind him.

"There they are! Get them!" Mordis shouted.

Gasping, Tenya peered over her shoulder in time to see the old woman and the giant running out of the mouth of the ravine towards them.

"Hold on!" the little man shouted.

He leaned forward over the neck of the beast and the creature responded to his urging with a burst of speed. Tenya hung on for dear life as they raced into the night, away from the ravine. She could hear Mordis flinging curses after them, but, suddenly, she didn't care. They had escaped! The creature's giant, loping strides took them farther and farther away from the terrible old woman and her simple-minded slave.

The little man in front of her glanced over his shoulder and white teeth flashed in a grin. Facing forward once more, he urged the beast to even greater speed, and they raced long into the night.

They rode for hours and Tenya soon lost all track of time. Although she began to become accustomed to the creature's swaying gait, she still clung to the little man's cape to make certain she would not slide off. The dark country looked strange and unfamiliar to her, nothing like the gentle countryside cradling her tiny village.

Numerous rocky ravines like the one they had left behind pitted the landscape. Stunted, twisted trees rose black against the sky. The creature pushed through stands of rustling ferns taller than its own height by several feet, and slogged along the wet, marshy edges of swamps.

After a while, the constant jogging gait began to take a toll on Tenya. Her backside hurt and her muscles cramped from trying to maintain her seat. The adrenaline that had surged through her during their escape had drained away. Even those first hours of new discovery, the excitement of traversing strange lands, had faded, leaving her weary. Now, she wanted nothing more than to slide from this creature's back and stretch her cramped, aching legs.

"Please, can we stop soon?" she pleaded.

The little man glanced back. "There's a small clearing just up ahead," he said. "We'll rest there."

Indeed, not much farther on, they arrived at a small, peaceful clearing and the man brought the beast to a halt. Inside the circle of trees, Tenya slid from the animal's sloping back and winced as her sore muscles groaned in protest.

The little man tied the beast to a tree, and then came over to Tenya. "Here, drink this," he urged, holding out a small water skin.

She took it gratefully, pulled out the stopper and drank. The cool water refreshed her parched throat. She handed the water skin back to him, noticing he watched her with bright, inquisitive eyes.

"Are you all right?" he asked, his voice kind.

Tenya nodded. "I think so. But, I'm very confused."

He chuckled. "I'm sure you are. I'd wager no one in your village has ever talked about Zardonne, the Master of the Dark Rift."

She shivered slightly. "I hadn't even heard of him, until now. That horrible old woman, Mordis, was bringing me to him. She kidnapped me from my village. She said Zardonne is planning to take over the whole world and make everyone submit to his will."

"I'm afraid that what she told you is true. Zardonne is gaining strength every day. The Death Riders have been seen as close as the Ferrish Wood and his Guardians have been noticed flying over the

Jamal Mountains. There are many stories of villages and towns being laid to waste by Zardonne's minions all along the borders of the Plain of Naryn."

"Mordis told me about the Guardians," Tenya said. "But what are the Death Riders?"

"Zardonne's harbingers of death," he answered grimly. "They're demons from the Rift that do his bidding. They ride terrible mounts called targs, and spread death and destruction wherever they go. They, as well as the Guardians, are Zardonne's eyes and ears."

Dazed and bewildered, Tenya sat down on a fallen log. "Tell me more."

"Zardonne is from a place of evil that lies just beyond the boundaries of our world. Many years ago, he managed to create a Rift in the fabric that separates our world from his black pit of hell and he invaded Tellaron with an army of demons. Although he was very strong, the Mistress of the Wind was able to command a cyclone powerful enough to lift him and his minions and fling them back into the Rift. Spells were used to seal the rip between our world and his but, unfortunately, it was not enough. A few years later, the Demon Master again rose from his pit. The Mistress of the Wind nearly succeeded a second time in capturing him, but that time Zardonne was much stronger, and he won the battle."

"He imprisoned her?" Tenya asked, quietly.

The little man glanced at her. "You know what happened?"

She shook her head. "Not all of it. Mordis only told me bits and pieces."

She wondered if she should reveal her suspicions–that she believed the Mistress of the Wind to be her mother, Elea, and that she had seen the tower of ice in a vision. He would no doubt think her completely mad. After all, Mordis had not admitted outright that Elea was the woman who had challenged Zardonne those many years ago, although her sly insinuations had certainly led Tenya to believe it.

"Zardonne could not completely destroy the Mistress, even with his newfound strength," the little man continued. "The best--or worst--he could do was to banish her to a place where she could never escape."

The tower of ice! If only she could see inside that tower…

As if in response to her silent plea, a snowflake brushed her cheek. She looked up, startled. The dark clearing had disappeared, replaced by a stand of icicle-laden trees at the base of the gleaming tower of ice.

CHAPTER 5

Tenya's eyes watered from the silent wind raging about her. She could barely make out the outline of a small door at the base of the tower. She made her way to it, grasped the handle with numbed hands and struggled to open it. The door would not budge. Whimpering in frustration, she pounded on the hard surface. "Mother, are you in there?"

The wind ripped the words from her mouth and shattered them on the frigid air. She stared up at the smooth, gleaming walls. Stinging snowflakes battered her upturned face, freezing on her eyelashes and filling her mouth. "Mother!"

As quickly as the vision had come, it vanished, and the clearing swam back into focus.

The little man sat studying her curiously. "Are you all right?"

She did not immediately answer, thoughts racing madly through her head. Had she actually summoned the vision this time with her silent plea?

The first time the image had come to her, she had seen only the tower and not the door. This time, she had actually touched the icy walls and tried to get inside. A faint energy had emanated from the tower. She'd felt it through the bitter cold of the walls. Had it come from Elea?

Tenya became aware of the little man's intense scrutiny and drew a deep breath, trying to control the tight excitement of her thoughts. "I'm fine now," she said. "I-I just felt faint for a moment. All the tension and fright, I suppose."

He nodded. "That's understandable. You should rest now. It'll be dawn soon, but we're far enough away from Mordis that we should be safe. Just to make sure, I'll cast a concealment spell to hide us."

"Are you a sorcerer?" Tenya asked, startled.

He grinned quickly. "Let's just say I'm a wandering stranger with a few tricks up my sleeve. By the way, my name is Sindril."

"Mine is Tenya. Thank you for rescuing me from Mordis." She shivered. "That old woman terrifies me. And that man, Falgar. He does whatever she commands without question, like some kind of brainless monster."

Sindril nodded grimly. "He is exactly that, I fear; enslaved by Zardonne to do Mordis' bidding whenever she commands. And, without a conscience, he has no qualms about doing it, no matter how atrocious the task might be."

43

"That's terrible! What about Mordis? Why and how does she serve Zardonne?"

"It's thought that she has been with Zardonne since the first time he entered Tellaron through the Rift. She's one of the many wicked, depraved humans who were seduced by his evil and power. Now, she's his supplier of prizes--beautiful young women or sometimes children. He needs fresh, young blood to replenish his dark powers and keep him strong. She roams the countryside in search of likely victims and brings them back to his domain in the middle of the Plain of Naryn."

Tenya shuddered. Had Dianis known the motives behind Mordis' agreement to the abduction? Or, had she just been so anxious to be rid of her bothersome stepdaughter that she'd not even asked the old woman what she intended to do with her?

Tenya preferred to think the latter was true.

She wanted to ask Sindril more questions about the Mistress of the Wind, but exhaustion from the long, perilous ride quite suddenly caught up to her. Fatigue replaced the nervous energy that had kept sleep at bay since their escape from Mordis in the ravine, so she took Sindril's advice and curled up under a tree, her head pillowed on her arm. Oddly, she felt safe with the little man. He had promised to protect her while she slept and she trusted his word.

She slept well into the afternoon and woke with the sun shining in her eyes. She sat up slowly, blinking and stretching... and instantly became wide-awake.

The little man and his strange beast had disappeared.

Panic surged inside her. Where had he gone? She had foolishly trusted him, and he'd left her without a word, stranded in a desolate, treacherous land. What would she do now? She had no idea where she was or how she could protect herself. What if Mordis found her? And, what other evil creatures roamed this unknown land?

She was lost and alone and abandoned...

Tears were gathering in her eyes one second, and the next second she nearly screamed. Hot breath fluttered on the back of her neck. Whirling, she found herself face-to-face with the strange beast she'd ridden the night before. Its rainbow eyes swirled with brilliant colors.

She looked up. Sindril sat on the animal's broad, sloping back, concern furrowing his brow. He slid off the animal's back and hurried toward her.

"Did I frighten you? I'm very sorry. I was hoping to get back before you woke up, so you wouldn't be alarmed if you found yourself alone."

Tenya sagged in relief, her fright dissipating. He hadn't abandoned her after all.

He held up something small and furry. "I found us some supper. I thought you might be hungry."

She nodded, suddenly quite ravenous.

"I thought you'd left." She watched the little man deftly skin their supper, and smiled weakly. "I was trying to decide what I should do."

He glanced up for a moment. "I would not rescue you from Mordis and then leave you unprotected," he said, faint reproach in his tone.

"I'm sorry." Her cheeks warmed in embarrassment. "I should not have jumped to the wrong conclusion so quickly. I suppose I panicked when I woke up and found you gone."

His infectious grin reappeared. "No apology needed. I should have let you know I was going hunting."

He had a fire snapping in no time and skewered the meat on a stick to cook over the coals. The smell of roasting food made Tenya's mouth water.

Later, as they tore off delicious chunks of the cooked meat and devoured them, Sindril said, "You deserve an explanation for what's been happening. I know you must be very confused, right now."

She stared at him, incredulous. "You can explain what's going on? But, how do you know?"

"How much did Mordis tell you?" he asked.

"Only that Zardonne had sent her to kidnap me. She insisted I'm a threat to him–or will be, one day. She said I have some kind of powers and warned me not to try using them against Zardonne." She licked juice from the meat off her fingers. "I have no idea what she's talking about. Believe me, if I possessed magical powers, I certainly wouldn't have spent my life hoeing potatoes and hanging out the wash for my stepmother."

Sindril studied her for a moment. "My rescue of you was not entirely coincidental. As it happens, I was headed for your village to fetch you myself, when I spotted that notorious old woman and her slave with what appeared to be a prisoner in their cart. I decided to follow them for a while, determined to thwart the old witch and free the poor soul she'd captured before continuing on my journey. Imagine my astonishment to discover it was *you* she had abducted! I knew then you were in grave danger. It was doubtful Mordis simply happened upon you in her search for young prizes. I feared Zardonne must have learned of your existence and sent her to kidnap you, to bring you back to his domain." He grinned. "It gave me double the pleasure to relieve Mordis of her most valuable prize."

"You were coming to my village to fetch me?" She frowned. "Not-Not to kidnap me, too...I hope?"

He looked up sharply. "No. Not to kidnap you."

"Then...why? What did you–what do you want with me?"

The little man sighed. "You may find my words hard to grasp, considering how sheltered your life has been, but it's essential that you believe what I'm about to tell you. The future of our world depends upon your conviction of who you are."

Her heart began to thump with nervous anticipation and the oddest sense that she knew what he would say next settled over her. "Tenya, the Mistress of the Wind is your mother. She's being held prisoner by Zardonne in a tower of ice, at the far northern end of the Plain of Naryn. The Demon Master was somehow able to confine her powers to the tower. She has been unable to communicate with the wind, which is the source of her strength. However, she has managed to communicate in other ways, of which Zardonne, fortunately, is unaware. One of those is by sending visions to her daughter– you, Tenya. Your mother has been trying to reach you all these years through the strange dreams you've been experiencing."

"Then...she *is* still alive," Tenya breathed. What was more, her mother possessed extraordinary powers and had battled an evil being who had imprisoned her for the last sixteen years. Though she'd already nearly convinced herself she was the daughter of the woman held prisoner in the tower of ice, she'd had no real basis for her belief.

Until now…

"Yes, she's alive," Sindril continued. "And Mordis is right– you do possess powers that make you extremely dangerous to Zardonne. Small wonder he sent the old woman to abduct you, as soon as he discovered your existence."

"But...I don't *have* any powers!" Tenya cried. "I thought Mordis referred to the visions, but even those are not of my doing." She shook her head in frustration. "I don't know what to believe anymore."

Sindril regarded her with bright eyes. Without warning, he lifted the short staff and pointed it at her. A narrow, bright beam of red flashed from the dark jewel on top.

Startled, she instinctively threw up an arm to protect herself and a soft, white light suddenly surrounded her body, oddly warm and tingling. The beam from the staff deflected harmlessly off the white shield in crackling sparks.

Tenya sat frozen, unable to believe her eyes. She stared at the white radiance enveloping the arm she held in front of her face and, as she watched, the glow slowly faded away.

Sindril leaned on the staff, his dark eyes watching her with an unreadable expression.

Slowly, she lowered her arm and gaped at the man, shaken as much by his sudden attack as by the extraordinary shield of light that had erupted around her body. Fear sharply pricked her. Up until now, the little man had shown her nothing but kindness and concern. Did this unexpected attack indicate his true nature?

"What happened?" she managed to ask at last. "Why did you try to harm me?"

Sindril had a pleased expression on his face.

Anger began replacing her fear and she glared at him. "Well?" she hissed through clenched teeth.

He grinned again. "That was merely a little test. And, you passed it brilliantly."

"A test?!" she exclaimed hotly. "You could have *killed* me!"

He shook his head. "Not at all. The beam of light from my staff was harmless. It would only have touched you lightly without serious effect. The real test was to see what your reaction would be."

Tenya was only slightly mollified by his reassuring words. "You might have at least warned me."

He shook his head again. "I couldn't. The result might not have been the same. I had to see what your response would be to an unexpected danger."

"I don't understand," she said, her anger now fully replaced by bewilderment. "Where did the white light come from?"

"You summoned it in response to what you perceived to be an attack. It was your way of protecting yourself."

"But, *how* did I summon it? I don't remember doing anything but raising my arm in front of my face when I saw the beam from your staff."

"I'm sorry. I can't explain how your powers work." His grin broadened. "But, at least I've proven to you that you do possess them."

She frowned skeptically. The little man could perform many strange and mysterious feats; that much she'd witnessed already. Was it possible *he'd* made the shield of white light appear around her himself? But, what reason would he have for doing so? Why would he want her to think she possessed some kind of magical powers if she really didn't? On the other hand, if she'd done it herself, then *how* did she do it?

"I see that you still don't believe me," Sindril said.

"I could never *do* something that before!"

"Actually, you were never *aware* that you could do it. You had no cause to use your powers; therefore, they lay dormant inside you." He leaned forward. "It's very important you believe in your abilities, Tenya. If you allow doubt to rule you, you'll continue to deny them, and that could leave you in grave danger. Zardonne has already made one attempt to capture you. I'm certain he won't stop until he has found you again and eliminated the potential threat you present to him."

She remained silent for a moment. "What about my mother? Can she be freed from her prison?"

Sindril regarded her gravely. "Zardonne is very powerful, and he has many spies and servants throughout the lands. It's doubtful we would be able to get close to his domain without his being aware of it, but there is a good possibility we may be able to overcome enough of his obstacles to free the Mistress."

"Then, we *are* going to try to rescue her?"

"I daresay we must. Your powers are still so young and untried. We will need her help if we are to defeat him. And, we must do so soon. Time is running out. Zardonne continues to grow in strength and, if he's not stopped soon, those images you have seen of catastrophes beyond imagination will unfortunately come true. But make no mistake...this will be a very dangerous undertaking."

CHAPTER 6

Sindril explained that they were presently on the fringes of the Targon Plains and Zardonne's domain was located several leagues to the east and south of their present position. Although the Plains were desolate and empty in places, he assured her he'd been across them several times and knew routes that passed close to scattered oases of trees and water.

"We can probably reach the far end of the Plains in two days. But, we must travel at night and sleep during the day," he said.

"Why do we have to travel at night?" Tenya asked.

"If we traveled during the day we would have to contend with the sand beetle, and that, I assure you, would not be at all pleasant."

"What is the sand beetle?"

"It's a voracious little creature no bigger than your thumbnail. They come out during the day by the

52

thousands and spread across the Plains, until it looks as though the land is covered by an endless, black moving carpet."

Tenya shuddered slightly. "And, these beetles bite?"

Sindril smiled faintly. "Oh, they do more than bite. They will devour any living animal that happens across their path...fur, flesh, bones and all."

"They sound horrible!"

"Indeed, they are. They're the reason most creatures on the Plains only come out at night. It's not safe during the day."

Tenya felt nauseous. "But, if the animals only come out at night, how do the sand beetles survive? There would be nothing for them to eat."

Sindril shrugged. "Oh, there's always the odd, hapless creature who ventures out when it shouldn't. And, if no such foolish creature is available, the sand beetles eat each other."

Tenya shivered in revulsion. In the Ardis Valley, the closest thing to a dangerous beast was the tiny rock lizard, which could deliver a very painful–but non-fatal–bite, and then only when severely provoked.

Another thought suddenly came to her. "But, if it will take us two days to cross the Plains, how can we hope to elude them?"

"For some unknown reason, the sand beetles avoid the small oases scattered about the Plains. They will carpet all available rock and sand but will leave the patches of grass and trees alone. That's why it's very important that we reach one of those oases before the first rays of the sun appear. Once under the shade of the trees, we'll be safe from the beetles. But, you must never, *never* leave the oasis, or the sand beetles will make very short work of you."

"Are you certain these beetles only come out during the day?" she asked doubtfully.

"I'm very sure. I've crossed the Targon Plains many times–always at night–and I've never encountered a sand beetle in all my travels. We'll have to travel swiftly and stop just before the sun rises. That way, we can cover as much ground as possible because, believe me, we don't want to linger on the Plains any longer than we have to."

Tenya had her doubts, but as Sindril had said, he was living proof that one could cross the Targon Plains and survive. He'd done so several times...or so he said. Ah well, she would just have to place her trust in him.

"What lies beyond the Plains?" she asked.

"There is a narrow corridor known as the Windy Tunnel that leads to the foothills of the Jamal Mountains. The winds blow constantly there. On the other side of the mountains is a mystical forest called the Ferrish Wood. Zardonne's domain begins just beyond the Wood; a land reeking with corruption and evil so fathomless, it oozes from the very pores of the earth. Nothing grows there–no trees nor grass nor flowers. Only a black, foul-smelling soil covers the land, with stagnant pools of poisonous green water, here and there. It's not a pretty place."

Tenya remained silent. The journey did indeed sound dangerous and daunting, but if the remotest possibility existed that she could find the tower of ice and free her mother, she would willingly undertake the task, no matter how cowardly her heart tripped in her chest.

Sindril smiled warmly. "Are you rested enough to start across the Plains tonight? It will be dark shortly and there will be a full moon to give us plenty of light."

She took a deep breath and nodded her head decisively. "Let's go before I change my mind."

They set out as soon as they doused the fire, mounted as they'd been the night before–Sindril in front, Tenya behind. The sun had already sunk toward the bottom of the sky, leaving trails of orange and red amongst the purple. Night was not long off in coming.

The animal seemed to need little guidance from Sindril. It picked its way delicately and surely across the darkening land.

"Why have you crossed the Targon Plains so often, if it's such a dangerous place?" Tenya leaned forward to ask Sindril.

He chuckled. "My passion for adventure, I guess. I'm a wandering man by nature."

"Don't you have any family to worry about you?"

He shook his head. "I have none."

"You must get very lonely sometimes."

Sindril patted the shaggy long neck of the beast they rode. "I have my friend here. He's all the company I need."

"What kind of animal is he? I've never seen anything like him."

"He's a murbeest, more swift and sure-footed than a horse and very handy to have around on my travels."

They continued on in silence for a while. Tenya tried to determine the lay of the land, but the encroaching darkness made visibility difficult. She could only discern that the surroundings appeared to be very flat and the stands of trees less numerous. Nervousness tingled up and down her spine.

"Are we on the Plains yet?" she asked quietly.

"We're just on the fringes. Within a half hour, we'll be on the Plains themselves."

She lapsed once more into silence, searching the darkness for heaven knew what--perhaps, a black carpet of scurrying beetles, all hungrily clicking their voracious little jaws.

Presently, the ground beneath the murbeest's hooves turned to fine red sand, with odd clumps of coarse grass defiantly sprouting here and there. As Sindril had predicted, a full moon rose in the night sky and shone with a soft luminance, enabling Tenya to clearly view the daunting Targon Plains.

As far as she could see, blood red sand stretched toward the dark horizon, undulating gently in rippling dunes. Dark patches scattered about proved to be striated rock that had a purplish sheen in the moonlight. Aside from the sand and rock, nothing else could be seen. Tenya could detect no signs of life, though Sindril had told her that at least twenty different species of animals inhabited the Plains; all of which, with the exception of the sand beetle, came out at night to hunt and feed.

The further they traveled across the intimidating expanse of sand and grooved rock, the more apprehensive Tenya became. She longingly looked back over her shoulder, but she could no longer see the dark outlines of the last stand of trees they had left.

Nervous tension overtook her, causing her leg muscles to quiver, and she had to force herself to relax. Sindril seemed completely at ease, his body moving in sync with the murbeest's long-legged rhythm, and she took comfort from his unconcerned attitude.

Soon, she began to nod off, put to sleep by the swaying pace of the murbeest.

SCREEEE!

A shrill, discordant scream penetrated her light doze and Tenya bolted upright, heart pounding in her chest.

"What was that?" she cried, clutching Sindril tightly.

"Merely a beast of the Plains," he said, soothingly. "Don't be alarmed. It's not close. And, it won't be interested in us. That scream means it's already found prey."

Tenya again tried to relax, but all desire for sleep had fled. She remained wide awake and alert, searching the unrelenting sand and shadows for signs of other wildlife. Nothing moved in the moonlight, but somehow that didn't comfort her.

They rode for hours. There seemed to be no end to the Plains. Wherever Tenya looked, only sand and more sand stretched off into infinity. She wondered

how Sindril could tell where he was going.
Everything looked the same to her.

That thought brought on a bout of alarm. What if
Sindril *didn't* know where he was going? What if
they became hopelessly lost and confused? What if
they were caught out on the sand when daylight
came? What if...?

With a tremendous effort, she quelled her rising
hysteria, though she found herself watching anxiously
for a dark clump that would indicate one of the oases
Sindril had mentioned. She also watched the sky,
looking for a hint of pale gray that would announce
the approach of dawn. She had no idea how long
they'd been riding, but surely dawn could not be far
off.

"Shouldn't we be looking for one of the oases?"
she suggested, tentatively.

Sindril grinned over his shoulder at her. "We're
coming up to one now."

Tenya peered past him but could see nothing
different ahead. Still, Sindril seemed certain... *And, he
has traveled these Plains many times before*, she
reminded herself.

Finally, a dark clump of trees loomed in front of
them, just as the sky over the eastern horizon took on
a definite light gray color, heralding the coming of
dawn.

Tenya's whole body slumped in relief.

The oasis proved to be surprisingly extensive.
Twenty or thirty tall trees surrounded a clear, cold
stream running through thick, soft grass. She was
surprised at the vast difference between the oasis and
the surrounding expanse of relentless sand and

likened it to a little island of fertility in a red sea of desolation.

Sindril dismounted and led the murbeest to the very center of the oasis, where the trees grew thickest and the stream bubbled up out of the ground. Tenya slid wearily from the creature's sloping back and sank down to the ground.

"We'll be safe here," Sindril assured her. "You should rest now. We'll leave again at nightfall."

Tenya nodded doubtfully, certain she would not be able to sleep with her nerves in such knots. But, whether from total exhaustion, or from a spell cast by the little man, she dropped off in a deep sleep immediately after she lay down beneath one of the trees, her tired body cushioned by the cool carpet of grass.

CHAPTER 7

Hours later, Tenya awoke, stirred from sleep by a foreign sound. The sun blazed down on the hot sands beyond the oasis, sending waves of heat shimmering up into the breathless air. Beneath the canopy of trees, however, the shade was cool and refreshing.

She looked over and saw that Sindril still slept, his outlandish hat pulled low to cover his eyes and the short staff held tightly against his chest. The murbeest also seemed to be asleep, standing on his feet with translucent membranes over his eyes.

Tenya rose quietly to her feet. She went to the stream and took a long drink of the clear water. It felt like cool velvet on her tongue.

As she straightened up, a faint clicking and swishing sound caught her ear again. She stood still for a moment to listen, cocking her head slightly. She tried to identify the sound and its location. It seemed to be coming from beyond the trees. Tentatively, she moved in its direction, away from the stream toward the outer fringes of the trees. The noise became louder.

Click. Swish. Click. Swish.

She stepped up to the edge of the trees where she could finally see and– "Oh!" She leaned against the trunk of one of the trees to steady herself, her legs abruptly threatening to give out.

There before her was the most horrifying sight she could imagine. A vast, slowly moving carpet of black beetles covered the sand surrounding the oasis for as far as she could see. The swishing sound came from their steady, relentless movement forward, and thousands of tiny pincers and mandibles busily searching the air for prey caused the clicking.

The entire plain seethed with the creatures that covered almost every square inch of sand. Amazingly, not one of the horrible little beetles came near the edge of the oasis. A stretch of bare red sand, perhaps a foot or two wide, extended from the edge of the thick, green grass. It seemed as though an invisible line, or barrier, prevented the beetles from venturing into the oasis.

Even Sindril's description had not prepared her for the paralyzing sight of thousands of tiny, loathsome insects mindlessly bent on devouring any living thing they encountered. She could not believe the incredible noise they made and stared at them in fascinated revulsion.

"Revolting little creatures, aren't they?" Sindril spoke beside her.

She started with a small gasp. The steady, monotonous noise of the beetles had masked his approach. "Now I see why we can't travel by day," she exclaimed. "This is incredible! I've never seen anything like it."

"Yes, it is incredible," he agreed. He laid his hand on her arm. "Come away now."

She allowed herself to be led back to the center of the oasis where the murbeest, now also wide awake, shuffled uneasily in response to the loud, relentless clicking and swishing of the vast army of beetles. His huge eyes whirled with a deep red color, which Tenya suspected was a sign of distress or agitation.

She went to the beast and gently placed a hand on his nose, thinking to comfort the poor animal. Suddenly, gazing into the spinning red of his eyes, she found herself *inside* his mind, probing gently through the confusion and distress. She placed soothing mental fingers on his jangling nerve ends, and the beast's spinning eyes gradually slowed, changing to their normal rainbow colors. The trembling in his broad, dun-colored body ceased and the animal snorted softly, rubbing his head against her shoulder. She withdrew gently from his quieted mind.

"You've made a friend." Sindril, who had been silently watching, smiled faintly.

Tenya absently stroked the murbeest's soft nose, shaking her head in astonishment. "How did I do that?" she asked. "It felt like I was actually inside his mind. I could see his distress whirling like brightly colored ribbons. And, somehow, I knew that all I had to do was reach out with my own mind and stroke the ribbons away."

"You're frightened by the idea of having such a power?" Sindril asked, gently.

"Not really frightened. More like...confused," she said slowly. "Everything is happening so quickly. It's all so new, so...*strange*."

He smiled. "Once you get used to your abilities, they won't seem so overwhelming."

She grimaced. "I don't know if I'll ever get used to the idea of possessing powers. Just when I've resigned myself to being able to do one thing, I seem to discover some new ability. What will come next?"

He shrugged. "Who can say? You are the daughter of the Mistress of the Wind and she possesses extraordinary talents. Your powers, although still very young, are no doubt as great."

"But, how do I control them? They just seem to happen."

"You'll learn," he replied. "Once you realize what you can do, practice and patience will be your guides to controlling your abilities." He held up a warning finger. "But, you must be careful not to use them indiscriminately or unwisely. You may be unpleasantly surprised at the results."

"Like pointing my finger at a tree and having it burst into flames?" she grinned.

But, Sindril didn't join in her amusement. "It's very important that you understand how dangerous such powers can be in the hands of an untrained person. They are not something to be trifled with. You must not succumb to the temptation to play with them without knowing what the results will be."

"This is scary," she complained. "I don't know which is worse, being Dianis' drudge, or possessing unknown powers of uncertain strength."

Now, Sindril smiled sympathetically. "I know this has all been very strange for you—not to mention frightening. But then, these are strange and trying times for everyone. Zardonne's threat has thrown all the lands into turmoil and chaos. His destruction is essential if we want to live in peace and harmony."

"Do you believe if we can free my mother from her prison, she'll be strong enough to defeat him this time?"

Sindril remained silent for a moment. "She's been a prisoner on Zardonne's land for many years. It's possible her powers have been weakened in the midst of so much evil. On the other hand, she's been working to strengthen them. Zardonne's vigilance has been slack; we know that because of the messages she's managed to send. Once he imprisoned her, he felt confident he had eliminated her threat and has virtually ignored her all these years. However, we cannot know if she has retained her abilities, or strengthened them, until she is free to communicate with the wind."

Tenya sat quietly thinking. It was difficult to believe that only a few days ago she had been hoeing dusty rows of potatoes and bemoaning her existence as Dianis' slave. Now, she was embarked on a bizarre journey with a strange little man, bent on rescuing the mother she had not seen for sixteen years; a mother who, it seemed, possessed incredible powers. What amazed her even more was the discovery that she herself possessed powers that no ordinary human being could even imagine.

She sighed, overwhelmed by everything she had learned in such a short time. At the same time, a strange singing flowed through her veins at the thought of seeing the woman who had remained hidden in the recesses of her mind since she was a child.

Sindril seemed to read her whirling thoughts, for he smiled kindly and said, "It's still early in the day. Try to get some more sleep. We'll leave as soon as the sun goes down."

She shuddered slightly. "I'll never be able to sleep, listening to those little monsters out there. What if they sense us here and swarm into the oasis, looking for food?"

"They won't. Try to sleep. You'll be surprised how easily you'll be able to block out the noise of the beetles, if you try."

Skeptical, she laid down under the tree once more, prepared to spend the next few hours lying rigid and tense under the cool canopy of leaves. Closing her eyes, the clicking and swishing grated on her nerves, but gradually the noise receded to the back of her mind and she drifted off to sleep.

She awoke to a hand gently shaking her shoulder and opened her eyes to see Sindril bending over her. He grinned, his white teeth flashing in his dark face.

"It's time," he said.

She sat up abruptly, realizing that darkness had descended on the oasis. She could barely make out the dim figure of Sindril heading over to the pale shape of the murbeest. She listened intently but could no longer hear the relentless, insistent clicking of the sand beetles beyond the trees. Although the lack of noise brought some comfort, apprehension still clung to her as she rose to her feet. She hurried over to join Sindril.

"They're gone," he said. He sounded so certain and calm that her fears immediately evaporated.

"I'm afraid we don't have much to eat. But, this should keep you going for a while." He handed her a piece of cold meat from their supper the night before.

Despite the hunger that gnawed at her, she chewed each bite slowly, making it last as long as possible. Sindril had filled the water skin with fresh, clear water from the underground spring and this, along with the small pieces of cold meat, comprised their supper.

After eating, Tenya went to the murbeest and tentatively placed a hand on his nose. She looked into one of his large, bright eyes and willed her mind into his. Instantly, she found herself inside the animal's head--a warm, calm place now with no trace of distress or fear. Soft, golden waves of affection flowed from the animal's mind into her own, along with an absolute and unquestioning trust that touched her deeply. The murbeest snorted softly and rubbed his head against her shoulder.

She withdrew gently from the animal's mind and smiled into his rainbow colored eyes.

"You've gained his trust and love," Sindril said from behind her. "It was easier touching his mind this time, wasn't it?"

Tenya smiled. "Yes, it was. I knew what to expect and it wasn't such a shock. It's still a strange feeling, though, to be able to see inside another creature's mind."

"I imagine it is." Sindril chuckled.

They mounted the murbeest and started out once more on their journey.

Tenya found the broad, sloping back of the creature less awkward to sit, now. She settled herself comfortably behind Sindril, swaying with the smooth, powerful muscles of the animal beneath its shaggy, dun-colored coat.

She experienced a momentary flash of panic as they left the darkening shelter of trees and moved out onto the vast expanse of sand. Yet, as Sindril had pointed out, the sand beetles had completely disappeared, as though they had never existed. Tenya wondered for a moment if perhaps she had only dreamed them.

"How much further do we have to go?" she asked.

"We should reach the other side sometime near dawn," he said. "You'll know when we're getting close, for the eternal winds from the Windy Tunnel can be felt on the fringes of the Plains."

"How dangerous is the Windy Tunnel?" she asked warily, thinking about the horrors of the Plains over which they traveled. What monstrosities could she expect to encounter in the Tunnel?

Sindril seemed to hesitate for a moment before answering. "I won't lie to you, Tenya. I think it's better if you know exactly what we will be facing."

Tenya tensed at the ominous words.

"The Tunnel is quite formidable. The winds there blow constantly and they're not just gentle breezes.

Sometimes, they can be so strong that large trees are uprooted and flung through the air. The corridor is very narrow, so much so in places that a person can touch the walls on either side by stretching out his, or her, arms. Some say the wind blowing through the Tunnel is not a wind at all, but the howling voices of a thousand ghosts."

"Do you believe that?"

He shrugged. "I've encountered stranger things. But, I've never had the inclination to linger in the Tunnel long enough to discover if the tales are true or not."

"What about other creatures?" Tenya asked, thinking of the horrible little sand beetles she had seen earlier that day.

"No monsters like our hungry little beetle friends," he replied. "There are only the constant winds. But, believe me, they are enough to make us travel as quickly as we can to the other side."

They continued on in silence for a while and Tenya used the time to think. She wondered what would have happened to her if Sindril hadn't come along when he did to rescue her from old Mordis. Perhaps she would have been drugged by the taraweed, forced on her by the old woman, and would have made the journey to Zardonne's domain only half aware of what was happening to her. Or, worse still, perhaps she would have been forced to continue her abduction alert and aware of the inescapable fate awaiting her.

How ironic, she thought. *I was terrified when I found out Mordis was taking me to Zardonne, yet here I am heading to the domain of the Demon Master of my own volition.*

Life could certainly be strange sometimes.

CHAPTER 8

On this night, the full moon hid behind scudding clouds, only emerging now and then to bathe the landscape in brief luminance. Despite the daunting darkness, Tenya felt more relaxed and calm than she had been the night before. She no longer doubted Sindril's ability to find his way across the Plains, for he seemed to know exactly where he was going. And, aside from the chilling scream of the beast that had roused her from a troubled doze the previous night, they encountered none of the other nocturnal inhabitants of the desolate Plains.

The hours passed uneventfully. Lulled into a light sleep, Tenya slumped against Sindril's back, rocking in time to the murbeest's plodding gait through the deep, soft sands.

She awakened a short while later at the sound of Sindril's low voice, alerted by a note of tense urgency in his tone. At the same time, she became aware of an insistent wind tugging at her clothes and pulling strands of hair from her braids. The murbeest stood still, his shaggy sides trembling beneath Tenya's legs.

"I think we're in trouble," Sindril said, quietly.

She looked over his shoulder and gasped. Ahead, the clouds rushed across the sky in the wake of the strengthening wind and unsteady flashes of pale, ghostly moonlight revealed a terrifying sight.

Several yards away, a creature with coal-black fur and gleaming orange eyes crouched in the moving shadows. Two long, pointed fangs protruded from either side of a bristling muzzle and saliva dripped from its teeth to fall in glistening drops on the red sand.

"Wh-what is it?" Tenya managed to whisper, not daring to move in case she provoked the dangerous-looking animal.

"It's called a demon beast," Sindril whispered back.

It did, indeed, look like a creature straight out of the pits of Hell. She stared at it, almost afraid to breathe. It still crouched silently, its fierce orange eyes glittering in the fitful moonlight.

Tenya licked her dry lips. "What do we do? Will it attack us?"

Sindril's low answer hardly reassured her. "I don't know. They're very unpredictable. Perhaps if we remain very still, it will eventually go away."

"Can't you do something?" she whispered, desperately. "You have magic in your staff. Why don't you use it against the beast?"

Sindril paused for a moment, and then said, "We're on the edge of the Plains, near the Windy

Tunnel. The wind blowing around us comes from the Tunnel, although it is only a mild breeze compared to what awaits us in the corridor. Unfortunately, for some reason, the wind prevents me from using the power in my staff. I can do nothing."

Tenya's pulse raced frantically. The demon beast could attack at any moment and they had no power to stop it.

Even as she thought it, the beast suddenly came to life. A ferocious snarl issued from the creature's throat and its powerful muscles bunched in its stocky legs as it prepared to lunge.

Tenya's heart leapt into her throat and her breath locked in her chest. In front of her, Sindril tensed and the murbeest began to prance in panic and terror.

"Tenya, do something!"

Dimly, she heard Sindril's shout but, for a moment, she remained frozen, staring in dumb horror at the beast preparing to charge them. Then, suddenly, it seemed as though an island of calm surfaced in her mind and her terror disappeared. She saw the creature move as though in slow motion–it sprang forward, powerful legs bunched up underneath its bulky body.

She tingled all over and, still with that same strange sense of detachment, she saw a soft white light suddenly outline Sindril, the murbeest, and herself. A rush of adrenaline–and something else she could not define–pervaded her body.

Die!

The thought careened through her mind and her right hand lifted, as if of its own volition, to point at the oncoming creature. A vivid white light flashed before her eyes, so brilliant it momentarily blinded her.

Gradually, her vision cleared and she blinked uncertainly. The white glow faded from her body and that of her companions and the detached feeling of calm receded, leaving her shaken and dazed. Just a few feet away, the demon beast lay on its side, not moving, its head no longer recognizable. All that remained was a mass of charred, black pulp from which tendrils of smoke rose rapidly on the steady wind.

Tenya blinked at the dead creature, trying to understand what had happened. She became aware of Sindril staring back at her over his shoulder.

"Like pointing my finger at a tree and having it burst into flames," she said, shakily.

He grinned, white teeth flashing in his face. "Remind me never to anger you."

Tenya blew out her breath, releasing the last of her pent-up tension. She still couldn't believe she was responsible for the dead, charred body of the demon beast lying on the sands in front of them.

"I thought for certain we were done for," Sindril said, feelingly. He slid off the back of the murbeest and cautiously approached the still-smoldering carcass.

The creature lay appallingly close to the murbeest, who snorted and pranced nervously, prevented from running away by Tenya's soothing hand on his neck.

"You can see how close it came to us," Sindril said. He glanced back at her. "You put up your shield just in time. The beast bounced off it split seconds after you raised it. But, it was the flash of fire you threw that finished it off." The little man grinned. "I must admit, I was a little worried you wouldn't use your powers in time to save us."

"I almost didn't," Tenya admitted, ruefully. "Everything happened so quickly. I felt completely helpless when I first saw the demon beast start to charge, but then I was suddenly calm. In my mind, I told it to die– and it did!"

"Thank goodness." Sindril straightened from examining the dead animal and glanced around. "We'd better move on. The creature's mate may be somewhere nearby."

Tenya's heart hammered as she searched the swiftly moving shadows on the Plains. Did that shadow seem blacker than the others? Did wicked orange eyes gleam faintly in the midst of it?

"Oh, yes, please–let's go," she urged.

Sindril nodded and vaulted onto the back of the murbeest. He nudged the animal forward with his heels and the murbeest cautiously minced around the smoking carcass, continuing on into the face of the growing wind.

The fine red sands of the Plains gave way to rocky ground, coarse grass and stands of scraggly, bent trees. Winds whistled and moaned relentlessly through a narrow, rocky defile just visible up ahead.

Tenya enjoyed a sense of relief when they left the Plains and entered the trees, for, despite the constant wind that rushed past her face, the scanty protection of the trees seemed to afford more comfort than the wide-open vulnerability of the Plains.

"Are you ready to tackle the Tunnel? Or, do you want to rest first?" Sindril shouted back at her, the roar of the wind making normal speech impossible.

"Let's go!" she shouted in reply. "The sooner we start, the sooner we'll reach the other side."

He nodded and urged the murbeest forward. The animal pranced a little, reluctant to enter the noisy chaos of the narrow, rocky corridor.

Sindril had been right about the formidability of the winds of the Tunnel. They threatened to unseat them from the murbeest's back, rising and wailing around them like restless beasts on the prowl.

Tenya ducked her head against Sindril's back, trying to shield her eyes from the swirling clouds of windblown dust. Strong gusts slammed into her, as though powerful hands attacked, slapping, punching and grabbing to pull her body this way and that. She recalled Sindril's words and thought she could hear a faint voice in the howling wind, but blamed the fanciful notion on her imagination.

How much farther to the end of the Tunnel? How much longer would they have to endure the terrible ferocity of the wind?

Wait!

The wind…

Her mother's power came from the wind. She could command it to do her will. Was it possible, as Elea's daughter, she might also be able to communicate with it?

She closed her eyes, uncertain how to proceed. She started by willing her mind to become a calm, undisturbed place. *Can you hear me?* She thought, tentatively, and then more strongly, *I am a friend. Can you hear me?*

It could have been only her imagination, but the constant wailing seemed to hesitate for a fraction of a second, as though listening.

She tried to reach out with her mind again, repeating the silent words over and over. *We are your friends. Please don't harm us. If you can hear me, please talk to me.*

She felt a slight pressure in her mind and then recoiled from a sudden onslaught of such pain and despair that it nearly knocked her from the murbeest's back.

Help us! Free us!

Babbling, terrified voices assaulted her senses, pounding into her with unbelievable force. She clamped her hands over her ears, trying to shut out the clamor. "No, no, stop! I can't bear it. There are too many at once!" The assault abruptly ceased, the voices dying away to a rustling, waiting silence.

Slowly, Tenya lowered her hands, her mind strangely calm after the terrible battering of pain and terror. There seemed to be a vacuum of absolute stillness surrounding her.

Who are you? She asked. *Why do you need help?*

A tiny voice, so faint she had to strain to hear it, begged, *Can you free us?*

I don't know. Free you from what? Who are you?

She felt a feather-light touch on her cheek and the tiny voice said wearily. *We have been trapped here for sixteen years, helpless victims of the Demon Master. He killed our bodies and imprisoned our souls so that we can never find peace. We are forced to hunger and cry forever for that which we can never hope to attain.*

Why? Tenya asked. *Why did he do this to you?*

We helped the Mistress defeat the Demon Master in the first Great Battle. When Zardonne returned, he killed as many of us as he could find and left us to this fate...punishment for rising against him.

Then, the story Sindril had told her about the winds in the Tunnel was true. Ghosts did indeed inhabit the wind!

You are not the Mistress, the tiny voice went on, *but we sense great power in you.*

I am her daughter. Tenya answered. *Zardonne also imprisoned the Mistress. She's locked away in a tower of ice.*

The winds rustled softly, a collective sigh of sorrow and despair.

We wondered, the tiny voice said, sadly. We have waited these many years for her to free us, but she never came. Now, we know why. Perhaps, our situation is hopeless after all.

Such utter resignation and despair vibrated in the soft voice that tears stung behind Tenya's closed eyes. *No! There must be a way! I do have powers, but I'm not sure of them. I don't know if they're strong enough to free you, but I can try.*

Once again, feathery touches brushed her cheeks and her mind, so light they might have been imaginary.

We sense the goodness and strength in you. You feel our pain. We have faith in you.

The touches withdrew and the voices quieted. Tenya sensed a waiting calmness in the wind.

What do I do? She thought, desperately. *Oh, Mother, I need you now! I need your strength and your power and your wisdom. How can I free these poor, lost souls from their eternal prison and give them peace?*

In her mind, the tower of ice rose, looming before her, overwhelming in its terrible, stark beauty. Not a vision this time but her own desire to see the edifice that held her mother prisoner. She touched the gleaming cold walls and, at once, a faint power vibrated through the solid ice to tingle through her fingertips. Strength flowed through her body. Then, the tower vanished once more into the mists of her mind, taking with it her desperate sense of helplessness.

CHAPTER 9

Tenya opened her eyes. The Tunnel had disappeared. In its place, a gray mist swirled, its touch cold and malevolent. Dark shapes moved within its enveloping tatters, indistinct but unmistakably evil.

For a moment, uncertainty and fear assailed her. Surely, these could not be the desperate, forsaken souls that had pleaded with her to help them. Or, had those tiny voices deliberately deceived her in order to trap her here in this foul mist?

As though reading her thoughts, the feathery voice that had spoken earlier warned, *Take care, Daughter of the Wind! The Demon Master has left guards to watch over us. They will try to destroy you.*

The shadows hissed and growled menacingly, swaying closer to her. She could feel the evil radiating from them in waves.

You are not welcome here, sorceress!

She wanted nothing more than to run from the overwhelming horror that threatened her, but Tenya stood her ground, a warm, singing power running through her veins.

A dark shape rushed at her from out of the mists. In response, a strong, white fire sprang from her fingertips. Struck by the fire, the thing shrieked horribly and disappeared in a brilliant flash.

She spun swiftly around, sensing movement behind her. Again, white fire streaked from her tingling fingertips. Another of the creatures vanished with a shrill wail.

Give up, sorceress, a voice rumbled.

Never! Tenya cried, her gaze darting from one to another of the encroaching shapes in the swirling mist. More white fire flew from her fingertips, scorching the mist and sending dark shadows scattering, yelping in pain.

You cannot defeat us all, the deep voice growled. *You are too weak! Your powers are too young.*

Her breath caught between heartbeats. Did the creature speak the truth? Was she too weak to defeat all of Zardonne's minions? Each time the white fire flashed from her fingers, she experienced an instant of fatigue, and the singing in her veins grew fainter.

Terror welled in the pit of her stomach. So many of the evil beings surrounded her now; their vague, dark shapes rushed at her. They cautiously leapt away when the flames shot from her fingertips but not for long.

I will fail, she despaired, trickles of perspiration stinging her eyes. More shapes came at her and she had to keep spinning to face them. How much longer could she do this before exhaustion overtook her?

In the midst of all the chaos, she heard the tiny voice as though from a great distance. *The chains grow weaker! You have the power to free us!*

A newfound strength surged through her veins, replacing her budding panic with cold determination. Straightening her shoulders, she redoubled her attacks on the dark shadows, feeling the power surge once more through her veins. No matter how often the darker force of Zardonne's guardians of the winds repelled her, she fought back, destroying them one after the other. More than once, she gasped for breath, her lungs burning as though on fire, but she refused to give up. With each shadowy creature she vanquished, the mist weakened and the dreadful power of the Demon Master loosened its hold on the winds.

At last, only one dark shape remained in the wavering tendrils of gray mist. It was much larger than the others, its vague shape hulking and menacing. Tenya could see the fiery gleam of its eyes.

So, sorceress, it comes down to us. The grating voice belonged to the one that had spoken to her earlier. *You are stronger than I realized. But, you will still fail.*

The creature's sudden, ferocious lunge forward drew a gasp of surprise from her. A dark wave of incredible force struck her in the chest and she staggered backward, shaken. She heard the monster's triumphant laugh.

Her veins sang with power again. She lifted her arms and strong, white fire streaked from her fingertips. The dark shape's laugh turned to a strangled cry, but it did not vanish as the others had. Its essence wavered and dimmed for a moment, and then its shape darkened once more.

I am stronger than you, sorceress. You cannot destroy me.

Evil can always be destroyed! Tenya cried, advancing on the indistinct shape. *There is no place for you here. Begone!*

Blinding flashes ripped through the gray mist, striking the sinister shape and driving it backward. Cries of rage and pain wrenched from the thing, but after wavering for an instant, it came back stronger than before.

A green light shot from the creature and struck her shoulder.

Tenya staggered and her whole arm went numb.

She and the guardian circled each other warily, each looking for weaknesses and openings in the other's defenses. The thing's vague shape made it difficult for Tenya to follow its every move, for it wavered in and out of the tattered tendrils of gray mist.

Give up! You cannot hope to win. The voice rumbled like two huge boulders grating together, making Tenya's skin prickle.

Exhausted and shaken, she tried desperately to track the creature's erratic movements. Zardonne's denizen of evil exuded terrifying power and she felt the uncertainty of her own strength eroding her determination to win. Fear that she would fail to free the voices in the wind from their prison shook her to the core.

Tenya, you have the power–do not give up!

A different voice this time–Sindril's voice–hammered at her, breaking down the bonds of despair and hopelessness. She lifted her hanging head, power once again flowing through her exhausted body.

The dark shape feinted to her right but she stood her ground, refusing to be drawn. Her whole body tingled and she raised both hands.

Flares of brilliant white fire, streaked with red, sparked from her fingers and tore away the last shreds of swirling gray mist. The black hulk in front of her shrieked horribly. The fiery red of its eyes suddenly winked out, the thing shuddered...then disappeared.

Instantly, the gray mist vanished. In its place, absolute stillness and peace reigned.

Tenya felt feather touches in her mind and the tiny voice spoke once more, its tone one of incredible wonder and joy. *We are free! You have saved us. We can now find the peace we have sought all these long years. Thank you, young sorceress.*

Then, the voices of the wind, too, faded, and total silence descended once more.

Tenya opened her eyes.

She saw the narrow, rocky corridor, its walls touched with the pinkish glow of the rising sun. The murbeest stood tethered to an outcropping of rocks off to one side, his swirling eyes slowly resuming their normal rainbow colors.

Not a breath of wind stirred in the Tunnel.

Tenya turned at a light touch on her shoulder. Sindril stood beside her, his wizened face smudged with dirt, his floppy hat askew on his head. The outlandish feathered cape looked rather the worse for wear, as though many of its bright, multicolored feathers had been plucked from it. Despite his disheveled appearance, the little man's irrepressible grin showed whitely beneath his gray-streaked beard.

"Your first victory over Zardonne's evil servants," he said, proudly.

Tenya's senses reeled from the exhausting violence of the confrontation she had just endured. Her left shoulder still tingled from the creature's paralyzing blast of green light. She massaged it gently, feeling the prickling sensation of returning circulation, and stared at the grinning Sindril.

"You saw what happened?" she asked.

"Well, some of it, at least," he replied. "The rest, I guessed at. One moment we were riding the murbeest, trying just to stay on his back, and the next, you had slid to the ground and had become very still, as though you were listening intently to something, or someone. Before I knew what was happening, there were streaks of white and green fire bouncing madly about the corridor."

"All I wanted to do was see if I could talk to the wind, perhaps quiet its fury a little," Tenya explained. "But, I found out a lot more than I bargained for. There were voices in the wind. They were souls imprisoned there by Zardonne after his second battle with the Mistress. They were being punished for taking her side in the first battle and they asked me to set them free. But I had to destroy Zardonne's guards first in order to do so."

Sindril nodded. "I could see only dark shadows flitting about the corridor, but they were obviously attacking you."

Tenya shivered, remembering the awful power of the dark shapes in the mist. "I didn't know if I was strong enough to destroy them all." She rubbed her shoulder. "There was one, at the end, who was much stronger than the others. It nearly overpowered me."

"I could see you hesitating," Sindril said. "I tried to encourage you to continue."

"I heard your voice, imploring me not to give up."

"I wasn't certain if you heard me or not, so I added my own magic to yours to help destroy the last of the dark shadows."

Tenya recalled the streaks of red light that had flashed within the pure white of her fire. That must have been Sindril's magic from his jeweled staff.

A thought suddenly occurred to her. "Wait a minute. Sindril, I thought you said your powers were useless in the Tunnel. How could you help me?"

He looked sheepish. "I, ah, I'm afraid I wasn't exactly truthful with you earlier, Tenya."

She frowned at him. "What do you mean?"

When he hesitated, understanding suddenly dawned on her. "The demon beast was another test, wasn't it?" she exclaimed. "Just like your attack on me earlier."

He looked aggrieved. "It was not an attack. I had no intention of harming you. As for the demon beast, well, yes, I suppose you could say it was a test."

"But, why?" she demanded. "We could have been killed! How could you know that I had the power to save us, and, more importantly, that I would know how to use it to destroy the creature?"

He grinned wryly. "I admit I did take a big chance. But, Tenya, you came through brilliantly!"

She refused to be appeased and glared at him, hands on her hips. "You deliberately put us in great danger just to see what I would do? If I hadn't used my powers when I did, we would both be dead now! You–You impossible little man! I ought to...to…!"

"What? Use your fire to strike me dead, as you did the demon beast?" Sindril asked quietly.

Her anger abruptly checked and she felt shaken and frightened. She recalled his earlier words about not being reckless with her powers. How close she had come to doing just that; striking out at him in her fury. He was right. She had to learn to control them.

She stared bleakly at him. "Sindril, I...I'm so sorry. I..."

He shook his head quickly. "No, Tenya, it is I who must apologize. You're upset and understandably so. I'll try to explain my actions and perhaps then you won't be so angry with me." He looked so beguiling that she had to smile at him.

His impish grin returned. "We were in danger, yes, but, if you hadn't killed the demon beast with your powers, I would have used the magic in my staff to destroy it. It would have been close, but I was willing to risk it. I wanted you to use your powers, Tenya. That's why I said I couldn't use mine. I had to take the chance that you would summon yours in time to kill the creature."

"But, I don't understand. Why was it so necessary for *me* to kill the beast?"

"It's very important that you use your powers and learn to control them. Even in the short time since

I rescued you from Mordis, you've grown stronger. Can't you feel it? Soon, you will master the magic in you."

Tenya had to admit there was truth in what he said. She *did* feel different–stronger, more alive, her body undergoing a subtle, rejuvenating change. She was finding it increasingly easier to summon the hidden powers within her.

"Zardonne is very powerful, Tenya," Sindril said quietly. "You had but a small taste of his strength a short while ago when you battled the creatures in the winds. You have not yet come up against the full force of his evil. Therefore, if we hope to destroy him, it will be necessary for you to develop your powers to the fullest. Together, with the Mistress, we can vanquish him from Tellaron."

"I suppose you're right," Tenya conceded. "But, Sindril, please, no more tests. I don't think I could take many more surprises like that."

He grinned. "I don't think it will be necessary any longer. You're learning quickly. You took the initiative upon yourself to challenge the shadows in the wind and you succeeded. True, you did falter a little, but only because you were unsure of yourself. Now, you have a better idea of what you are capable of, and the next time you will be much stronger."

"I only wish I had as much faith and confidence in me as you seem to have," she sighed. "Without you, I don't think I would have the courage to continue."

"Nonsense! You're much braver than you give yourself credit for. Come, let's continue on our way.

We should be able to move much faster now without the constant winds to hinder us."

It was true. The winds in the Tunnel had totally ceased. Tenya probed gently with her mind, trying to reach the imprisoned voices, but only silence greeted her. The lost souls had indeed been set free and would haunt the narrow, rocky corridor no more. Sindril laughingly said the name would have to be changed from the Windy Tunnel to something more appropriate.

The long corridor began sloping gently upwards and the murbeest had to pick his way carefully over the gravel floor. At times, the Tunnel narrowed so much that the rocky walls brushed against Tenya's knees.

"We're coming into the foothills of the Jamal Mountains," Sindril explained. "There is a small village called Tundel near the Dagas Pass, where we can stop and rest, and get something to eat. I know the tavern owner there. He's a good man and will look after us. Perhaps, too, he'll have news of Zardonne's latest exploits."

Tenya nodded. She had not realized just how tired and hungry she was until Sindril mentioned food and rest. The thought of stopping for a while appealed greatly to her.

CHAPTER 10

Tundel turned out to be a small, quiet cluster of rough, wooden buildings built into the side of the impressive Jamal Mountains. The murbeest emerged from the Tunnel onto a narrow, gravel road leading up to the village, and the sight of the towering peaks astounded Tenya. Their black-streaked orange faces shone like burnished copper in the rays of the rising sun. The gentle, rolling slopes of the hills surrounding the Ardis Valley could not compare with the rugged majesty spread out before her. The tops of the mountains were hidden from view by billowing white clouds that made them appear to vanish into the sky.

Tundel appeared deserted in the early hours of the morning. Neither man nor creature stirred, except for a few dogs lying in the dusty street. They jumped to their feet and slunk away, growling over their shoulders at the approaching travelers.

Tenya heard the faint tinkle of bells in the distance and spied a herd of goats on the mountainside near the far end of the village. A small figure moved about the fringes of the herd and she supposed it was the goat herder, up early to tend his flock. Aside from him, there were no other people up and moving around.

The murbeest's hooves clomped briskly down the hard packed village street. As they approached the first of the small, wooden buildings, Tenya thought she saw curtains move in some of the windows. It appeared that some of the residents had been aroused by their arrival, but oddly, no one came out to greet them. She caught glimpses of faces in other windows they passed, but those persons, too, moved quickly from sight when she looked in their direction.

Puzzled, she glanced around in growing apprehension. An almost tangible pall of fear seemed to hang over the silent village.

Sindril spoke quietly, echoing her thoughts. "There is something wrong here. I can feel it in the air. I know it's early, but you would think someone would be out on the streets by now, going about their business."

"I see people behind some of the windows," Tenya said, "but, whenever I look their way, they jump out of sight, as though they don't want to be seen."

Sindril slowed the murbeest to a stop. With the clop of his hooves silenced, the oppressive stillness deepened. "Something has happened here," he said, thoughtfully.

Suddenly, doors up and down the street burst open and villagers rushed forth. They all carried some sort of weapon, ranging from common garden implements to long, black staffs with jagged blades affixed. They quickly surrounded the murbeest, brandishing their weapons menacingly.

Startled, Tenya gazed upon their strained faces, grim with fear and determination. She clung to Sindril, frightened by the sudden, angry charge.

The little man's body was rigid, his short staff pointed downward into the threatening crowd.

"What do you want here, stranger?" a man's voice called out harshly.

"We seek only food and rest," Sindril replied calmly, despite the tension in his body. "We have traveled far."

"What is your business in these parts?" another voice challenged.

"We are merely travelers. We mean no harm to anyone."

A third man jabbed his bladed staff towards Sindril. "How do we know you speak the truth?" he demanded, his eyes narrowed in his weather-beaten face.

"You have my word," Sindril said.

"Why should we trust your word?" a woman in the crowd called shrilly. "You could be one of *them*, come in disguise, to wreak more pain and havoc on our village."

"I don't know who you mean by 'one of them', but I can assure you that my companion and I don't wish to cause any trouble. We merely seek a little hospitality and then we will continue on our way."

"He lies! Kill them now, before they can do us harm," another voice shouted.

Others growled and muttered in agreement, surging forward with weapons raised.

Tenya's heart leapt into her throat. She noted Sindril had tightened his hold on his staff, prepared to use its magic to repel the attackers, if necessary.

"Stop!" a commanding voice suddenly rang out.

The crowd subsided, reluctantly falling back. A broad-shouldered man with a bushy black beard pushed his way through the muttering villagers. He stopped beside the murbeest and grinned. "Sindril, you old goat, what are you doing back in these parts?"

Sindril relaxed, breaking into a smile. "Hurn, you old lizard, since when do you greet visitors to your village this way?"

The big man's grin disappeared. "It's a long story, my friend. Come down off that beast and I'll take you to the tavern. While you eat and drink, I'll tell you what has happened." His blue eyes slid curiously to Tenya. "Who's your friend?"

"That, too, is a long story," Sindril sighed, dismounting from the murbeest.

He held up a hand to help Tenya slide from the animal's sloping back. She did so reluctantly, eyeing the mumbling, shuffling villagers with trepidation.

The black-bearded man turned to the crowd and held up his huge hands. "All is well, good neighbors. This is a friend of mine. You have nothing to fear from him, I give you my word. He is not a Death Rider in disguise."

Sindril swung quickly to face him. "A Death Rider?"

"Part of the story, my friend," Hurn said. "Come, let us go to the tavern and I'll tell you all about it."

The crowd of villagers dispersed slowly, some still muttering and shaking their heads. Others continued to eye Tenya and Sindril with suspicion and distrust. A few of the men looked as though they might cause more trouble, but Hurn stared them down with a warning glower. One or two yet hesitated, but even they soon turned away, unwilling to contest the powerful tavern keeper.

"They are certainly upset about *something*," Sindril observed, quietly, watching the villagers slowly return to their homes.

"And, with good reason," Hurn replied, grimly.

He led them down the dusty street towards a long, low, wooden building set back against the burnished orange side of the mountain. Sindril tied the murbeest to a post beside the door and the three of them entered the dimly-lit tavern.

One lone girl, a young, dark-haired beauty, occupied the quiet taproom, stoking the fire in the huge stone hearth. She glanced quickly at Tenya and Sindril and fled through an open doorway into what was presumably the kitchen.

Hurn showed them a rough-planked, well-scrubbed table, and then went behind a long counter that ran the length of one side of the low-ceilinged room.

"We had a visit from a stranger a few days ago," he said without preamble, his bearded face grim. "The man rode in on a blood-red stallion, all smiles and jests and greetings. But rather than seek food or shelter, as one might expect, he rode his mount to the center of the village then lifted his arms and began to chant. None of us knew what he was about until the Death Rider came. The man had summoned him out of the mountains.

"Like a vision from Hell, he was, bringing with him thunder and lightning, though the evening was clear. Before we knew what was happening, he charged into the village on his terrible mount, right up to the stranger who had called him forth."

Horror at the memory was reflected in the strained muscles of Hurn's face before he continued. "The Death Rider reined in his mount and the stranger spoke to us. He said that the Demon Master was bringing his army through the mountains shortly and we should pledge our allegiance to him without fail or we would all die horrible deaths.

"Then, the Death Rider pointed to a young child and said, 'This will be your fate if you do not obey Zardonne.' There was a burst of fire and the child just disappeared. One moment, he was there and the next there was just a small pile of smoking ash where the boy had been standing. Before we could move or speak or even think, the Death Rider rode off, back into the mountains, taking the stranger with him."

The tavern keeper's voice fell silent. Tenya stared at him, unable to believe her ears. Safe in the Ardis Valley, she had been blissfully unaware of the extent of evil and corruption that marked the other lands. Dianis' cruel treatment of her dimmed in comparison to what she had learned so far about the Demon Master, Zardonne.

Hurn took a deep breath and went on, "Since then, the villagers have been living in constant fear, terrified that the stranger, or the Death Rider, would return to further terrorize them. When they saw you approaching, they thought their fears had been realized and more horror would be visited upon the village."

"But, who was the stranger?" Tenya asked.

Hurn shrugged. "He was one of Zardonne's minions acting as a messenger. There are many who willingly serve him."

"Now, I can understand the villagers' greeting to us," Sindril said. "I haven't visited here for quite some time and likely most of the people didn't recognize me. Naturally, after what you just told us, they would be afraid of strangers."

"I almost didn't recognize you myself at first," Hurn said, wryly. "That outlandish outfit of yours made it difficult to identify you."

"Outlandish? I'll have you know this is the height of civilized fashion, my friend," Sindril huffed in pretended offense.

He ruined the moment with a grin, and nodded his thanks as Hurn placed a tankard of ale in front of him. "It doesn't bode well that a Death Rider has ventured this far through the mountains. That means Zardonne's army is not far off."

Hurn nodded grimly, sitting down at the table with them. "I'm afraid so. I've heard tales that have made my blood run cold. Though the Ferrish Wood is safe from his powers, Zardonne has been ravaging villages on this side of the Belisar River. I've talked to people fleeing their homes. They say that, for miles around, the land is a desolate wasteland, charred and destroyed by the Demon Master's terrible fire. Whole villages have been laid to waste. Men, women and children alike are slaughtered to satisfy Zardonne's monstrous appetite for destruction."

He turned towards the doorway through which the young girl had disappeared. "Sarath, bring food for our guests!"

Facing Sindril and Tenya once more, he continued, "I've heard there's been resistance against Zardonne. A troop of horsemen from the Coros Region and the Shetii Clan from the Ferrish Wood formed an army of two thousand strong. But, though they have won small skirmishes, not even the legendary strength of the Coros horsemen or the magic of the Shetii Clan have been able to send Zardonne scurrying back to the Plain of Naryn with his tail between his legs."

At that moment, the young girl appeared, carrying a tray of freshly baked bread, cheese and fruit. She approached the table timidly, as though prepared to drop the tray and run at the slightest provocation.

"This is my daughter, Sarath," Hurn said to Tenya. He noticed the young girl's apprehension and smiled up at her, patting her gently on the arm. "Sarath, there's no need for fear. You remember Sindril, don't you? He's been here before. He looks rather odd, I know, but he's entirely harmless."

Sindril again pretended affront. "Odd? Well, I must say, that's a fine way for a friend to talk." His dark eyes twinkled up at Sarath. "The last time I saw you, Sarath, you were climbing a tree, had scrapes on both your knees and smudges of dirt on your freckled face. I believe you were about eleven at the time."

The young girl stared at him for a moment and then a shy smile touched her lips. "Now, I remember you," she said, softly. "You helped me when I fell out of the tree. I cut my leg and you touched it and all the pain and blood went away. You were very kind."

Sindril grinned. "Yes, I do seem to have a habit of rescuing young maidens in distress." He glanced over at Tenya.

Hurn caught the inference and asked Tenya curiously, "How did you happen to meet up with this scoundrel, young lady? You look familiar, but I don't recall ever seeing you here before."

Tenya hesitated, wondering how much she should reveal to this man. Though he and Sindril seemed to be on amicable terms, he was still a stranger to her. Would it be wise to tell him she was the daughter of the Mistress of the Wind?

She looked to Sindril for help. He seemed to sense her dilemma and smiled gently. "I think you can trust him, Tenya."

She caught Hurn watching their brief exchange with a puzzled frown and decided to tell him everything. If Sindril didn't feel it would be dangerous to reveal her identity to his friend, then she shouldn't, either. She may have known the little man for only a short time, but she trusted his judgment implicitly.

CHAPTER 11

By the time Tenya finished her tale, the morning had nearly passed and she was drooping with fatigue. In the charged silence that followed, Hurn and Sarath stared at her in astonishment.

"You really are the daughter of the Mistress?" Hurn asked at last, intently studying her dirt-smudged face and disheveled hair. She endured his scrutiny with quiet composure.

"You do look very much like her, with your dark hair and green eyes," he finally said. "I only saw her once, many years ago, but her beauty is not something one easily forgets." His bearded face took on an expression of restrained hope. "And, you really think you can free her from her prison?"

"I have to try," Tenya said, quietly.

"But, how do you propose to go about it? It'll be difficult to get past Zardonne's defenses and reach the tower alive. He'll know of your presence the moment you set foot on the Plain of Naryn."

She sighed and glanced at Sindril. "I know it sounds impossible, but what choice do we have? I've only recently learned of my powers, and don't know the full extent of them or how strong they are. I haven't used them enough to battle Zardonne on my own. We have to try to free my mother and, hopefully, our combined powers will be enough to vanquish him once and for all."

"I must admit, I'd almost given up all hope that something could be done to stop Zardonne. He grows stronger every day." Hurn covered Tenya's small hand with his much bigger one. "You have my promise, little one, that I will do everything I can to help you."

She smiled. "Thank you. You're very kind."

"And now, I think our brave young lady here needs to sleep," Sindril declared, speaking for the first time since she'd begun her tale. "We can talk more after we've both rested. Are your beds still as soft and inviting as I remember them, Hurn?"

"Certainly, my friend, you shall have only the best that I can offer."

Sarath led Tenya up steep, narrow steps to a tiny loft at the far end of the room. Only a dimly glowing lantern and a low bed furnished the space, but the thick, soft mattress, covered with a bright, multicolored quilt, beckoned invitingly.

Sarath smiled shyly at Tenya, offering to take her clothing and clean it for her; offering, as well, the use of one of her nightgowns in the meantime.

Tenya thanked her and gratefully shed the rough tunic and trousers encrusted with grime and dirt. Sarath went back down the narrow steps, promising to return shortly with the nightgown. While she waited, Tenya sat on the low bed, and imagined this must be what it felt like to sink into a soft, downy cloud. From the taproom below, she heard the two men talking, their murmuring voices drifting up to comfort her. So relaxed did she become she'd nearly fallen asleep before Sarath returned with the nightgown and a basin of hot water, but she managed to rouse herself long enough to wash away the travel dust of the last few days.

The young girl had also thoughtfully provided a hairbrush and Tenya undid her disheveled braids. Her tresses cascaded in waves to her waist and she brushed them until they shone like polished ebony in the glow of the dim lantern. Sighing with pleasure to be clean again, she quickly donned the plain, fresh-smelling nightgown and sank once more on the downy mattress. Within minutes, she fell fast asleep, her dreams quiet and undisturbed.

When she awakened, late afternoon had arrived, judging from the warm golden light streaming through the one tiny window in the loft. The delicious aroma of roasting meat wafted up to where she lay drowsily on the soft bed. Whereas earlier the tavern had been empty, the room below now hummed with the muted voices of many patrons.

She found her clothes neatly folded at the foot of the bed, freshly cleaned and pressed. On the floor beside them sat a serviceable pair of slippers. She'd been so sound asleep, she hadn't heard Sarath return and place the clothes on the bed.

The deep sleep had refreshed and revitalized her. She quickly donned her tunic and trousers, slipped on the shoes, and gave her hair a quick brush, leaving it hanging loose down her back. Sarath had left another basin for her and Tenya splashed cool water on her face, chasing away the last vestiges of sleep.

The smell of the roasting meat stirred her stomach into hungry rumbles so she hurried down the steep, narrow steps to the taproom. At the bottom of the stairs, she hesitated, gazing out into the crowded, noisy room. Several men sat at the tables drinking ale from huge tankards. Their conversation buzzed in low-pitched, excited tones, like the sounds of a thousand bees.

Over by the huge stone fireplace, Hurn turned the handle of a long spit. Several chickens skewered along the length of the spit sizzled appetizingly over the bed of hot coals, their skins already a crisp, golden brown. Sarath hurried from table to table with tankards of ale and mugs of mulled wine.

Tenya saw Sindril sitting at a table near the large, dusty window at the far end of the room. She hesitated, wanting to slip unobtrusively past the filled tables to reach him. The villagers' hostile greeting earlier that morning still left lingering traces of unease in her.

She no sooner stepped down from the last rung of the stairs on to the wooden floor of the tavern when a tall, thin man at one of the nearby tables noticed her. He pointed a bony finger her way and said loudly over the buzz of conversation, "There she is now!"

She froze, her heart fluttering beneath her breast, as all eyes in the tavern turned to where she stood at the foot of the steps. She worriedly searched the faces of the men, but could see no hostility or menace in them. Indeed, they all stared at her with a kind of reverent awe and expectancy.

Uneasy and wondering at their reaction, she looked to Sindril for help. He smiled slightly and rose from the bench, threading his way through the other tables until he reached her side.

"There's no need for fear, Tenya. These people won't harm you."

"I don't understand," she whispered. "Why are they all staring at me like that?"

"It's not every day that a young sorceress comes into their village. They're understandably in awe of you."

She stared at him. "But-But, how do they know...?"

At that moment, Hurn walked up, his bearded face slick with perspiration from tending the hearth. He grinned sheepishly. "I'm afraid it's my fault, Tenya. I couldn't keep such news to myself. The visit of the Death Rider has struck terror into the hearts of the villagers. They dread the coming of each day because it means that Zardonne and his army are that much closer to Tundel. Who knows when he and his evil horde will come charging down out of the mountains, bringing death and destruction in their wake? You are like a salvation to us."

The weight of Hurn's expectations fell on her shoulders like a ton of bricks. She dreaded the thought of the villagers relying on her to destroy the Demon Master. "But, I can't...I-I don't know..."

Sindril's dark eyes, filled with kindness, settled on her. "Tenya, you are no longer the young girl hoeing potatoes in the Ardis Valley. You have grown far beyond that now. You're frightened by what lies ahead of you, but the important thing is that you must develop your powers to the fullest and use them to the best of your ability. That's all anyone will ask of you."

She stared at him, troubled, and started nervously when several of the men jumped up from their benches and crowded around her, asking questions and talking simultaneously. Her head reeled with confusion and babble. Instinctively, she sidled closer to Sindril for protection.

Hurn held up his greasy hands. "Quiet! Quiet, everyone! Give the poor girl room to breathe. You're frightening her."

Gradually, the noise subsided and the men fell back a few paces, though anticipation still shone on their faces. Tenya wondered anxiously what they expected of her. She had no idea what to say to them.

Sindril came to her rescue once more. "Even sorceresses need nourishment," he said, lightly, taking Tenya's arm and guiding her through the men to the table by the window. "Please, let the girl eat before you bombard her with your questions."

Reluctantly, the men returned to their tables, allowing Sindril and Tenya to sit and partake of their meal. Yet, their excited chatter still filled the room.

In their relatively peaceful corner of the tavern, Tenya felt her pulse slowly return to normal. The zealous assault by the villagers had been almost as overwhelming as their earlier hostility.

"Sindril, these people seem to think I'm a supreme being of some kind," she said, in a low, worried voice. "They think I can just wave my hand and save their village."

Sindril's dark eyes glinted impishly. "Perhaps you can."

She frowned at him. "Don't laugh at me."

He smiled warmly. "I'm not laughing at you. I see that I have still not fully convinced you that you are not just an ordinary young woman. You have the potential for extraordinary powers. I don't know exactly what form those powers will take, but they would seem to be different from your mother's. She captures the strength and force of the wind, while you seem to be able to use fire. But, even as inexperienced as you are right now, you do have the means to be a great threat to Zardonne."

At that moment, Sarath came to their table with a platter of succulent roasted chicken, freshly baked bread and creamy cheese. She set the platter down, and then left to attend to other customers.

Tenya gazed thoughtfully out the window. She could sense several of the men in the tavern throwing curious, awed glances her way, but she couldn't bring herself to meet their gazes.

"I'm frightened," she said quietly. "I don't know if I'm strong enough for what lies ahead."

He laid a hand on one of hers. "You are. You must believe that. When the time comes, your strength and courage will help you meet whatever challenge comes your way."

At last she was able to return his smile. "You're always so encouraging, Sindril. Where were you when Dianis was forcing me to do all those boring, deplorable chores?"

He chuckled. "You see? If you could survive that, you can survive anything."

"I have a feeling this is more dangerous than hoeing potatoes in the hot sun. It's certainly more frightening." She shook her head. "To think I used to feel my life was so miserable and harsh, when everywhere else people were suffering–even dying– at the hands of Zardonne. I never realized how much evil and corruption there was outside of my village."

"You couldn't know. That was one of the reasons your mother chose that particular village, because it was so far away from the outside world. She wanted to raise you in a peaceful place where she could teach you to use your powers when you came of proper age. It was never in her plans to be separated from you. Now, she feels you can help her, even untested as you are."

"She feels... How do you know?" Tenya whispered excitedly. "Does my mother communicate with you, as well? Does she send you visions?"

Sindril tipped his head in a slight nod. "She remains in contact with me...not through visions, but through my jeweled staff. Fortunately, the Demon Master is unaware of our communications. As I told you before, he has taken his attention from her these last few years. Now that he spends his time preparing for his siege of the world, she is virtually ignored in the tower of ice. As I said, she feels you are ready to help her in the battle against Zardonne. That's why she sent me to fetch you."

"Oh! Can you contact her now?" Tenya begged, her pulse bumping erratically.

"I'm sorry, Tenya, but I dare not." He shook his head regretfully. "I truly wish I could, for your sake. I know how anxious you must be, but she has refrained from contact these last several days. She fears Zardonne might discover our communications if we use them too often, and she doesn't want your journey jeopardized in any way."

Her disappointment was sharp, but at the same time Tenya had to concede the wisdom of her mother's plans.

Sindril smiled gently. "You will see her soon, Tenya. Never fear."

"All my life, Dianis delighted in telling me that my mother had abandoned me. She said my mother had deliberately run away because she no longer wanted the responsibility of a husband and a young child. I never believed it, not for one moment. I was only three when she left, but I can still remember her. I've kept her memory alive in my mind for sixteen years. I never knew the real reason for her disappearance until now, but I always knew it was not something she had done because she didn't love me."

Tenya's eyes glistened with unshed tears and Sindril touched her hand, his small, dark face compassionate.

"Elea had no other way to speak to you from her prison, but she hoped the visions she sent would prepare you for the time when she would send for you. Believe me, Tenya, your mother has never once forgotten you, not even for a moment."

Tenya smiled and dashed a tear from the corner of one eye. "You love her, too, don't you, Sindril? I can hear it in your voice when you speak of her."

His wizened face held a gentle expression. "I have been with her from the beginning. I was by her side in the first Great Battle and in the second one as well." His face grew grim. "I tried to save her from being taken prisoner by Zardonne, but my magic was too weak. I wanted to try to rescue her from the tower, but she urged me not to do so. She said that I would be more useful to her if I remained free and out of Zardonne's reach. I was not to risk my life any further by attempting to free her."

Tenya reached over and touched his hand. "She was right, Sindril. How else would she have been able to send someone to guide me safely to Zardonne's domain? You must not blame yourself."

His quick grin flashed. "You are very much like your mother," he said, and Tenya felt a thrill at his words.

"How much farther is it to the Plain of Naryn?" she asked, suddenly anxious to continue the journey.

"Several days," he answered, breaking off a piece of roasted chicken and chewing on it. "Once we are through the mountains, we'll have to proceed with extreme caution. If what Hurn says is true, Zardonne's army is on this side of the Belisar River and heading this way. If we make it to the Ferrish Wood, we'll be safe there, for Zardonne's powers are useless in the Wood. We may even be fortunate enough to encounter some of the members of the resistance against Zardonne. They could be very useful to us in helping to free the Mistress."

He had no sooner finished speaking when a tremendous commotion exploded outside the tavern. It sounded as though the heavens themselves had split open, releasing a torrent of booming thunder that rolled deafeningly off the orange rocks of the mountains.

And, above the high-pitched screams and shrieks, someone shouted, *"A Death Rider!"*

CHAPTER 12

A Death Rider?" Tenya started up from the bench, a terrible sense of foreboding sweeping through her.

Beside her, Sindril's face registered shock. The other occupants of the tavern ceased their conversations and leapt up from their tables.

Hurn reached the tavern door ahead of the first man and threw it wide open. Immediately he staggered back, his bearded face blanching. "Heaven save us all, it's the Death Rider back again!"

The men in the tavern quailed and gasped, staring at each other in shock. The clash of thunder from outside charged through the open door, bringing with it a wind that smelled strongly of burning metal and ash. Dust from the tavern floor swirled into tiny, stinging whirlwinds and tankards sitting on the counter rattled along its length.

Tenya flung up her hand to protect her eyes from the blowing dust. Her heart felt as though it had suddenly stopped beating. A Death Rider! Back again to terrorize the little village? Or, did its visit have another purpose?

Her sense of foreboding grew until it threatened to suffocate her. Somehow, she knew the Death Rider's appearance had to do with her. But, just as suddenly, the dread disappeared and she felt oddly calm and detached. She started toward the open door.

Sindril grasped her arm, trying to hold her back. "Tenya, what are you doing? Don't go out there."

"It's all right. I know what I'm doing," she heard herself say, as though someone else spoke through her.

She strode to the open door, pushing against the violent wind that swept through it. Outside, she could see terrified villagers crouching in the dusty street, shielding their faces from the thunder and wind. Two demonic figures stood in front of the tavern.

The Death Rider's gigantic, black body was covered in bristling spines and deformed lumps. Yellow eyes with vertical black slits glared from a face straight out of a nightmare. Spiked teeth gnashed in an oversized jaw that jutted out from underneath a flattened, bulbous nose.

The rider's mount was just as loathsome, a bizarre combination of half-lizard, half-horse. The targ had the body of a horse, but terrible, slavering jaws filled with rows of teeth dominated its huge, scaled head; a forked tongue flicked rapidly in and out of its gaping mouth. Clawed hooves and fiery red eyes completed the grotesque creature.

Tenya took all of this in at a glance. She still felt strangely detached, as if set apart from the unfolding events.

"GIVE ME THE GIRL!" A deep, sepulchral voice boomed from the black demon, overriding the deafening furor.

"We don't know who you mean!" a woman screamed shrilly. "Please, go away and leave us alone."

The Death Rider ignored the woman. "GIVE ME THE GIRL!"

Tenya heard Sindril come up behind her. He pulled at her arm. "Tenya, come away," he urged. "If the Death Rider sees you..."

"He has come for me," she said, remotely.

"Then, all the more reason you should hide," he hissed. "You will do your mother no good if you are seen by one of Zardonne's Death Riders."

Tenya smiled faintly. "On the contrary, I think I will do my mother much good."

Indeed, she knew with sudden certainty she must go out in the street and confront the Death Rider. Her veins sang with that wondrous, enticing power once more, emboldening her. This encounter needed to take place, for only by facing–and defeating– one of the Demon Master's most powerful servants could she know the extent and strength of her own powers.

She slipped from Sindril's restraining hand and stepped out into the chaos of the street. She stopped, facing the black figure and his slavering, snorting mount.

"I'm the one you want," she said clearly, and waited.

The Death Rider's huge head swung toward her, his black, slit eyes blazing. For a moment, her pulse beat erratically and a flicker of uncertainty sparked through her brain. She quelled it quickly, allowing calmness to wash over her once more.

The world around her receded until only her and the Death Rider existed. Even the thunder and voracious wind could not penetrate the vacuum of highly-charged tension surrounding them.

The demon's hideous mouth twisted. "SO, YOU ARE THE ONE? YOU DO NOT SEEM VERY DANGEROUS."

Tenya permitted herself a small smile. "Appearances can be deceiving."

"YOU ARE BUT A PALTRY GIRL," the Death Rider mocked.

"Perhaps, but obviously a girl of whom Zardonne is afraid."

The gigantic monster stiffened perceptibly. "THE DEMON MASTER FEARS NO ONE!"

"Then, why he is so anxious to be rid of me?"

"YOU ARE MERELY A NUISANCE HE WISHES TO EXTERMINATE. HE DOES NOT FEAR YOUR PUNY POWERS."

"I see," Tenya said dryly. "It seems he's going to a lot of trouble simply to rid himself of a *puny* nuisance. How did you find me, by the way?"

"THE OLD WOMAN, MORDIS. SHE CAME SLINKING BACK TO OUR OUTPOST WITH THE NEWS OF YOUR RESCUE BY A LARGE PARTY OF ARMED ASSAILANTS. BUT TRACKING YOU WAS SIMPLE. ZARDONNE HAS EYES AND EARS EVERYWHERE."

Tenya nearly laughed out loud. Trust Mordis to try and save her skin from Zardonne's wrath by embellishing the truth of Sindril's rescue. The old woman certainly would not want to admit that one little man in an outlandish floppy hat and feathered cape had bested her.

"What do you intend to do now?" Tenya asked.

"I WILL TAKE YOU TO ZARDONNE. HE WILL DECIDE WHAT MUST BE DONE WITH YOU."

"Perhaps I will not let you take me to Zardonne."

The yellowish glow in the demon's slit eyes blazed brighter. "YOU DO NOT HAVE A CHOICE!"

"Oh, but I do," she countered softly. If fear existed within her, it was buried too deep to affect her now. A vital, surging power sung through her body, tingling in her fingertips. She would not give in meekly to the demon.

The Death Rider stirred on his hideous mount, as though sensing the leashed power within her. "YOU ARE A FOOL IF YOU BELIEVE YOU CAN DEFEAT ME," he warned.

Tenya did not answer. She made herself appear calm and relaxed, unafraid of the daunting creature before her. In reality, her body vibrated tightly with anticipation, eager to unleash the white fire burning in her veins.

The Death Rider suddenly lifted a hand covered in black spines and pointed at her. A huge ball of green lightning streaked through the air, accompanied by a loud crack of thunder.

Tenya's white shield sprang into being around her body as she leapt backward. The ball of fire missed her and several shocked faces at the open door of the tavern jerked quickly out of the way of the deadly green streak of light. It struck a post by the front door of the tavern, splintering it, and reducing it to a pile of smoldering ashes.

Tenya crouched slightly, watching the Death Rider through narrowed eyes. The white shield tingled around her and she wondered briefly if it would have been strong enough to deflect the Death Rider's murderous ball of fire if she had not leapt out of the way.

The Death Rider hissed in anger, pulling roughly on the reins of his targ as the beast snorted and pranced jerkily. Again, the demon's finger pointed at Tenya and fire flashed from it. Once more she leaped aside, countering with a streak of white fire from her fingertips. It struck the Death Rider fully in the chest and knocked him backward, though not quite unseating him. His glowing yellow eyes blazed to a blinding intensity.

Tenya felt a thrill of satisfaction.

"YOU DARE STRIKE ME?! YOU WILL PAY DEARLY FOR THAT, GIRL."

White fire danced from her fingertips, striking the Death Rider and his mount in several places. The targ screamed as patches of its skin erupted in flame. It jerked convulsively, nearly throwing the Death Rider from its back.

Tendrils of smoke drifted from her strikes on the Death Rider's deformed body. He howled in terrible rage, and flung multiple streaks of green fire toward her. The air thrummed violently with the acrid odors of burning metal and ash and the crack of raging thunder.

Tenya could not dodge all of the Death Rider's fire, but those streaks that made contact bounced harmlessly off her sparkling white shield. Before he could summon more malicious power, she called on the full strength of the white fire in her veins and sent it spinning brilliantly toward the black figure. His horrible shriek rent the air as both he and his mount burst into flames.

For a moment, tongues of bright fire clearly delineated the two hideous figures. The demon's phosphorescent eyes glared out at her in disbelieving fury. Then, a crackling inferno consumed both the Death Rider and his targ, and within seconds, they completely disappeared, smoking ashes scattering on the vicious wind left behind in their wake.

CHAPTER 13

Tenya stared at the spot where the Death Rider had been, vaguely aware of the white glow receding slowly from her skin. She felt marvelously alive and strong, her senses heightened to a fever pitch.

Gradually, she became aware of silence around her and looked up. The thunder and roaring wind had disappeared. The sky had returned to normal, the late afternoon sunlight slanting down from the clear blue. No sound broke the sudden silence that had descended on the village and Tenya noted the frozen faces of the huddled villagers, their shocked expressions and disbelieving stares.

"Tenya, are you all right?" Sindril was the first to move, charging out of the tavern with the feathered cape flapping about his wiry body, his wizened face drawn in anxious lines.

"I'm fine," she replied calmly.

"Whatever possessed you to confront the Death Rider?" he reproached her. "You could have been killed!"

"You're the one who is always urging me to test my powers," she reminded him gently. "Besides, somehow I knew it was important that I challenge him. I'm not certain I can explain it."

Sindril stared at the black spot on the dusty street; the only thing that remained of the formidable Death Rider and his mount. He shook his head in wonder and admiration. "I don't know how you did it, Tenya. Zardonne's creatures are almost impossible to destroy. And, yet, in only a matter of minutes, you reduced one to nothing."

"I feel as though there is something awakening within me; a sense of control and authority...and power. At first, the thought of facing the Death Rider terrified me. I wanted nothing more than to run and hide, hoping it would go away. But then, the fear just disappeared, and in its place I felt this-this great surge of confidence. It's difficult to explain, as I said, but I felt I could challenge the Death Rider and win."

Sindril stared thoughtfully at her. "Your mother will be pleased with how you've grown. Not that she ever doubted your capabilities. She always knew that, someday, those tiny seeds within you would germinate into a wealth of power. That was unquestionable; it was only a matter of time. That's why she didn't summon you sooner. She wanted to give your powers a chance to grow and expand before she called upon you to help her vanquish Zardonne."

Hurn and a host of villagers rushed up to surround them, their faces shining with awe. The tavern keeper laid his hands gently on Tenya's shoulders and looked down into her eyes.

"There is no doubt in anyone's mind, now, that you are who you claim to be, little one. We are all at your service. Tell us how we can help you."

Tenya hesitated, uncertain what to say. The confrontation with the Death Rider had occupied the whole of her attention and she'd forgotten about the villagers, how they would witness the violent encounter and the display of her powers. Some of them stared at her now, dread mingling with their awe. That she could instill such fright in others saddened Tenya, and she wanted to reassure them they had nothing to fear from her.

"My friends," she called to them, raising her voice to reach everyone surrounding her, including those that hung back on the fringes, uncertain and wary. "Twice now, you have been subjected to the terror of a Death Rider's visit. A child of your village has been destroyed by their presence and the rest of you frightened beyond belief. Zardonne and his army are fast approaching, destroying everything in their path. And, he must be stopped."

The only sound heard was the faint tinkling of bells from the goat herd on the side of the mountain. The people of the village waited patiently and silently for her to continue.

"Some of you have been told that I am the daughter of the Mistress of the Wind. Well, it's true. Elea is my mother. You witnessed my battle with the Death Rider so you know that I possess powers, but they are not yet strong enough to destroy Zardonne. I must free my mother from her prison so that, together, we can stop the Demon Master's conquest of the world and send him back through the Dark Rift, once and for all. But, we can't do it alone. We'll need your help."

The crowd murmured. She could see stark fear reflected on many of the weather-worn faces.

"I know you're frightened. Zardonne is powerful...but he is not invincible. If enough of us fight against him, we *can* destroy him. The Mistress defeated him once. She can do so again. If we raise a powerful army to help her, we can put an end to the Demon Master's reign. Many people have already raised arms against him, the Shetii Clan and the horsemen of Coros. Do you wish to sit back meekly, waiting for Zardonne to overrun your village and destroy your children and homes? To force you to submit to his evil will? Or, do you wish to show him that you will fight for the right to peace and harmony, for the right to live in a world free from evil and fear?"

The crowd erupted in shouts and fist shaking.

"We must protect our homes and children!"

"Zardonne must be destroyed!"

Tenya raised her hands, calling for silence. "There's not much time. We must make ready to repel Zardonne's forces when they come through the mountains." She turned to the black-bearded man beside her. "Hurn, you asked what you can do to help. You can be a leader for your people, and the people of the other villages nearby. Organize and prepare them for Zardonne's attack. He won't be expecting resistance, but you must make certain that he encounters it. Sindril and I must continue on our journey to the Plain of Naryn and free the Mistress."

Hurn nodded. "I will send messengers to the other villages and raise an army. We will try to hold off Zardonne for as long as we can, to give you and the Mistress time to plan your attack." He laid a huge hand on Tenya's shoulder. "You have much courage, little one, for one so young. But, be careful. There will be much danger in your journey." He turned to Sindril. "Take good care of her, Sindril."

The little man nodded. "I intend to protect her to the best of my ability."

"That's good enough for me," Hurn said and turned back to the murmuring, shuffling crowd. "You have all heard Tenya's words. We must show Zardonne that he cannot take over the world without a fight from us. I'll need some volunteers to take messages to the other villages and to help organize our forces. Rath, I appoint you as my Second-In-Command. Doron, you will be the Master-Of-Arms. We need to gather as many weapons as we can."

A gangly youth of perhaps seventeen stepped forward out of the crowd. "Hurn, I want to be one of your messengers. I can run very fast."

Hurn smiled at him and clapped him on the shoulder. "So be it, Arabar. I'll compose the messages I want you to take to the other villages and you can be on your way shortly. We must not waste any more time hiding under our beds."

Shouts of agreement went up from the crowd. It amazed Tenya how quickly the villagers had changed from a frightened, cowed people to a people charged with zeal and fighting fever. The Demon Master would not have an easy time of subduing these villagers.

Sindril touched her arm. "Come, Tenya, we must be on our way. With Zardonne's army so close to the mountains, we have no time to lose."

She nodded. Before she could turn to follow him, Hurn's daughter, Sarath, rushed over, handing her a large bundle. "I packed some food for your journey and a woolen cloak for your travel through the mountains," she said. "Please be careful."

Tenya gave her a quick hug. "Thank you, Sarath. I'll be careful, I promise. We'll see each other again soon."

Once more mounted on the murbeest, Tenya and Sindril headed up into the mountains, leaving the small village bustling with activity. Tenya glanced back and saw Hurn standing in the middle of the dusty street, shouting orders right and left, and villagers scrambled to obey him. Satisfied that Tundel was in good hands, she faced forward again.

The narrow, rocky path they followed–that Sindril told her was called the Dagas Pass–wound up the orange mountains in a twisting, serpentine fashion. At times, it hugged the burnished sides of the mountains, dropping off into sheer, dizzying nothingness on one side. The murbeest picked his way carefully over the shale-covered ground. Sindril often crooned to the animal in a soothing voice, encouraging him when he hesitated and calming him when the sheer drop to one side made the beast balk.

Tenya found herself closing her eyes in white-hot fear when the path seemed scarcely wide enough for the murbeest's hooves. She waited with bated breath for the animal to slip over the crumbling edge and send them all plummeting straight down several hundred feet to the spiked tops of the trees far below. She tamped the fear down, telling herself that if she could face a powerful Death Rider without qualm then she could certainly endure this trip up the mountainside.

The trail wound higher into the mountains until it seemed as though they'd climbed into the clear, azure sky itself. The air became noticeably cooler and thinner, with the crisp smell of snow teasing their nostrils. Tenya shivered slightly, feeling the chill penetrate the thin tunic she wore, and rummaged in the bundle Sarath had given her. She pulled out the woolen cloak and wrapped it tightly around her shoulders.

They had only traveled a few hours more when darkness descended rapidly, falling like a thick, cold blanket over the mountains. Sindril's jeweled staff emitted a soft red glow, illuminating the rocky path in front of them.

"We must find shelter for the night," he said. "It would be foolish to travel through the mountains in the darkness, even with the light from my staff."

Tenya agreed. One misstep and they would all end up dead on the rocks and trees in the valley far below.

Sindril found a dark depression in the side of the mountain that proved to be a wide, shallow cave, large enough for the three of them to enter. He tied the murbeest to an outcropping near the entrance and entered the dark cave, Tenya right behind him. His staff dimly illuminated the hard-packed floor and black-streaked walls.

"It's not very luxurious." Sindril grinned. "But, at least it will give us some shelter from the cold night."

They prepared for sleep immediately, foregoing supper and a fire. Sindril didn't want to risk attracting any of Zardonne's servants who might be lurking in the mountains. The knowledge that the Death Rider had so quickly tracked them to the village of Tundel disturbed him, and he didn't want to make it any easier for Zardonne's spies to find them again.

Tenya hugged the warm cloak tightly about her and laid down on the rock floor. She could see the silhouette of the murbeest against the entrance of the cave, his tissue-thin ears flicking on either side of his tapered head. He snorted softly and Tenya sent a silent message to him, reaching out with tendrils of calming thought. The creature immediately became silent, rainbow eyes turning in the darkness to look at her. A wave of quiet trust flowed from the murbeest across the cave to where she lay on the hard ground and she smiled softly in the darkness.

Although she had calmed the uneasy murbeest, she found it more difficult to soothe her own troubling thoughts. Sleep eluded her as she recalled what had happened earlier in the village, and she wondered what lay ahead beyond the mountains. She recalled Hurn's disturbing words of the chaos and destruction in the villages Zardonne's army had attacked, his description of the Demon Master's relentless push forward through the land weighing heavily on her mind.

One unsettling thought burned brighter than the rest. What if, by the time she reached Zardonne's domain, found a way to avoid the deadly traps and monsters that infested his land, and freed her mother, it was too late? The Demon Master might have already forced his evil presence on all the lands. It would be virtually impossible to overcome him then.

She stirred on the hard ground, unable to find a comfortable position to accommodate her restless mind. Beside her, Sindril lay quiet, his face hidden in the folds of his feathered cape.

Mordis' description of the Plain of Naryn had been chilling– quicksand and strangling vines and the Guardians; hideous creatures, half-bird and half-human, that could tear a person to pieces in seconds. According to the old woman, these terrible creatures patrolled everywhere on the Plain. How could she and Sindril slip by them unnoticed? It was too much to hope that word of her escape from Mordis had not yet reached the ears of the Demon Master. Surely the Death Riders had informed him by now. And, surely he would increase the guard around the tower of ice.

She tried to empty her mind for sleep and had barely closed her eyes when a spine-chilling shriek split the night air, sending her upright in panic. Beside her, Sindril jumped to his feet, his small, wizened face a pale blur in the darkness.

Over by the entrance, the murbeest snorted and pranced, jerking against his tether.

"What was that?" Tenya whispered, her heart thudding hard.

"Stay here," Sindril commanded. He crept to the entrance of the shallow cave. Tenya could barely make out his hunched form against the darker rock wall.

Another unearthly wail rent the air and Tenya jumped again, the sound sending shivers of dread down her spine. She had never heard anything like it before. What sort of creature made such a sound?

Despite Sindril's warning to remain where she was, she felt compelled to crawl to the entrance and see what shrieked so horribly outside.

She dropped down beside Sindril's still figure. He glanced quickly at her but said nothing.

At first, she could see only thousands of tiny pinpoints of glittering light in the dark sky. Nothing moved on the narrow, rocky path in front of the cave or to either side of it. The far edge of the path disappeared in a sheer drop, and she could not imagine any kind of creature being able to cling to the vertical cliff wall.

"What is it, Sindril?" she whispered. "What made that awful noise?"

Silently, the little man pointed to the star-sprinkled night sky.

Then, she finally saw it.

The creature's wingspan was wide and almost blocked out the moon that hung like a glowing ball in the inky sky. The gigantic head looked nearly human; long ropes of hair streamed behind it as it flew. The wings beat ponderously and the strange being cruised slowly past the cave entrance where she and Sindril crouched. Its eyes suddenly lit up with yellow phosphorescent beams, and swept the sides of the mountains like twin torchlights.

"Get back!" Sindril hissed, drawing Tenya abruptly away, deeper into the dark recesses of their shelter. The two beams of light narrowly missed them, raking the top of the entrance instead.

Tenya lay on the hard ground under Sindril's slight weight, her heart beating painfully against her ribs. Though she'd never seen one before, it occurred to her what the creature might be, and dread nearly suffocated her.

Sindril's next words confirmed her suspicions.

"It's one of Zardonne's Guardians."

CHAPTER 14

I t seemed like hours that she and Sindril lay on the hard-packed floor of the shallow cave, not daring to move. All the while, the Guardian flew slowly back and forth across the face of the moon, searching with its beaming eyes. Every now and then, it would emit its terrible shriek and Tenya's skin would crawl.

She concentrated on soothing the agitated murbeest's mind, trying to keep the animal calm so that he wouldn't attract the attention of the dreadful flying creature. Neither she nor Sindril had any doubt as to what, or more specifically, for whom, the Guardian searched.

The sparkle of stars had faded from the lightening sky when, at last, the ponderous Guardian emitted one last shriek and swung away toward the southeast, its huge wings beating the air with dull, rhythmic thuds. They waited until the creature became a mere speck in the pale gray sky, then they sat up, gazing at each other.

"Obviously, your escape from the Death Rider has not gone unnoticed by the Demon Master," Sindril said.

"Do you think he'll realize we're heading for the Plain of Naryn?" Tenya asked, worriedly. "I'm afraid he'll set up such a heavy guard around the tower of ice that we'll never get close enough to free my mother."

"Perhaps," Sindril said thoughtfully. "But, perhaps not. The Demon Master may be so certain of his powers that he'll believe he and his army can stop us before we get near the Plain of Naryn. He may think it unnecessary to guard the Mistress's prison."

"Do you think the Guardian will come back?"

He shook his head. "I don't know. But, we must be very cautious from now on. We're advancing farther into enemy territory, and Zardonne is certain to have more of his servants searching the countryside for us."

"Maybe we should continue on our way. I couldn't sleep now, in any case."

Sindril nodded. "Yes, I think you're right. We should move on while we still have a bit of darkness to conceal us. Later, when it's light, we'll have to be extremely careful to keep ourselves hidden as much as possible."

They rose from the rocky floor and dusted dirt from their clothes. "How much farther do we have to go?" Tenya asked.

Sindril went to the murbeest and untied him. "Let's see. It'll take at least a day to reach the Sandos

Peak. From there, we follow Morgana Pass down the other side of the mountains. That will take another day, unless there's a lot of snow…"

"Snow? In the summer?"

"Mountain seasons are quite different. Summer here means possibly a foot or two of snow in the pass, which will delay us perhaps another day. In winter, the pass is buried in deep snow and almost impossible to travel through. The Ferrish Wood lies roughly three miles from the foot of the Pass. We'll stop there for a rest and to plan our rescue attempt of the Mistress. There is someone in the Ferrish Wood I want you to meet. Besides, we'll be safe there from Zardonne. His power can't penetrate the Wood, much to his great disappointment, I imagine."

Tenya tried to contemplate his words amidst her own impatience and frustration at the thought of traveling another two or three days just to reach the Ferrish Wood. Then, they still had to cross the Belisar River before they even approached the fringes of the Plain of Naryn. She shuddered to think how far Zardonne's army could march before she and Sindril could attempt to free her mother.

Although they both kept a sharp eye out for the Guardian, they didn't see any sign of it during the long, tiring climb to the top of the mountains. Tenya hoped the creature had given up its search and returned to its home on the Plain of Naryn. She wondered uneasily how Zardonne would react to the news that she had not yet been captured. Despite Sindril's reassuring words, she still worried that the Demon Master might harm her mother or put so many obstacles in their path that it would be impossible for them to free her.

Dawn eventually arrived in earnest, bright and sunny. The path became steeper and the air thinner and colder; so cold, Tenya feared her nose would freeze and fall off. She wrapped the woolen cloak tightly about her body, but still the frigid air cut through her clothing to tease her shivering skin.

Fortunately, the trail no longer skirted the side of the mountain in a dizzying ribbon. Solid rock loomed on either side of them, offering a false sense of security. They encountered no dangers that day as they climbed toward the summit of the towering mountains. Nothing seemed out of the ordinary.

"Sandos Peak, where we are headed, is the highest peak in the Jamal Mountains chain," Sindril told Tenya, as the murbeest picked his way carefully along the rock path. "From there, one can see for hundreds of miles in every direction. All, except for the Ferrish Wood, that is."

"Why can't you see the Ferrish Wood?" Tenya asked. "I thought you said it was only three miles from the bottom of the mountains."

"There is a spell placed on the Wood so that–to most people–it appears to be a vast, empty plain, devoid of life. Very few have ever seen the real Wood."

"That's curious. Have you seen it?"

"Oh, yes, I'm pleased to say that I have. My magic is apparently strong enough to see through the illusion, and I've even had the pleasure of meeting some of the Shetii Clan. Believe me, it is a great honor when one is chosen to communicate with them.

They keep most of the world out by their magic. Only a select few are allowed access to them."

"Will I be able to see the Wood?"

Sindril grinned. "Oh, indeed, you will. Your mother was born of the Shetii Clan."

Astounded, Tenya could only stare at him. "Why didn't you tell me this before?"

He shrugged. "I didn't want to overwhelm you with too many revelations at once."

The Ardis Valley and Dianis, with all her petty hatreds and jealousies, seemed far removed, now. Even her father Bentar, for as much as she loved him, had receded into the background of her thoughts. There'd been so much to learn in such a short time. And, apparently, there was more to learn still!

Her life had changed so quickly–and so unexpectedly. *She'd* changed. She was no longer the shy, quiet girl afraid to open her mouth for fear Dianis would strike her. Nor was she the lonely girl who wept for the mother she'd never known and the father she'd lost to depression. She was the child of a magical people, endowed with powers that seemed to grow stronger with each passing hour. She'd done battle with evil forces and had survived. She'd traveled into unknown and dangerous territories, planning ahead for more battles that could spell her own death. Yet, she did so willingly–even eagerly–her concern more for her imprisoned mother than for her own safety.

Her thoughts turned to the small, mountain village they'd left far behind. "Sindril, do you think your friend, Hurn, will be able to gather enough people and arms to fight Zardonne?"

Sindril nodded decisively. "Hurn is a good man and a brave one, too. He'll see that Tundel and the other villages are ready to meet Zardonne's army when it comes. Not all of the Demon Master's minions have magical powers. He commands a great many mortal beasts, some of which, I'm ashamed to say, are even humans. Those can be killed with ordinary weapons. If enough people rise against them, they can do a great deal of harm to Zardonne's troops."

He brought the murbeest to a halt. "Let's stop for a short rest. I don't know about you, but I'm starving."

They huddled close against the shaggy side of the animal, trying to keep warm as they munched on bread and cheese from the bundle Sarath had given them. When their hunger was somewhat sated, they remounted and continued on.

In a few places, the steep pass through the mountains forced them to dismount the murbeest and lead him on foot up the rocky slopes. Tenya didn't mind the exercise. It kept her thoughts off the troubles that lay ahead, and the relentless, biting cold that penetrated her garments. Silently, she thanked the young girl, Sarath, for her thoughtful gesture of the cloak. Without it, she would be suffering a great deal more.

By nightfall, they had reached Sandos Peak, an impressive, towering edifice covered with a cap of glistening snow. A howling wind snapped Tenya's hair and cloak viciously about her. She hid her face against the murbeest's shaggy shoulder, shielding her eyes from the stinging pellets of snow whipped up by the wind.

"This way!" Sindril shouted in her ear, the words almost carried away by the savage gusts of wind. He had to hold his floppy hat tightly squashed against his head with one hand or lose it to the mountain.

Another cave became their shelter for the night. Taller and deeper than the one they had stopped in farther down the mountain, it seemed to run far back into the orange rock, with several dark tunnels branching off in many directions.

Tenya entered cautiously, straining her eyes to see through the darkness. Despite Sindril's staff lighting the way, she feared going in too far, in case they couldn't find their way back to the entrance. She was also afraid that some kind of dangerous creature claimed the cave as home. Yet, Sindril seemed to know exactly where to go. He led them to one of the tunnels, slightly wider and taller than the others.

The red glow from his jeweled staff lit up the glistening rock walls. A short distance from the entrance, the tunnel opened into a fairly large cavern. The white, ashy remains of a dead campfire lay in the middle of the rocky floor and a pile of dried wood and branches lay heaped against one wall. Obviously, this cavern had been used as a shelter before.

"Do you know this place?" Tenya asked.

"Yes. I often seek shelter here in my travels through the mountains. Not the most lavish of quarters, but certainly better than sleeping out in the cold and blowing snow."

They made a small fire, confident the glow from the embers could not be seen from outside. The crackling tongues of flame comforted Tenya and she crouched close to them, warming her chilled hands and toes. Although cold pervaded the cavern, the absence of the wind was a blessing.

When her body had thawed sufficiently, Tenya rummaged in the bundle that Sarath had given them. In addition to more bread and cheese, she found two of the delicious chickens that Hurn had roasted, and a flask of red wine.

Between her and Sindril, they devoured one of the chickens, half a loaf of bread and a huge wedge of cheese, washing it all down with sips of cool wine. The murbeest contentedly munched on a pile of dried grasses heaped in one corner of the cavern. Sindril had obviously prepared the cavern well, with food for the animal as well as wood for the fire, for it would have been extremely difficult to find either on this snow-covered peak.

After eating, Tenya sat on the hard ground drowsily staring into the flames of the fire, her mind pleasantly quiet and peaceful. There would be time enough tomorrow to deal with the unsettling thoughts that had crowded her mind for the last several days. Fatigue had settled deep into her bones and she wanted to think of nothing other than sleep.

Ever kind and thoughtful, Sindril said, "Sleep now, Tenya. I'll take the first watch."

She nodded gratefully. "Wake me when it's my turn."

"I will," he assured her.

Tenya lay down beside the fire, pulling the cloak tightly about her, and almost instantly fell asleep, despite the hardness of the cold, stone floor.

She awakened much later to find the fire had gone out and her body had stiffened from the cold. Sindril sat across from her, a dark silhouette against the cave's wall.

"How did you sleep?" he asked, when she sat up.

"Surprisingly well," she moaned, her cramped muscles protesting movement of any kind. "What time is it? Is it my turn for the watch?"

Sindril stood up. "It's time to leave."

"I thought you were going to wake me so I could take a turn at the night watch." She narrowed her eyes suspiciously. "Did you sleep at all last night?"

"Now I know why I like to travel alone," he complained. "No one can nag me, then."

Tenya sighed and shook her head. "What am I going to do with you?"

"You can help me pack our things and load up the murbeest." He gave her an impish grin.

Outside the cave, sunlight on the brilliant white snow almost blinded them after the relative darkness of the cavern. The howling wind from the night before had abated, but a stiff breeze still raised tiny whirlwinds of snow from the crusty blanket.

Sindril moved away from the mouth of the cave. "Come, Tenya. I want to show you something."

She followed him to the edge of a rocky promontory that seemed to hang out into space. With some trepidation, she moved up beside him, and then caught her breath in stunned fascination.

A breathtaking vista of forest and plains stretched out before her. From this height, the trees appeared like a green, uneven carpet, and the streams like bright, silver threads woven through it. She could see for miles and miles, the view so overwhelming that she held her breath at the sight.

Looking down, she saw the narrow trail they had followed earlier, winding up through the burnished orange rock like a twisting black serpent. From this distance, she couldn't see the small village of Tundel nestled at the foot of the Pass, but farther away, half-concealed by the trees, she could just make out tiny clusters of houses–other villages in the surrounding countryside.

"It's beautiful!" she managed at last, releasing her pent-up breath in a frosty puff.

"Come and see the view from this side." Sindril led her across the crisp blanket of snow to the other side of the peak. She followed eagerly, expecting to see much of the same.

Looking down, the spectacle that awaited her on this side astounded her; a glittering, emerald-green forest that stretched as far as the eye could see. The golden rays of the rising sun touched the tops of tall, thin trees and the forest seemed to shimmer in the still morning air. A faint mist blurred the edges and rose in gentle swirls to disappear against the brightening sky.

The brightness of the foliage against the pink-gold sky and the soft trails of mist along the edges gave the impression of an otherworldly place rising magically out of the quietness of the morning air. Peace and tranquility caressed her as she gazed raptly into the enchanted forest.

"Is that the Ferrish Wood?" she breathed.

He nodded. "Beautiful, isn't it?"

"It's incredible! And, you say most people can only see a desolate plain down there? It's so hard to imagine, when all I see is the most extraordinary sight I've ever beheld."

"That's because you belong there, Tenya. You feel a kinship with the forest and its magic, so it is visible to you."

She stared down at the Wood, a strong, powerful pull tugging at her soul. She could hardly wait to reach it and enter its cool, ethereal depths.

CHAPTER 15

As Sindril had feared, snow had fallen in the Morgana Pass. The way was not impassable, but the going was more arduous. In places, the drifts piled so high that it took them the better part of an hour to force their way through...only to find another, even higher drift to contend with on the other side.

By the evening of the first day in the Pass, Tenya found herself exhausted and soaking wet. Her feet felt like two blocks of ice and it seemed to take all her strength to move one in front of the other. While she had been pushing her way through the deep snow, the cloak had helped to deflect some of the cold and she had worked up a warm sweat. Now, with the dark blanket of night descending around them, and the leaden exhaustion that dragged at her body, the insidious cold seeped back into her bones. Wet and chilled, she shivered uncontrollably.

Sindril, on the other hand, seemed little affected by the deep snow or the bone-chilling cold. His unflagging cheerfulness served to keep Tenya from giving up totally and sinking wearily to the frozen ground in submission.

They spent the first night in the Morgana Pass in a huge snowdrift they hollowed out into a shallow cave. The absence of wood prevented them from lighting a fire, but Sindril's jeweled staff gave off a faint, glowing heat that sent small rivulets of condensed snow trickling down the sides of the snow cave.

Though she insisted she was too tired to be hungry, Sindril convinced Tenya to eat some of the cold chicken. Their trek on the morrow would be no easier, he'd reasoned, and she would need to keep up her strength for the ordeal.

Afterward, she lay huddled in the meager warmth of the woolen cloak, wondering tiredly if the night would again be shattered by the screech of the searching Guardian.

With a soft snort, the murbeest folded his legs and lay down beside her, his rainbow eyes whirling in the dim red glow of Sindril's staff. Tenya snuggled close to the animal, burying her face in his soft, dun-colored fur. The animal's warm breath fanned her cheek and she smiled wearily, allowing fatigue to pull her down into the dim netherworld of sleep.

The next day dawned gray and overcast. Great piles of ominous clouds shrouded the towering peaks above them.

Sindril sniffed the air like an animal. "I think we're going to get snow today. We'd better make as much progress as we can before the storm comes."

Tenya nodded, trying to ease her cramped, cold muscles. The thought of pushing through endless drifts of snow once more did not appeal to her at all. "Why don't I use my fire to melt *all* of the snow?"

Sindril's white teeth flashed in his grin. "That's a good idea. But, you don't have to melt all the snow– only the deeper drifts to allow us to pass through."

She was finding it much easier to call upon the white fire that burned in her veins. Her control over the ability was improving. But, she used it only when necessary to melt paths through the larger snowdrifts, afraid she might lessen its power by wielding it in wanton abandonment. In the very near future she would have need of its full strength.

"Why didn't I think of this yesterday?" she said, at one point. "I could have saved us a lot of slogging through deep snow."

"Hardship is good for a person," Sindril replied, cheerfully. "It helps to build character."

"You *would* say something like that," she groaned, picking up a handful of snow and throwing it at him.

The storm that had been building all morning on the mountaintops descended on Morgana Pass early in the afternoon. At first, only a few lazy flakes fell from the sky. Then with frightening speed, they increased in number and gathered into a blowing white fury that cut off all view of the winding path that led down the mountainside. Tenya and Sindril clung tightly to the furry sides of the murbeest and trudged on into the stinging wind, Tenya trusting the guidance and instincts of Sindril to keep them going in the right direction. She could see nothing of the trail and the blinding snow made it almost impossible to keep her eyes open.

"Should we stop?" she shouted at Sindril.

"This won't last long," he shouted back over his shoulder. "These mountain storms soon blow themselves out. We'll keep going."

As usual, the little man proved to be right. By late afternoon, the wild snowstorm had spent itself, easing off once more to a few lazy flakes, and then stopping altogether.

"How much further is it?" Tenya asked, as they trekked through the freshly fallen snow.

"We're about halfway down the Pass. I estimate we should reach the valley floor the day after tomorrow. That is, if we don't have to contend with any more snowstorms."

Disappointment pricked her. The lure of the Ferrish Wood burned strongly in her veins. She could hardly wait to see the birthplace of her mother and the magical people who were her kin. Still, not much could be done to hurry their progress down the steep, snow-smothered trail.

The third night on the mountain turned out to be as cold and miserable as the first two, and Tenya was beginning to wonder if she'd ever be warm again. Snuggling against the furry side of the murbeest helped some, but the frozen ground still made sleeping a light, fitful affair. She brightened somewhat when Sindril assured her they'd soon be out of the snow and down on the warmer slopes of the mountains.

The next day, they didn't encounter any more snowstorms as they continued through the Pass, and, as Sindril had promised, the going became easier and warmer when they left the higher elevation of snow-capped peaks and descended to the lower slopes. Tenya even found she could shed the heavy cloak.

Scraggly, stunted trees grew out of cracks in the orange rock, along with patches of coarse grass for the murbeest to nibble on. Occasionally, they'd stop for a rest, sitting on sun-warmed boulders and gazing down into the valley below. On one such occasion, Tenya noticed a dark smudge against the far, shimmering horizon and stared curiously at it. "What is that, Sindril?" She pointed.

He shaded his eyes and peered toward it. After a moment, he lowered his hand. "No doubt that's smoke from a burning village," he said, grimly. "The Belisar River lies in that direction."

Tenya stared at the smudge, agonizingly recalling the purpose of their journey. For a short while, she'd been able to forget the Demon Master and his evil, in the face of the long, hard trek through the snowy Pass. Now, it came home to her again, a brutal reminder that Zardonne and his army were wantonly destroying families and homes.

That night, they built a small fire and ate a supper of chicken, bread and cheese. The murbeest munched on the clumps of tough grass that grew on the fringes of the little clearing where they had made their camp.

"What will we do once we reach the Ferrish Wood?" Tenya asked, as they sat by the crackling fire.

"We must contact Hanifar," the little man replied. "He's the leader of the Shetii Clan. He'll be able to tell us what progress the resistance has made against Zardonne and how far his army has advanced. Also, I plan to ask him for volunteers to help us in our rescue attempt of the Mistress. Just the two of us alone will not be enough, I think."

Tenya nodded, trying not to think too deeply about the deadly traps on the Plain of Naryn. At the back of her mind gnawed a little nagging doubt that her powers had not developed enough to combat the Gate of Death, strangling vines and the Guardians. She dared not voice this doubt to Sindril, for fear he would think her weak and cowardly. She couldn't be certain she could live up to his total confidence in her, nor to that of the villagers they had left behind. They looked upon her as the savior of their village.

Sometimes, she thought wearily, *being a person gifted with magical powers is not as enviable as one might think.*

"This time, Sindril, I will take the first watch," she said, firmly. "You will get some sleep. And, that's an order."

"Nag, nag, nag," the little man complained good-naturedly. He pulled his hat down over his eyes and wrapped himself in his feathered cape, falling asleep almost immediately.

Tenya hugged her knees to her chest and glanced about. A deep silence had descended on the night. The stars had not yet appeared in the inky sky and only darkness showed beyond the wavering circle of light cast by the small fire.

Despite the quiet, she felt a pinprick of unease. Even with Sindril only a few feet away and the murbeest still busily cropping grass off to one side of the clearing, she felt very much alone in the dark night.

She scanned the sky, but could see nothing against the thick blanket of clouds. Even had the Guardian been up there, cruising slowly in its ponderous flight, she doubted she would have been able to spot it, unless its eyes were lit up with their yellow beams.

She listened intently, but no sound save the faint munching of the murbeest came to her ears. She glanced toward the animal. He seemed quite calm, his rainbow eyes bright with their natural, vibrant colors. Surely, if something dangerous lurked out there in the darkness, the animal would sense it and react.

Tenya relaxed a little. A warm breeze riffled through her long, dark hair and the last of the winter chill left her bones. As beautiful and majestic as the mountains were, she didn't know if she would want to repeat the journey she and Sindril had just made through them.

She glanced toward the murbeest again. This time, the animal appeared to be asleep, translucent membranes covering his large eyes. Again, she felt that lonely sensation of being the only creature awake on the entire mountainside.

She stared into the fire, mesmerized by the flickering flames. Every now and then, she would rouse herself to scan the dark skies or the surrounding shadows. Nothing stirred. Faint snores issued from the huddled form of Sindril a few feet away.

She glanced at him, smiling faintly. She had grown quite fond of the strange little man since his dramatic rescue of her. She could understand why her mother placed such faith and trust in him. He had proven over and over again to be a loyal and steadfast friend.

A soft snuffling noise came from behind her. She started and glanced over her shoulder. Relief flooded through her when she realized the sound had been made by the murbeest stirring in his sleep, one of his tissue-thin ears flicking in time to his dreams.

Tenya forced herself to relax the tightly strung muscles quivering across her shoulders. Of course, it would not do to relax *too* much, she realized. She still needed to remain alert, but at the same time, she didn't want to be jumping at every little noise or shadow.

The mountains really are magnificent, she decided. Tucked away in the Ardis Valley, and never venturing far from it, she had never seen such strange and beautiful country as she and Sindril had traveled this last week. Of course, it had its drawbacks–the hideous little sand beetle of the Targon Plains, the demon beast, the cold and snow of the upper mountain reaches.

If the nature of their journey had not been so serious, she reflected, she would rather enjoy traipsing around the countryside with Sindril and the murbeest. It would be a great adventure, without the threat of Zardonne and his army to contend with. She could even put up with the sand beetles and other dangerous creatures because their deadliness did not spring from the ruthless cruelty and conscious evil of the Demon Master and his minions.

She added another stick of wood to the fire, which sent sparks flying up into the still night air, and settled back to contemplate the orange flames once more.

What will tomorrow bring? She wondered, a little uneasily. Up until now, she and Sindril had encountered only isolated and individual elements of Zardonne's evil, which so far she had been able to defeat. But, what would happen if she met up with several of the Demon Master's servants at once, or, worse still, Zardonne himself? The white fire seemed to be strong and her ability to use it grew steadily every day, even every hour, but would it be powerful enough to stand up against the concerted powers of the Demon Master or his Death Riders?

These questions milled constantly in her mind, coming back again and again to haunt her. Always, that nagging doubt and uncertainty concerned her. *After all,* she thought wryly, *discovering that one is the daughter of a sorceress of the Shetii Clan, and is gifted with strange and dangerous powers, takes some getting used to.* Not to mention, the idea that everyone expected her to battle the creature of terrible evil and save the world from his destruction. If that wasn't a weighty burden to bear...it seemed to her she could be forgiven the misgivings and doubts that assailed her.

A slight noise came from her left, among the dark shadows beyond the flickering light of the fire. She started up nervously, searching the darkness for the source of the sound. She couldn't see anything and the noise didn't come again. She glanced first at Sindril, then the murbeest, and noted that both still slept soundly. She wished that she, too, could close her eyes and drift off into that blessed oblivion, but that would be selfish. She had been on watch for only a few hours and Sindril deserved to sleep as much as possible, having spent the majority of their journey through the mountains wide-awake and on guard.

She stood up and stretched her arms and back to relieve the stiffness and tension. Still on her feet, she tilted her head back to view the towering edifice of rock that rose darkly up into the starry night sky. She shivered slightly at the sheer grandeur and majesty of the peaks, feeling tiny and insignificant before them.

Again, she heard a noise behind her and whirled, searching the shadows. Beside a flat rock that looked like a table balanced on a pointed pedestal, she thought she detected a brief flash of movement. She stepped forward, cautiously, heart pounding and eyes searching the shadows by the unusual rock formation. The movement came again. Something, or someone, definitely lurked behind the rock.

Tenya hesitated, wondering if she should awaken Sindril. Yet, what if it turned out to be only a harmless mountain creature, drawn by curiosity to the fire? Sindril needed his sleep and she hated to wake him unnecessarily.

Another movement; a flash of white behind the rock, but she couldn't get a good look at it. Her pulse beat erratically. She knew the shield and white fire could be summoned easily if necessary, but she didn't know what kind of creature threatened her, if indeed it posed a danger at all.

She took a few more hesitant steps forward, eyes intent on the black shadows where she had seen movement. Suddenly, she heard a rushing sound behind her and whirled in time to see an apparition in filthy rags dart out from behind a cluster of rocks to where Sindril lay beside the fire. Cackling insanely, the creature plucked the little man's jeweled staff from the ground and delivered a sharp kick to his side. He came awake with a startled grunt.

Before Tenya could react, a powerful grip seized her from behind, knocking the breath from her. Dangling limply from her assailant's huge arms, she stared in shock at a triumphant, leering Mordis, who clutched Sindril's staff in both her grimy hands.

CHAPTER 16

Tenya cursed herself for having allowed the old woman and her giant slave to sneak up on her and Sindril. She should have been more alert, instead of gazing dreamily into the fire and letting it mesmerize her.

Mordis leered at Sindril, who stood quietly, his small, wizened face showing no expression. "Ah, ha, you little toad!" she crowed, triumphantly. "I've got you now! You ain't so big and brave without this here little stick, now, are you?"

Sindril said nothing. He glanced at Tenya, hanging limply from Falgar's powerful arms. "Are you all right, Tenya?" he asked quietly.

She grimaced. "Yes, I'm fine. I'm sorry, Sindril. I should have been more alert. She used Falgar as a diversion to lure me away from you."

The old woman cackled gleefully. "That was a good trick, wasn't it?" She sidled over to where Falgar stood and glanced slyly up at Tenya. "Thought you could escape old Mordis, did you, girlie? Not on your life! The Demon Master wants you and I'll see that he gets you."

Tenya stared down at her wrinkled face and wondered why she had once been so terrified of the old woman. She was nothing more than a pathetic, filthy, old hag. Of course, at the time of her kidnapping, Tenya had never realized that she possessed magical powers and had no reason to be frightened of her abductors.

Mordis believed she had gained the upper hand by taking Sindril's jeweled staff that–to her way of thinking–contained all the magic she feared. The old crone didn't realize how much Tenya's powers had grown since the last time they'd seen each other. Even now, the leashed power in her body tingled faintly. She could call upon it at any time. Mordis, however, seemed completely unaware, reveling in the recapture of her most valuable prize.

"You and this little toad have led me a merry race across the countryside," the old woman said. "But, I've got you now and you're not getting away this time." Her wrinkled face darkened. "I endured a lot of abuse over you, girl. Zardonne's Death Riders almost killed me when they found out you had escaped. I had to do some fast talking to get free of that trouble." She poked Tenya in the ribs with Sindril's staff. Tenya didn't flinch.

"No escape this time, girlie. The Demon Master awaits his prize and old Mordis intends to see that he gets it, and that I get my reward." She cast a wicked glance upon Sindril. "As for you, little man, I think I'll let Falgar here have a little fun with you first before he kills you." Her dark eyes glittered fiercely. "That'll teach you to interfere with me."

Sindril stared back at her, saying nothing. He seemed quite unconcerned by the threat. That only made Mordis angry and her face flushed an unbecoming shade of dark red.

Tenya decided the time had come to end the old woman's gloating; time to let her know that she did not have the upper hand as she believed, and that she, Tenya, was no longer the confused, frightened girl of a week ago.

Her body tingled with just enough white fire to infuse a painful shock into Falgar's thick arms. Grunting in surprise, he released her to grab his arms and vigorously rub them. Tenya fell to the ground. She looked up and, for the first time since she'd met him, saw a startled expression on his round, disfigured face.

Mordis gaped. "What are you doing, you fool? Why did you let her go?"

The giant shook his head slowly, his wet, slack lips opening and closing without sound. He backed away from Tenya.

"She'll run, you idiot!" Mordis hobbled over and grabbed Tenya's arm–and yanked her hand away just as fast. She stared at her skin, shock flitting across her wrinkled face before she turned a glare on Tenya.

"That's right, Mordis." Tenya calmly stood, her skin glowing faintly from the white fire pulsing though her veins. "My powers are no longer ineffective. They've grown considerably since last we met. You could subdue and frighten me then, but no longer."

"I don't believe you," Mordis snapped, her gaze narrowing. "This is just some kind of trick." She turned to the hulking Falgar. "Grab her before she gets away, you fool! What's the matter with you? She's only a small girl."

The simple-minded giant, so accustomed to doing the old woman's bidding, shuffled toward Tenya, holding out his huge hands to snatch her up once more.

Without moving, Tenya sent a circle of white fire to surround him. He stopped abruptly, flinging his hands up in front of his face to shield it from the silent flames. He whimpered softly, abject terror flooding his disfigured features. Tenya steeled herself to ignore it. He was no doubt a helpless pawn in the hands of the horrible old woman and the Demon Master, but he had to be stopped.

Mordis' wrinkled face twisted with impotent rage. She held up Sindril's staff, pointing the jeweled end at Tenya. "You're not the only one with magic, girl," she hissed. "I have the toad's magical staff."

"Do you know how to use it?" Tenya challenged.

Mordis scowled. "I'm a quick learner."

Obviously, it had never occurred to her that she might have to use it. She probably thought the mere threat of possessing the staff would be enough to make Sindril and Tenya cower. She continued to brandish it menacingly, hoping, no doubt, that something would trigger the magic.

"Give up, old woman," Sindril said, cheerfully. "You know you're beaten."

"Shut up!" Mordis spun on her heel to include him in the fierce glitter of her eyes, swinging the staff between him and Tenya. She shot a quick glance at Falgar, who still cowered inside the glowing circle of white fire. Obviously aware she could expect no help from him, she shook the jeweled staff furiously. "Work, you stupid stick!"

Tenya exchanged an amused glance with Sindril. Now that the initial shock of Mordis' and Falgar's ambush had subsided, and Tenya knew that her powers would be strong enough to overcome any tricks the old woman might have up her filthy sleeve, she could actually find some humor in the situation. One thing she had to give the horrid, old creature credit for was tenacity. Despite all the odds being against her, she still refused to give in.

"Well, Tenya, what do you think we should do with these two?" Sindril asked, conversationally.

"I think throwing them over the side of the mountain would be an appropriate fate," she answered.

A momentary flash of fear in Mordis' eyes rewarded her. The old woman licked her lips and then scowled once more. She jabbed the staff menacingly at them, but Tenya noted with amusement that she also moved back a step.

Sindril shook his head. "No, no, that would be too quick." He tapped his pointed chin with one finger. "I think a more fitting punishment would be to tie them to some rocks and leave them to the mercy of the mountain creatures."

"Are the mountain creatures particularly nasty?" Tenya angled her head toward him, purposefully baiting the old woman and ignoring her at the same time.

"Oh, yes, some of them definitely are. I'm sure Mordis knows what they're like, through her extensive travels. They can be quite dangerous."

"You don't scare me," Mordis blustered, shaking the staff. "Don't pretend you're not helpless without this thing. You're just trying to bluff me."

"Then, what about your friend Falgar there?" Tenya pointed out. "How do you explain the circle of fire?"

"It's just a trick, an illusion! He's such a brainless idiot, he doesn't realize it." She brandished Sindril's staff. "This is where the real magic lies. You're too young to have any real powers. I'm not afraid of you. But, *you* should be afraid of *me*, now that I have this staff."

She touched the dark jewel on the tip of the staff. A flash of red light and an audible crackling caused her to drop it with a startled cry; she stared at it as though it had turned into a fanged-serpent.

Quick as a flash, Sindril darted forward and snatched up the staff. He waggled a finger playfully in front of Mordis' shocked face. "You see? You really shouldn't play with something you don't understand. It's liable to turn on you when you least expect it."

Her toothless mouth opening and closing in wordless fury, the old crone appeared to be on the verge of stamping her foot, like a spoiled, willful child thwarted in her efforts to have her own way. Tenya sent another circle of silent white fire to surround her, and the furious old woman screeched and covered her face.

"A somewhat realistic illusion, wouldn't you say, Mordis?" Tenya asked her.

Sindril chuckled. "Well, now that *that* nonsense is over with, what *will* we do with these two?"

"Why don't we leave them here just as they are in their prisons of fire? This is probably the route Zardonne's army will take up into the mountains, isn't it? Then, when they encounter Mordis and her friend in their present predicament, it will serve as an example of my powers. Zardonne will realize that we won't be taken easily without a fight."

"Good idea," Sindril approved. His dark eyes glinted impishly at the cowering Mordis in her circle of fire. "That is, if the mountain creatures don't get to them before Zardonne and his army do."

Mordis' face blanched. "You can't just leave us here like this. We'll be helpless against the predators!"

"Now you know how your *prizes* feel, you horrible old woman!" Tenya hissed. She had no intention of telling the woman that the beasts of the mountains would not be able to penetrate the circle of fire–not unless they possessed magical power that could counteract her own. She also kept hidden the fact that the beasts– fearing fire–most likely wouldn't come near her or Falgar. Let the old harridan experience some of the terror and panic she'd been instilling in her victims since she'd been in service to the Demon Master.

Tenya glanced at Sindril. "Can we leave now? The air around here has a distinctly rotten odor to it." Through the screen of shimmering white flames, she caught Mordis' offended glare.

Sindril grinned. "By all means, let's start on our way. But, have you had any sleep yet?"

She shrugged. "I'm not that tired. I can always sleep later. Right now, I'd like to get away from this place as soon as possible. These monsters make my skin crawl."

"You think you're so smart now!" Mordis shrieked. "Wait until you meet Zardonne. Then, we'll see who your master is. You won't be able to escape him, girlie. He'll teach you to dare oppose him."

Tenya and Sindril ignored the raging woman and prepared to leave. They mounted the murbeest and set off down the Pass, Mordis' vile curses following them, but growing fainter as the distance between them grew. Dawn had almost arrived, making visibility fairly good, and the more level terrain allowed Tenya and Sindril to ride the murbeest instead of having to proceed on foot.

As they descended the mountainside, Tenya's sleepless night caught up with her and she dozed lightly behind Sindril. When later she stirred, she discovered that morning had bathed the land in a bright light. The sun slanted down on the Pass, teasing her eyes so that she had to blink and rub them.

The trail had flattened somewhat and many more trees grew here than on the higher slopes. Her pulse quickened at the thought that they must be closer to the Ferrish Wood. She leaned forward, peering eagerly over Sindril's shoulder and he turned to grin at her.

"Ah, good, you're awake. I wouldn't want you to miss your first entrance into the Ferrish Wood."

"Then, we're almost there?"

"It's about another half hour."

They traveled faster now, having left behind the steep slopes. Now, they moved through the gentler foothills of the mountain range.

We can't be in the Wood yet, Tenya thought, *the trees are so ordinary and unexciting.*

She had imagined that the trees of the Ferrish Wood would be special. From high up on the mountaintop, the forest had seemed to possess a magical beauty that far surpassed the rather mundane quality of the land they'd traversed so far.

Then they rounded a massive jumble of orange boulders...

CHAPTER 17

The full spectacle of the ethereal forest spread out before her like a sudden, wondrous mirage.

Tenya could hardly draw a decent breath. She could sense the life in the Wood even before they reached the fringes of it.

Sindril halted the murbeest at the edge. Tenya slid from the animal's broad, sloping back and walked slowly in among the tall, silver-barked trees.

Tennnyaaa.

The soft whisper sang through her mind and vibrated up through the soles of her feet as she walked across the warm earth. She pressed a palm against the cool trunk of a nearby tree and could feel its heartbeat pulse beneath her fingertips.

Gossamer strands of pale pink moss festooned many of the silver-barked trees and, everywhere, riotous carpets of flowers of every imaginable hue spread across the ground. Sunlight, like liquid gold, slanted through the screen of emerald leaves and the trailing curtains of soft mist.

Tennnyaaa.

"You know who I am?" she whispered.

A light breeze stirred and the tree seemed to lean closer to her.

You are home.

Her eyes filled with tears and her heart brimmed to overflowing with the richness of the emotions flooding her. The forest welcomed her. It folded itself around her in a gentle, protective cocoon as real and comforting as the woolen cloak that had protected her from the bitter cold of the mountaintops. Never before had she felt more secure or loved than she did at that moment.

The brilliant foliage of the trees rippled in soft whispers and brushed lightly against her.

Welcome, daughter.

She spun around. "Sindril, do you feel it? Can you hear them?" She wanted to share the incredible joy with him.

The little man, still astride the murbeest, smiled down at her. "The Wood recognizes one of its own. It has opened its secret places to you, Tenya."

She emitted a small laugh. "Only a week ago, if you had told me I would be talking to trees, I would have said you were mad. But, now, it seems so-so natural, so right. I can feel their life. I can hear their voices and it doesn't frighten me."

"You've grown, Tenya. You've discovered that life holds mysteries and secrets you never could have dreamed of in that little village in the Ardis Valley. As Rondilar once said, *'Open your mind to the magic and you shall walk in the realm of reality. Close your mind and you shall walk forever in illusion.'* "

"Who is Rondilar?"

"He was one of the ancient leaders of the Shetii Clan and was very wise and revered. His teachings are still followed today by his people."

"Speaking of leaders, how do we find Hanifar?"

Sindril chuckled. "Never fear. *He* will find us." His dark eyes searched the rustling, dappled shadows of the forest. "In fact, I wouldn't doubt that our presence has already been noted by the Clan."

Tenya spun around. "They're somewhere nearby?"

He shrugged. "They are aware of every movement, every breath, and every change in the forest. If they're not here yet, they will be very shortly."

No sooner had he stopped speaking than the forest sighed softly and Tenya felt her skin begin to tingle with the now-familiar power that stirred in her veins. She could hear no sound save the whispering breath of the trees, but somehow she knew they were not alone.

"I think they're here now," she said, in a low voice, sensing the nearby presence of a power very much like her own.

In response to her words, the silver trees seemed to part and out of the wispy trails of mist a figure emerged as silently and eerily as a ghost. The tall man had snow-white hair and a handsome, strong-boned face with a calm, composed expression. A brown robe of a fine, rich texture and color clothed his spare figure in soft folds. He touched two fingers of his right hand to his forehead and then to his heart.

"Greetings, Sindril. It has been long since last we met." His quiet, somber voice sounded like the deep tones of a bell covered in dark velvet.

Sindril returned the gesture. "Greetings, Hanifar. Yes, it has been long. But, I'm pleased to see that you are looking well."

A faint smile tilted Hanifar's firm mouth. "And, you, my friend. I welcome you back to the Ferrish Wood."

Tenya stood still, staring at the leader of the Shetii Clan. She couldn't help herself. Looking into his distinguished face seemed like looking into a mirror that reflected an older, male version of her face and green eyes.

Hanifar strode toward her and placed his hands on her shoulders. His eyes, as wise and venerable as time itself, gazed down into hers with an expression that seemed both infinitely sad and happy at the same time. "Tenya," he murmured.

"You know who I am?" she whispered, staring up at him in wonder.

He smiled slightly. "Does a tree not know the branch that sits upon its trunk or a bird the feather that adorns its wing? You are of my people, Tenya, the daughter of my daughter."

Tenya's pulse quickened. "You're my mother's father, the father of Elea?"

He nodded. "And, you are my granddaughter."

Though she wasn't quite sure why, this fact came as no surprise to her. That her mother was the daughter of a great and wise leader of a mystical people seemed only fitting.

"Welcome home, my child," Hanifar said.

Tenya's eyes filled with tears. For years, she'd longed for the warmth and love that had always been denied her by the bitter, vicious Dianis and her sad, melancholy father. Now, she could feel it emanating in strong waves from this tall, compelling stranger who claimed to be her grandfather, and it filled her to bursting with sweet wonder and joy.

Hanifar lifted a hand from her shoulder to gently touch her hair. "You look very much like her. You have her beauty; I can sense your strength. And, I can feel the power in your blood. But, it's a different power than hers. You have the gift of the white fire, as I do." He looked pleased.

He turned to Sindril, who had dismounted the murbeest and stood watching them with a faint smile. "Sindril, my friend, I thank you for bringing my granddaughter safely to the Wood. In these troubling times, there's much danger for one such as she, who possesses the power of the Shetii Clan."

Sindril chuckled. "How well I know, Hanifar. We've already had more than one taste of that danger."

Hanifar's dark brows drew together into a slight frown and he turned once more to Tenya, his strong hands tightening slightly on her shoulders. "Are you alright, my child? Have you been harmed in any way?"

She smiled up at him, touched by his concern. "I'm fine," she assured him. "As Sindril said, we did encounter a few troubles..." She grimaced slightly.

"And, a few unsettling signs of Zardonne's far-reaching evil. But we managed to escape unscathed."

"I'm afraid Tenya is being far too modest," Sindril said. "Your granddaughter battled Zardonne's guards in the Windy Tunnel and defeated them. The poor lost souls trapped there have been freed and are now at peace. And, what's more, she confronted one of Zardonne's Death Riders and reduced it to ashes scattered on the wind in a matter of minutes."

Hanifar's left eyebrow lifted a fraction. He regarded Tenya with respect and admiration. "I knew you had your mother's strength and courage," he said, proudly. "Now, come, let us go to the village. There are many questions that need to be asked and answered, and many years to be talked about. Your people await you, Tenya. They're anxious to welcome you, as the forest already has."

He moved off into the ethereal trails of sunlit mist, Tenya and Sindril following. The silver-barked trees stirred and moved back to let them pass.

"Sindril, why didn't you tell me Hanifar was my grandfather?" Tenya whispered, fiercely.

The little man remained unperturbed by her irritation. "Well, let's just say that such a fact is not common knowledge, at least, not until now."

She frowned. "What do you mean?"

He nodded at the tall figure in front of them, winding his way through the trees and mist like a ghost gliding from dappled shadow to sun-sparkled clearing. "Not even Hanifar knew of your existence." Sindril frowned, thoughtfully. "Elea must have contacted him recently and told him about you."

"My mother never told her people about me before now? Why?"

Sindril shook his head. "After the first battle with Zardonne, your mother went away to the Ardis Valley with your father. She wanted to live a simple, normal life, away from the magic and madness of the world. She gave birth to you and kept you a secret, for she wanted nothing at all to harm you. Alas, Zardonne's rise through the Dark Rift a second time necessitated her return to the world she had hoped to forget. She couldn't just sit back quietly in her safe little valley, allowing the Demon Master to take control of the world. Her conscience, and her heart, wouldn't let her. Then, when she was captured by Zardonne, the secret of your existence became absolutely essential, for she knew that he would stop at nothing to destroy one of her offspring."

"But, surely she could trust her own father to keep my existence secret?"

"It wasn't a matter of trust, Tenya. There are always spies about, and Zardonne employs some of the most talented, able to ferret out even the most carefully kept secrets. She could trust Hanifar to keep silent, but not everyone around him, and if any should have sensed your existence..."

"But, she's told him of me now."

"Yes. And, the Demon Master knows of you also." Sindril looked grave. "I suppose the Mistress hopes that Hanifar and his people will be able to protect you from him."

As though in response to his words, the trees rustled sympathetically and emerald leaves pressed a little closer to her.

She didn't have a chance to speak further with Sindril, for Hanifar halted and waited for them. Here, the trees had thinned out to reveal what seemed to be a huge clearing, pierced with spears of golden sunlight through the trails of mist. Feathery ferns, taller even than Hanifar, towered over the vivid carpet of flowers covering the ground.

As Tenya approached her grandfather, she nearly jumped in alarm when several other people suddenly materialized behind him, as though out of thin air. She hadn't seen or heard their arrival. One moment, only Hanifar stood in the clearing, and the next, at least thirty or more people surrounded him. She glanced quickly at Sindril to find him grinning.

"The Shetii Clan can take some getting used to," he said, his voice pitched so only she could hear him. "They tend to appear and disappear quite suddenly."

Hanifar held out a hand to her. "Welcome to Phantasm, my child."

Tenya put her hand in his, looking about in bewilderment. "This is your village? But, where are the houses?"

Hanifar's green eyes twinkled. "Close your eyes for a moment and then look around."

She did as he instructed and, when she opened her eyes, she could not help gasping. Set among the straight trunks of the silver trees were square and rounded golden structures that seemed to be constructed of nothing more than cobwebs and gossamer. All had windows and doorways covered with curtains of braided wildflowers.

"Phantasm," Hanifar said, quietly.

The wondrous sight enthralled her. Like the forest itself, the village seemed incorporeal, as though belonging to another time and place. The buildings appeared fragile, delicate, scarcely like dwellings at all, but anything else would have been unnatural in the exquisite beauty of the forest.

She turned her attention to the gathered people. Men and women alike possessed a delicate beauty that matched their village and wore flowing robes of various shades of brown and green. Some had dark hair, while others had hair the color of pale sunshine in a summer meadow. Still others possessed the white hair and wise features of the elderly. No children could be seen, but Tenya caught whispers of movement and faint giggles in the treetops and wondered if the children crouched up there, peering shyly down through the canopy of emerald leaves and streamers of pale pink moss.

The strange feeling of belonging intensified. The village and spare, wooden hovel in the Ardis Valley no longer felt like home. This living, breathing forest of unsurpassed beauty and splendor did.

"She looks like Elea," one of the women said, coming forward. She bore a distinct resemblance to Hanifar, although her features were more delicate and refined. Clear gray eyes regarded Tenya with curiosity and warmth, and a pale hand reached out to touch her hair. "Welcome, Tenya, daughter of my sister. I am Felina."

Tenya's throat tightened. "I-I'm glad to be here," she said, softly. Never before had she felt as cherished and loved as she did at this moment, in this magical forest with its enchanting people. And, the joyous thought whispered across her mind, *I'm home.*

CHAPTER 18

Tenya soon learned that Phantasm wasn't the only village in the Ferrish Wood. Several others like it existed throughout the forest, each run by an elder called the *Shano*. Hanifar held the title of *Shanogen*, the overall leader of all the forest villages. Before him, his father Tolon had been *Shanogen* and, before *him*, it had been his grandfather Rondilar, whom Sindril had mentioned to Tenya.

"Most of my people have gone to do battle with the Demon Master," Hanifar explained, his wise eyes reflecting concern. "Zardonne doesn't have the ability to penetrate the magical properties of the forest, so those of us who remain here are safe from him. However, my people are in danger outside the Wood's protective confines. Zardonne's magic is powerful, as evil is everywhere. The Shetii Clan are only so many and can do only so much to prevent destruction and death. So far, we've had no reports of casualties, but they are in constant danger the longer they remain outside the Wood. Zardonne will seek to destroy as many of them as he can."

The three of them sat around a table in Hanifar's conical-shaped dwelling. The room was light and airy with simple, yet beautiful, furnishings. Tawny sunlight cascaded through the large open windows to pool on the polished wooden floor. A sweet fragrance lingered on the warm air perfumed by the braided curtains of pink and white wildflowers. Sadly, the foreboding words of Hanifar marred the peace and serenity of his home.

"How strong is the resistance against Zardonne?" Tenya asked.

"It was two thousand, a few days ago. But, the numbers have now risen to three thousand, with the people from the Delmas Valley joining our ranks."

"The villagers from Tundel and the other villages to the west of the Jamal Mountains will join," Tenya said. "They are already organizing an army to fight against Zardonne."

"Thanks to Tenya's brilliant rallying speech." Sindril chuckled. "Hanifar, I'm certain many a man from Tundel would follow your granddaughter to the very ends of the earth if she asked them to, such was the strength of her inspiring words."

"As usual, Sindril exaggerates," Tenya brushed off his declaration. "I think the villagers were already prepared to fight without my intervention. Look how they greeted us, Sindril–bristling with weapons and prepared to string us up by our heels."

At Hanifar's raised eyebrows, she went on to relate to him all that had happened at the village of

Tundel days before their arrival. He seemed impressed by her account of the confrontation with the Death Rider.

"Elea was wise in calling for you now," he said. "She obviously has faith in your abilities and it appears her confidence in you is well-founded. She was not much older herself when her gifts matured enough for her to master them." His wise eyes searched Tenya's face. "Would you like to speak with your mother?" he asked, quietly.

Tenya's breath caught in her throat. "Is-Is that possible?"

Hanifar nodded. "We keep our contact to a minimum, in order to prevent Zardonne from discovering us, but I think, in this case, we can risk a calling."

Tenya's heart beat faster. "H-How do I speak to her?"

Her grandfather rose from his chair and held out his hand. "Come with me."

He led her to another doorway on the other side of the room where hung a braided wildflower curtain. Sindril followed, his wizened face beaming with pleasure. No doubt he, too, looked forward to speaking once more with her mother.

Only a narrow table made from the same golden wood as the furnishings in the main room occupied the small, windowless alcove. On the table stood a dark red stone, similar to that on the tip of Sindril's short staff, but much larger, providing the only illumination in the room. Its many facets radiated a soft, ruby glow.

Hanifar approached the stone and lightly caressed its luminous surface. "We'll call your mother through this."

Tenya moved slowly to join him, staring at the rich dark color of the stone. As she came closer, she could see what appeared to be thin strands of white light undulating deep within the glossy facets of the jewel. "What do I do?" she asked, excitement building in her veins.

"Place both of your hands on the stone, like this." Hanifar guided her hands to either side of the jewel.

To her amazement, instead of the cold hardness that she expected, the stone radiated warmth under her palms and seemed to pulse faintly just below the gleaming surfaces.

"Now, close your eyes," he commanded. "Let your mind become a calm and relaxed place."

She did as instructed and tranquility washed over her.

Hanifar's next words seemed to come from far away. "Think of your mother. Picture her in your mind."

Tenya conjured up the image she kept safely stored in the far reaches of her memory. Almost instantly, she felt a subtle difference in the dark jewel beneath her hand. The faint pulsing grew stronger and the warmth increased. It felt alive, but instead of being frightened by the thought, she experienced an unbearable jolt of excitement throughout her body.

"Open your eyes," she heard Hanifar say.

She obeyed...and found herself staring down into the wavering image of her mother inside the jewel. The thread of white light had expanded to a soft glow and, in the midst of it, her mother's face smiled out at her. Long, black hair floated softly about her delicate features like a nimbus.

"Tenya," her mother said softly, the sound like the music of a summer stream. "My child, you're safe."

Tenya leaned closer, pressing on the dark stone as though she could touch her mother through its warm, pulsing surfaces. "Mother?" she whispered in a hoarse voice.

The glowing image smiled tenderly. "You've grown into a lovely young woman," she praised. "How I wish I could have been there to watch you." She sighed, a breath of wind through cobwebs. "But, that was not to be. I've tried to follow your progress through the years, but it's been very difficult. Locked away as I am here, my powers have been severely curtailed."

Tears stung behind Tenya's eyelids. The stark loneliness and pain reflected in her mother's soft voice prevented her from speaking. It must be terrible for this lovely, spirited woman to be locked away for so long in such a desolate prison, unable to communicate with her husband and daughter.

"Tenya, my child, I ask your forgiveness. Those lost years can never be recovered. I can't blame you for any resentment or anger you might harbor against me. I abandoned you at a tender age and left you to grow up as best you could on your own."

At last, she gained her voice. "Mother, don't say that! You didn't abandon me. You did what was necessary. You could no more allow Zardonne to take over the world than you could stop breathing. I don't hate you for doing what was right."

The glow around the wavering image seemed to flare brighter as her mother smiled sadly. "These many years I have chastised and blamed myself for my actions. I feared I had destroyed all hope of your love and understanding. I couldn't bear that you might despise me."

"I've never despised you," Tenya assured her. "I knew there was a good reason why you left as you did, despite what Dianis always said."

"Ah, yes, Dianis; sad, bitter Dianis. And, what did she tell you?"

Tenya's face flamed as she recalled the cruel, cutting remarks Dianis had always made about her mother. "She said you were selfish and thoughtless and too much of a dreamer. That you made up stories to get attention and used your beauty and wits to do the same." She paused to allow her simmering anger to cool. "She said you never cared about Father or me. Why else would you run off without any explanation and leave us behind?"

"And, yet, my daughter, you didn't believe her?" her mother asked, gently.

"No. I could never understand her bitterness, but she couldn't make me hate you as she did."

Elea sighed softly, her lovely face saddened. "There is not much love or compassion in Dianis for anyone, not even herself. I knew her for only a short time, but she considered me her enemy from our first meeting." She fell silent for a moment and then haltingly asked, "How is...your father?"

Tenya hesitated, wondering how much she should say. Her mother bore enough pain and guilt already. Should she add to it by telling of her father's decline into melancholy and depression? Should she tell her that the spiteful, bitter Dianis was now his wife?

Tenya understood now why Dianis had married her father. Spite and jealousy had driven her to it. A viciously calculated act of revenge against the beautiful woman she deemed her rival. What better way to punish Elea than by stealing her family from her?

Tenya took a deep breath and plunged ahead, telling her mother everything but trying to speak of it in a way that would not wound her too deeply. Elea's face reflected sorrow, but not the abject pain and guilt Tenya had feared.

"I suppose it was to be expected," her mother said. "I can't blame your father. What else was he to think or do when I left and didn't return? I wanted only to protect you and him. I wanted to keep you both safe in the valley, away from Zardonne and his madness. I intended to return immediately after I had vanquished Zardonne, but I foolishly underestimated him. He was much stronger than he had been the time before. He couldn't be pushed back as easily, or as quickly, into the Dark Rift. Then, I was captured, and I couldn't get word to your father. He had no way of knowing what had happened. Gradually, I was able to strengthen my powers so that I could communicate with my father and Sindril through this stone, and I was also able to send visions to you. But, that was a poor substitute for being able to see you and talk to you, and tell you how much I love you."

Tenya's heart constricted at the thought of her mother's desperate loneliness and grief. How she must have suffered in her cold, lonely prison, knowing that her husband and daughter were hurt and bewildered by her unexplained absence; unable to reach out to them to assure them of her love.

"That's all in the past now, Mother," Tenya said firmly, swallowing the lump in her throat. "We must concentrate on how to free you from the tower. Zardonne grows stronger every day. We must overcome him *soon* or he will reign supreme over all the lands."

Her mother's image smiled. "You have made my prison a better place already, my child, just by the knowledge of your forgiveness. And, you are right. We must put all of that aside for now. Is Hanifar there with you?"

"Yes." Tenya moved aside to make room for her grandfather.

"My father, I trust you are well, and Felina, too?" Elea asked him.

Hanifar nodded. "Yes, my child. We're both fine. But, as Tenya pointed out, the news of Zardonne is not good. Jessen came yesterday with a report from the village of Marget, on the eastern fringe of the Delmas Valley. One flank of Zardonne's army is headed that way. The people of the Valley have organized themselves to attack the enemy before they arrive. They are being supported by a troop of five hundred horsemen from the Coros Region. Jessen reported that the day before yesterday the resistance was attacked by several of Zardonne's Guardians. Our side managed to destroy four of the hideous creatures, but not before there were numerous casualties. None from the Shetii Clan were killed, but the battle was fierce and bloody. And that is only one area of trouble. There are similar reports from the north, south and east."

Elea's face reflected worry. "What of Zardonne himself? Where is he?"

"He was seen several times at the head of his main force, which is converging on the Jamal Mountains, but Jessen tells me that he has now returned to his fortress on the Plain of Naryn."

"Then, he will be well guarded. It will be difficult to approach the Plain without his being aware."

"Hanifar, if I may?" Sindril asked politely, stepping forward.

The older man nodded graciously, surrendering his place in front of the red stone to the little man.

Sindril leaned forward, his small, dark face lit with pleasure. "Mistress, it's good to speak with you again."

Elea's face softened. "Sindril, my old friend, I'm pleased to see you once more. I wish to thank you for guiding Tenya safely to the Ferrish Wood. Did you encounter much danger?"

"Nothing we couldn't handle," he said airily, flicking an impish glance at Tenya. "Your daughter was remarkably brave and heroic, even if she doesn't believe it herself."

Tenya made a slight face at him but said nothing.

"Mistress, I have a plan, if I may offer it. Granted, it's very simple and one which may not work, but I feel it's worth a try."

Her mother nodded encouragingly. "Go on, my friend. What is your plan?"

"If Hanifar can spare one or two, perhaps even three, of his people to accompany us, Tenya and I will try to slip past Zardonne's forces to the northern end of the Plain of Naryn. From all reports, he is concentrating his efforts on the more populated southern and western lands and has not many forces operating in the less populated, inaccessible north. With such a small group as we would be, we might stand a chance of slipping by unnoticed. Also, I thought we might keep Zardonne's attention focused elsewhere by spreading false rumors of Tenya's whereabouts. If we can keep his spies busy on wild goose chases, we might be able to enter his domain unhindered."

Hanifar nodded slowly, his face thoughtful. "It might work. I can have my people spread the rumors, making it seem as though the new sorceress, Tenya, is appearing at several known locations of resistance and encouraging them to fight against Zardonne."

Her mother's image glowed pensively as she considered Sindril's plan. "It's worth a try, my friend. If you were to attempt to enter Zardonne's domain with a large army, it's highly likely you would fail. His powers are strongest in his own lands, and he has many deadly traps to protect himself." She smiled faintly. "But, for the last few years, he has relaxed his vigil on me, for he believes my powers have been steadily declining here in my prison. Such was his boast when last he saw me. He's unaware that, on the contrary, I've been concentrating solely on strengthening myself. There's not much else to occupy my time and I won't give up. I'm certain he still has guards around the tower and there are always two outside my rooms. But, I have confidence in your ability to get past them, Sindril."

"I will do my best."

Her mother's image shimmered. "Tenya, my child, are you still there?"

Tenya moved back in front of the stone. "I'm here, Mother."

"My child, I know I'm asking a great deal of you, perhaps too much. If I could have kept you safely in the Ardis Valley forever, I would have. And perhaps, even now, I don't have the right to ask you to carry out this dangerous venture. I couldn't bear it if I lost you."

"Mother, you said you have never given up in your prison, that you have never lost faith in your belief that someday you would be free again," Tenya reminded her quietly. "Then, like you, I will never give up until I have made every effort to free you. I love you. Dianis could never take that away from me. You are the Mistress of the Wind, but you are also my mother. How could I live with myself if I turned and ran back to the safety of the Ardis Valley, only to save my own skin? No matter how dangerous this venture may be, I, too, will never give up."

CHAPTER 19

The communication with her mother ended at that point. Tenya would have liked to talk with her longer, she had so many questions to ask, but she understood the wisdom of keeping the contacts short. As her mother explained, any moment one of the guards–or Zardonne himself– might enter her rooms and discover her secret. Since the red stone was her only link with the outside world, she didn't want to risk losing it.

"We shall see each other in person soon," her mother had promised before her image had faded within the deep red facets of the stone, replaced by the thin threads of white light once more.

Tenya's heart was bursting with what she had just experienced. Instead of the hatred and resentment her mother had feared, she felt only an incredible love for the woman who had mothered her for such a short time, but whose unseen presence had been a constant companion throughout the long, lonely years. Not even the poisonous venom of Dianis had flawed that perfect image she'd held in the back of Tenya's mind.

She became aware of Hanifar's eyes on her and smiled warmly at him. "Thank you for letting me speak to her. It meant a great deal to me."

"As I know it did for her, as well," he replied. "She feared you would loathe and despise her for leaving you without an explanation and then not returning. She is a strong woman and her spirit can never be completely broken, but it has been a very difficult time for her, living with her anguish and distress. Hearing you say that you love her and forgive her has, I'm certain, lifted a considerable burden from her shoulders."

"I'm glad," Tenya said, her eyes glistening with tears. "I had no idea she was suffering so much these many years, and, all because of me."

"Only because she loves you so much," Sindril quickly reassured her. "As long as she was aware that you were well and safe, she could claim a small measure of happiness. And, as Hanifar said, there is a strength and vitality in your mother that can never be destroyed, no matter how much pain or grief she must endure."

"Now," Hanifar said briskly, pushing aside the curtain of wildflowers, "we must talk of our plan to rescue her."

The three of them returned to the main room. Late afternoon sunlight slanted across the warm, golden floor. Tenya had been unaware of the swift passage of time while she had been speaking with her mother through the glowing red stone.

Seated once more at the table, Hanifar said, "Jessen is still here in the Wood. He has not yet returned to Marget in the Delmas Valley. He can be part of the group to go with you, as well as Felina. I know she will want to participate in the rescue of Elea. She and her sister are very close. And, I, of course, will go also."

Sindril glanced sharply at him. "Are you certain that is a wise decision, Hanifar? This will be a very dangerous mission."

Hanifar smiled faintly. "My friend, I am an old man, that is true, and my powers are not as strong as they used to be, but Elea is my eldest daughter and because of that she was chosen to lead the battle against Zardonne. Indirectly, I am responsible for her capture by the Demon Master and I intend to do everything I can to free her."

Sindril bowed his head slightly. "Enough said, Hanifar. You have the right to do what you wish, and I would welcome your company."

"When do we leave?" Tenya asked. Both men smiled at her eagerness.

"I know you are anxious to set out," Sindril said. "But, we must plan carefully. Zardonne won't give us a second chance if we fail the first time; therefore, it is imperative that we don't rush impulsively into this."

"I understand."

Hanifar rose from his chair. "I will ask Jessen and Felina to join us so that we may make our plans for the journey."

In a short time, all five of them sat around the table, ready to discuss the proposed venture. Jessen turned out to be a lanky youth, with sensitive features and a shock of blond curls. He'd smiled shyly at Tenya when he had entered Hanifar's dwelling. Her mother's sister, Felina, had given her a warm, gentle smile and taken a seat beside her.

Felina leaned toward her to touch her lightly on the arm. "I understand you have spoken to your mother," she said.

Tenya nodded, unbidden tears stinging behind her eyelids once more. Her heart twisted poignantly at the memory of her mother's exquisite features and melodious voice.

"I'm glad for you," Felina murmured.

Sindril began to outline his plan. The conspicuous murbeest would be left behind in the Ferrish Wood, and the five of them would travel to Zardonne's domain on horses. Their journey would take them northward, through the rough, treacherous land that led toward the Coros Region and the Tempest Sea.

Elea's prison of ice sat a day's journey from the northernmost fringes of the Plain of Naryn. The deadly flats of quicksand and reeking pools of green, poisonous water that characterized much of the Plain in this area dispelled the need for Zardonne to place a heavy guard around the tower.

"The way will be very dangerous," Sindril warned. "We must keep on the lookout for Zardonne's Guardians, for if one of them spots us, it will report back to Zardonne immediately. We will also have to be on guard for any of his Death Patrols. Although he seems to be concentrating mainly on the south and west, we know he has also sent a small number of his forces northward to capture the Coros Region."

"What happens once we reach the northern edge of the Plain of Naryn?" Tenya asked.

The little man grinned. "We rely a great deal on luck. Seriously, I believe the combined powers of the five of us should be sufficient to overcome any guards Zardonne has stationed around the tower. Once inside, we will divide up and search for Elea's rooms. She is aware of only two guards outside her rooms but there may be more. The Mistress's powers should return in full force once she has escaped the hindering influence of Zardonne's domain. We will then devise a battle plan to vanquish Zardonne and his army, once and for all."

"It sounds simple enough," Tenya said, wryly, "but, I have the feeling it won't be."

"If life were always easy, can you imagine how boring it would be?" Sindril said.

"You have a wonderful way of looking at things, Sindril. I really think you are good for me."

The little man beamed.

"When do you propose to leave?" Hanifar asked.

"Early tomorrow morning, just before sunrise," Sindril answered. "I don't relish the thought of daytime travel, since the risk of discovery by patrols is that much higher, but I wouldn't want to try blundering through that treacherous land in the black of night."

"I'm afraid you'll have to leave behind your cape and hat," Tenya teased.

He looked startled. "What do you mean?"

"Well, you must admit you stand out rather conspicuously in a crowd when you're wearing them."

He grimaced. "Yes, I suppose you're right. I'll have to exchange them for more mundane garb. Let's just hope this business is quickly finished."

Their journey began early the next morning in the still darkness just before dawn. The ever-present wisps of white mist wove eerie tendrils through the trunks of the trees as the small group mounted their horses in preparation for leaving the safety of the Wood. The rest of the villagers came out to see them off, handsome faces grave. Even the children accompanied the adults, their tiny delicate faces wide-eyed as they sensed the tension in the air.

Mounted on a sturdy gray mare, Tenya wondered, with a sharp pang, if she would ever see the Shetii Clan again. This journey would be by far the most dangerous of her travels, for now they would be entering Zardonne's domain where his powers would be strongest. It had taken nineteen years to make this homecoming to her mother's people, and, all too soon, she had to leave them again.

The little group of five had all donned dull, nondescript clothing–even Sindril, who gazed longingly at his feathered cape and floppy hat held in the arms of one of the villagers. Tenya and Felina had both tucked their long, dark hair up under floppy-brimmed hats, making them appear to be slender, young boys instead of comely women.

"My people," Hanifar addressed the silent throng of villagers. "We go on a dangerous journey, one fraught with much peril and risk. But, it is a journey that must be undertaken if we are to overcome the evil of the Demon Master. The Mistress of the Wind must be released from her prison to continue her battle against this monster, who will destroy the world if he is not stopped. Should we fail in our mission and none of us return, you, Dontar, as the son of my dead brother, will assume the role of *Shanogen*."

He pointed toward a tall, dark-haired man who bore a remarkable resemblance to Hanifar himself.

Dontar bowed his head slightly, acknowledging Hanifar's words. "I will do my best to follow in your footsteps if the need arises, my esteemed uncle."

Hanifar nodded. "Then, my people, we will say our goodbyes, for the time has come when we must start out on our journey."

The people moved back to let the horses pass. The trees, their emerald leaves rustling in soft whispers, brushed lightly against them as they rode by.

We wish you a safe journey, daughter.

Tenya felt the breezy tree voices in her mind and smiled faintly at the solicitous concern inherent in them. She reached out and gently pressed her fingertips against a silver trunk as she passed slowly by it.

It took all of the morning and a good part of the afternoon for the small group to wend their way through the Ferrish Wood. Every grove of silver-barked trees they passed whispered encouragement and support.

Little sound could be heard in the Wood, save for the sighing whispers of the trees and the faint thud of the horse's hooves on the warm, vibrant earth. The tendrils of white mist curled in lazy spirals among the tree trunks, rising from the carpet of vivid flowers like pale, silent ghosts.

The group passed several villages similar to Phantasm. Now that she knew what to look for, Tenya could easily discern the fragile, golden structures built between the trunks of the trees.

They made a brief stop at each village before moving on, for Hanifar wanted to inform his people of the mission being undertaken. Most of the villages contained mainly children and elderly people, for the majority of the inhabitants had left the Ferrish Wood to join the resistance against Zardonne. At each village, when the people learned of Tenya's identity, they accorded her the same warm, generous welcome the people of Phantasm had given her.

By late afternoon, they had reached the northeastern fringes of the Ferrish Wood. Through breaks in the emerald canopy, Tenya caught glimpses of black smudges staining the sky. She wondered uneasily if the smudges indicated clouds of smoke from burning villages.

Hanifar sent Jessen on ahead to scout the way.

Nearing the blurry edges of the Wood, Tenya began to experience a hammering panic in her veins. Soon, they would leave the Wood and begin their journey through the treacherous territory that led to her mother's prison–a territory teeming with the evil forces of Zardonne. Gone would be the tranquility and peace of the Wood. They would be flung into the chaos and madness of the Demon Master's world, and there would be no more peace until he was vanquished and sent back into the Dark Rift for good.

She flicked a quick glance at the others. Hanifar and Felina seemed unperturbed, their faces reflecting nothing but calm. Sindril caught her eyes on him and winked, his teeth showing in a white grin beneath his gray-flecked beard.

She inhaled deeply, taking courage from the others' composed attitudes. She forcefully quieted the thundering of her blood, telling herself sternly that she was the Daughter of the Wind and one of the Shetii Clan and should not allow herself to give in to fear and panic, but when Jessen appeared suddenly out of the spirals of mist, blond curls falling over his forehead, she started. He gave her a quick, apologetic smile as he reined in and turned to Hanifar.

"The way appears clear, Hanifar," he said, in a light, musical voice.

The older man nodded. "Very well, let's proceed."

They moved forward, passing through the last of the silver-barked trees that marked the fringes of the Ferrish Wood, and rode into the world beyond.

CHAPTER 20

The transition from the magical forest to the outside world hit her almost like a physical blow. Tenya nearly turned and fled, unprepared for such an astonishingly abrupt change. They had emerged near a square plateau of rock--so black, it appeared almost purple. The sun that had slanted through the emerald canopy of leaves in the Wood had disappeared, hidden behind billowing dark clouds rolling restlessly above the flat top of the plateau.

In the middle of the plateau stood a single, twisted tree, its gnarled branches reaching up to the dark sky. Tenya stared aghast at the black silhouette. The tree resembled a dreadful beast straight out of a nightmare, about to fling itself down upon them and rend them to pieces.

The rest of the land around the plateau was rough and rugged, rising and falling in a series of jagged steps that ran in every direction. Like the twisted tree, other trees grew in gnarled and crooked shapes, their bark blackened by fungus and mold. An oppressive, brooding atmosphere seemed to hover over everything.

Tenya glanced back over her shoulder at the shimmering trees behind her. They seemed to beckon her, tugging at her with their promise of tranquility. She wanted so badly to return to their protective embrace, but, with a great effort of will, she tore her gaze away and faced forward once more.

"We still have some daylight left," Sindril spoke up. "I think we should continue on a little farther to cover as much ground as possible."

Hanifar agreed and sent Jessen on ahead to scout for danger. The rest followed, picking their way carefully over the broken ground.

Tenya anxiously scanned the surrounding land. The twisted trees creaked and groaned incessantly, as though a hundred, disembodied voices moaned all about her.

The others gave no indication that the ghostly sound affected them. Their attention was focused on carefully navigating the uneven, ridged ground. Tenya determinedly did the same.

They passed the square, black plateau with its single, monstrous tree and continued on northward, skirting the edge of a huge stinking bog that lay at the plateau's ragged foot. A stagnant fog rose from the surface of bubbling muck and Tenya had to cover her mouth and nose until they had ridden well past it.

A little while later, she saw the ghostly figure of Jessen up ahead, returning from his scouting. He seemed as serene and calm as ever, but Tenya couldn't be certain whether that attitude was part of his normal disposition or if he had found nothing up ahead to disturb him.

He rode up to their little group and announced, "All clear."

She breathed a sigh of relief.

"I found a place where we can stop for the night, inside a circle of rocks. We could defend ourselves easily if someone should attack us during the night."

"Very good, Jessen," Hanifar said. He turned to Sindril. "Well, my friend, what do you think? Shall we stop for the night?"

The little man nodded. "It's getting dark. I think it would be a good idea."

Tenya doubted she would sleep much in this forbidding, brooding land, but she didn't voice her thoughts to the others. She would have gone farther on, so anxious was she to reach her mother's icy prison, but she had to concede to the others' wisdom. They knew the lands hereabouts, while she did not.

The horses climbed a high, jagged ridge of black rock. At the top, a circle of square, uneven stones surrounded a flat area. As Jessen had said, it would be an easily defensible position, for anyone trying to reach it would be exposed on the broken slopes of the ridge, and a silent approach would be nearly impossible.

They did not build a fire, fearing that Zardonne's Death Patrols might see the flames and pinpoint their location. Jessen volunteered to take the first watch as the others tried to find comfortable positions on the hard ground for sleeping.

Tenya lay down beside Felina and propped her head on her hand, gazing over at the older woman. "Please tell me about my mother," she said. "I only know what I've imagined all these years. My stepmother, Dianis, always talked about her with scorn and ridicule and tried to poison me against her. But, I never believed her words. Others spoke of her as a beautiful, gentle woman and that's the image I have protected fiercely all these years."

Felina smiled gently. "Then you must continue to think that way. My sister is a very special person, possessing a beauty and strength that is astounding. The sun smiles and the streams laugh where she walks." Felina paused for a moment and sniffled. "Since Elea has been imprisoned, the world has been darkened these many years...lessened. It's as though the sun has gone behind an endless black cloud and the richness of the earth is fading for lack of the sunlight that is Elea."

Tenya fought back tears of her own. "Do you think we'll be able to free her?"

Felina sighed heavily. "It will be difficult. We'll have to battle Zardonne in his domain, but no matter. What's important is that we must try, for the sake of those of us who love her and for the sake of the world."

Tenya nodded and laid her head down, pillowing it on her arm. She tried to block out the eerie moaning of the twisted trees farther down the slope as her mind sought the peaceful oblivion of sleep.

She awakened at dawn to the sound of voices and the clatter of saddles and bridles. Felina smiled at her and handed her a chunk of bread to eat for breakfast.

She chewed it quickly, swallowing it down with a drink from her water skin and then went to saddle her mare.

The day promised to be gray and baleful. The wind had died during the night, but now a silence as malevolent as a beast lying in wait for its hapless victims enveloped the land.

Tenya shivered despite the oppressive warmth. She couldn't help being affected by the strange atmosphere of the ugly land. She wished for the light and serenity of the Ferrish Wood and its fair inhabitants.

No one talked much as the small group prepared to leave the relative safety of the circle of rocks. A grim mood gripped everyone. Indeed, the very air vibrated with danger. Even Sindril's irrepressible good humor seemed dimmed by the disquieting grayness of the morning.

They descended the far side of the jagged ridge, working their way cautiously through the narrow canyons and ravines. The black, dull rock, quite unlike the burnished orange of the Jamal Mountains, seemed–to Tenya–to press in on them from all sides.

They had been riding for perhaps an hour when she spotted a black speck against the dull gray of the sky. She watched it curiously, and then, as it came nearer, her heart began to trip faster. A terrible sense of foreboding seized her and, all at once, she knew what the black speck was. She and Sindril had encountered one once before.

"Sindril, I think I see a Guardian!" she called urgently, spurring her mare up alongside his mount and pointing up at the sky.

Sindril squinted and shaded his eyes to get a better look. "Hanifar, Tenya's right! There's a Guardian heading our way."

"Quickly, we must hide!" Hanifar ordered, digging his heels into the sides of his horse and heading for a stand of gnarled trees several yards away.

The others turned to follow, but the Guardian had already spotted them. Its unearthly shriek split the still air. Two yellow beams streaked from its eyes and pinned the fleeing figures in a bright halo of light.

Heart pounding, Tenya bent low over the neck of the mare. She dared not look up, for she could hear the dull thudding of the Guardian's huge wings close overhead. In the next instant, a blast of hot air nearly swept her from the back of the mare, as a powerful wingtip flashed by her eyes.

"Tenya, come this way!" She heard Sindril's voice, faint above the thundering of the creature, and veered in his direction, urging the little mare to greater speed. She risked a glance upward and gasped. The Guardian was diving straight down toward Hanifar. At the last moment, her grandfather swung his mount in an abrupt circle and the Guardian hurtled by with a bone-chilling cry of rage.

The creature rose back up into the sky, its heavy, beating wings sending blasts of hot air and dust swirling madly about the horses. Fierce yellow eyes glared from the horrifying human head mounted on its long neck.

Tenya coughed and squinted against the whirlwinds of dust, trying to determine the location of the creature in the chaotic skies. It readied itself for another plunge, this time at Felina and her mount. Tenya cried out a warning, but the other woman had already seen the danger and urged her horse into a series of quick, sideways jumps to elude the creature's attack.

Tenya gritted her teeth, forcing down the panic and fear that had flooded her body at the Guardian's sudden appearance. *Mother, give me strength*, she silently pleaded, and sent a shaft of white fire streaking from her fingertips. It struck the Guardian on the neck just as the creature prepared to plummet toward Felina once more.

Puffs of smoke rose from its outstretched neck and the creature shrieked, its yellow eyes blazing. It checked its downward plunge abruptly, falling off sideways, and then straightening out. The gigantic head swiveled quickly, trying to find the source of the white fire. Before it had a chance to gather itself completely, Tenya raised a hand and commanded another streak of fire toward the ugly creature.

It opened its mouth in a furious shriek and plunged straight at her. The streak of white fire shot harmlessly by it into the air behind it. Tenya watched in horrified fascination as the Guardian hurtled toward her, the phosphorescent yellow beams of its eyes pinning her like a helpless insect.

Suddenly, a vivid combination of red and white flames streaked through the air and collided with the plunging creature, sending it tumbling head over heels. Gouts of flame erupted from the Guardian's body and wings and an unearthly glow surrounded it as it plunged out of control toward the ground. It crashed into a tumble of jagged rocks near the edge of a shallow ravine and the bright yellow beams of its eyes winked out.

The sudden cessation of noise and wind almost deafened Tenya. She stared in stunned disbelief at the body of the lifeless Guardian, pierced in several places by sharp pinnacles of rock and smoldering with the dying flames that had knocked it from the air. As she watched, the hideous creature assumed a greenish glow and disappeared, as though it had never been there at all. Only the echoes of its unearthly shrieks remained in the dust-laden air to assure her it had not been a nightmarish figment of her imagination.

"Is everyone all right?" Hanifar's calm voice brought her back to reality. He rode close to Tenya and her trembling mare. "Tenya, my child, have you been injured at all?"

She tore her gaze away from the spot where the Guardian had been. "I-I'm all right, Grandfather."

The others gathered about. Aside from grim, dirt-streaked faces, they had all survived the Guardian's attack unscathed.

Am I the only one whose heart is beating so strongly I'm afraid it'll fly out of my chest? Tenya wondered, envying the others their unruffled nerves.

"We must move on," Sindril said. "I don't know if the Guardian had time to report our location before we destroyed it, but we'll be safer if we leave this area as quickly as possible."

Tenya agreed heartily, still envisioning those phosphorescent yellow eyes staring into her with terrible purpose.

They set off quickly with Sindril leading the way. Jessen brought up the rear, his sharp eyes scanning the countryside–and the sky–for further dangers.

Later that afternoon, they came across the first evidence of Zardonne's campaign of destruction--a small village near the edge of a dense forest. Or, rather, what remained of the village's twenty wooden huts. They were nothing more than charred heaps, now. Only the blackened circle of stones in front of each pile gave evidence that a structure had once stood there.

A recent rain had formed puddles in the black ashes of the ruined village and a strong, acrid smell of soot hung heavy in the still air. The destruction had obviously occurred several days earlier, judging from the cold, smokeless ashes. Yet, the very air still hummed with the violence and death that had taken place.

They rode slowly through the ruins, shaken by the destruction. The horrible sight vividly brought to Tenya's mind a vision of a great, roaring inferno with a terrible, misshapen figure in its midst. She could picture Zardonne standing in the middle of the blazing conflagration of the little village, laughing triumphantly as the wooden huts went up in flames, and the inhabitants fled, screaming in terror. A palpable sense of evil quivered in the bitter air.

She spied something in the rubble and started when she recognized it, causing the little mare beneath her to jump sideways in alarm. Tenya pulled on the reins, bringing the animal back under control, all the while staring in horror at the charred remains of a body lying half under a blackened heap. A skull gaped up at her, its bony mouth open in a hideous grimace of pain and terror. A skeletal hand protruded from the rubble, pointing at her as though mutely appealing for help.

"Tenya, come away from there," Sindril said, gently.

Vaguely, she became aware of him riding up beside her and taking the reins of her horse to lead her away from the grotesque sight of the burned body.

It took several moments to shake off the frozen horror that gripped her. When she did, she fixed her gaze on Sindril, following him out of the village, refusing to look at any of the other charred heaps on the ground. She kept her eyes straight ahead and fought a suffocating rush of nausea that threatened to overwhelm her.

Now, the path of Zardonne's destruction became increasingly noticeable. The cruel land bore evidence of the passing of a large army, and Tenya and her companions came across several more burned villages. They hurried past them, not stopping to examine the devastation too closely. Not one living creature, man or beast, could have possibly survived.

At first, the sights sickened her, but as they rode farther, and damage and ruin continued to unfold before them, her anger against Zardonne grew...until it seemed as though a hot flame burned in her chest.

"How much farther?" she asked Sindril, moving her mare up beside his mount.

He glanced at her, his face grim. "By early tomorrow afternoon we'll reach the Plain of Naryn."

"Good. Zardonne shall pay dearly for this."

Sindril said nothing, but his dark eyes agreed with her.

They spent the night near the ruins of what appeared to have been a fortress of some kind. Partial sections still stood, while others had been destroyed, lying, now, in a vast heap. Tenya and the others took shelter within the angle of two corner walls, still adjoined, thus affording them protection from the back and sides and leaving only the front to guard.

Hanifar, Jessen and Sindril left to explore the ruins, seeking out any dangers that might be nearby. Tenya chose not to join them. She had no wish to encounter any more burned or mutilated corpses. She and Felina prepared a quick supper of bread, cold meat and cheese. Again, they did not build a fire to lessen the possibility of drawing attention to their location.

Later, sitting back against the cool rock wall, Tenya hugged her knees and gazed out into a night that descended rapidly on the land. She anxiously scanned the darkening sky for signs of more Guardians. Despite the fact that she could not detect anything, she still felt uneasy and restless, troubled by her thoughts and the disquieting atmosphere that seemed to lie like a pall over everything.

Tomorrow they would enter the Plain of Naryn, and the idea terrified her. What they had encountered thus far would pale in comparison to what awaited them in that vast, corrupt land.

For a few moments, she stared blindly at a faint greenish glow that showed above the ragged tops of the trees along the horizon. When awareness finally set in, she started up suddenly, heart tripping into her throat. "Felina, what is that?"

The other woman came to stand by her, looking in the direction of her trembling finger. "It's the glow from the Plain of Naryn," Felina said, quietly. "It comes from the pools of poisonous water that abound there."

A little while later, the men returned from their explorations. They reported that all seemed quiet and safe, and everyone settled down for the night. All except Sindril, who volunteered to take the first watch.

But, Tenya couldn't sleep. Her gaze was again drawn to the faint greenish glow above the black silhouettes of the trees. Just before she dropped off into a light, troubled slumber, she could have sworn the glow brightened for a moment...and she heard the distant rumble of demonic laughter.

CHAPTER 21

Her dreams that night troubled her greatly. Pillars of flame and demonical laughter wove among images of the tall, slender figure of her mother standing on a high hill with cyclones of wind spiraling from her fingertips. Grotesque creatures, fanged and clawed, howled at the foot of the hill, trying to reach her. Behind them stood a black figure, looming unbelievably tall against a roiling sky streaked with green lightning.

Tenya stirred and moaned in her sleep, trying to reach her mother's side to aid her. But, her feet seemed glued to the ground and she couldn't move. She cried out to the willowy figure on the hilltop, but the clamorous shrieks and howls of the demon-spawned creatures that scrabbled their way up the side of the hill drowned out her voice.

The gigantic black figure heard her cry, however, and turned slowly to look at her. She stared transfixed. Though the figure's face remained hidden in shadow, she knew with a sudden certainty that his visage would be unbelievably ghastly.

The thunder of her heart nearly deafened her as the terrible being started forward, its misshapen body and face slowly coming into focus...

She woke with a strangled cry, beads of perspiration popping out on her forehead. Instantly, arms encircled her and a soft voice crooned soothingly, "You're all right, Tenya. Hush. There is no danger. Hush now."

Tenya trembled in Felina's embrace, the vividness of her nightmare still with her. She could almost see the hideous countenance of the black figure as it had turned to stare at her with unseen eyes. "I-I'm fine now," she murmured. "It was just a bad dream."

Felina stroked damp hair from Tenya's forehead and smiled gently. "It's understandable. Being so close to Zardonne's domain can be quite disturbing. But, you're safe here with us. Try to sleep some more and I will stay by your side."

Tenya feared closing her eyes, lest she see the terrible figure again, but Felina's presence reassured her and, at last, she allowed herself to drift back down into that veiled world of sleep.

The rest of the night passed undisturbed. If she dreamt again, she couldn't remember. Certainly none had the terrifying quality of that first nightmare.

Once more, the morning dawned gray and dull. Sluggish, black clouds moved slowly across the sky like a herd of lethargic cattle half-heartedly grazing. Tenya rose and helped Felina prepare a quick breakfast. A heavy weariness enveloped her mind and body and she experienced a sudden stab of panic that her powers might not be quick enough or strong enough to battle whatever they encountered that day. Yet, when she reached for the magic within, it responded instantly with a faint singing in her veins, reassuring her.

Sindril came to her after breakfast, concern in his dark eyes. "Are you all right, Tenya? I heard you cry out during the night."

She quickly smiled. "It was nothing, only a nightmare. Felina chased it away for me."

"You're certain?" He searched her face.

She nodded, feeling rather guilty that she'd caused the little man to worry. But, his next words put her at ease.

"It's understandable that you should be troubled." He echoed Felina's assurance of the night before. "We all feel the wickedness and corruption staining this land. This close to Zardonne's domain, the taint is even stronger."

She shook her head. "But...you all seem so calm, so unaffected."

He grinned. "We find the calm within ourselves and use it as a buffer against the evil. In time, you will learn to shield yourself similarly."

Shortly afterward, they mounted the horses and left the scanty protection of the ruined fortress. Tenya watched the greenish glow above the treetops with growing apprehension as they rode toward it. Two hours later, they reached the Belisar River.

Tenya heard the river long before she saw it. For some time, she had been aware of a muted roaring noise that seemed to grow louder the farther they rode. Finally, as they came out on to a narrow shelf of rock that overhung a jagged canyon, she saw the source of the noise.

Far below, the tumbling, frothing river snaked through the bottom of the canyon. Silver spray hung in the air above the roaring water. Even from as high up as the canyon's lip, the little group could feel the fine mist and had to shout to be heard above the thundering of the river below.

"Do we have to cross that?" Tenya yelled, certain it would be suicide to attempt to swim across the raging torrent of water.

"We'll have to go down river!" Sindril shouted back. "There are easier crossings to be found there."

They turned around and left the overhanging shelf of rock, moving away from the canyon to where they could talk more easily.

"I'll go ahead," Jessen volunteered. "When I find a place where we can cross, I'll return for you."

He set off along the edge of the canyon, urging his horse as fast as he dared on the rocky ground, and soon disappeared from sight. The others followed at a slower pace.

No one spoke. The roar of the river, though slightly muted by the distance from the canyon's lip, still prevented normal conversation.

Half an hour later, Jessen returned, his blond curls disheveled from his hurried passage along the canyon edge. "I've found a place where we can cross. It's still fairly swift, but we should be able to swim the horses to the other side."

About a mile from the group's present position, the jagged canyon flattened out into coarse-grassed meadows on either side, flanked by scarred and broken ridges. Here, the river slowed its tumultuous rush somewhat, but to Tenya's fearful eyes, it still ran terrifyingly swift.

Sindril examined the river and the crumbling edges of the banks. "This will have to do. We don't have time to find an easier way. I'll go first and the rest of you follow."

"No, Sindril, let me cross first," Hanifar spoke up. "You know this area better than I. If something happens to me, you will still be able to lead the others to Elea. But, if something happens to you, our search will take much longer, and we don't have the time to waste on fruitless meanderings."

For a moment, the two stared at each other, each obviously reluctant to give in to the other. Finally, Sindril sighed and nodded. "Very well, Hanifar, you go first."

The older man nodded briskly and urged his horse to the bank of the river. The animal shied nervously away from the swift moving water, but Hanifar's firm hands on the reins calmed him. Tenya watched tensely as her grandfather's horse slid down the eroded bank and into the river. Immediately, the wicked current took the animal's hooves out from under him and the horse rolled his eyes in panic. Hanifar slid off his back and swam alongside, holding onto the pommel of the saddle.

Although the current carried them downstream a short distance, the horse swam strongly and steadily for the opposite shore. Tenya released her breath in a soft sigh of relief when the horse, with Hanifar still clinging tightly to the saddle, scrambled out on the far bank and stood dripping on the coarse grass.

Sindril turned to the others. "Who wants to go next?"

"I'll go," Felina said, her face tense. She urged her mare forward into the seething water, sliding off her back as Hanifar had done to help the animal swim better. Tenya saw her dark head go under the water for a moment and her breath caught with fear. But, Felina bobbed back up almost immediately, shaking her wet hair out of her face. An eternity later, it seemed to Tenya, the other woman made it to the far shore, joining Hanifar where he stood in his dripping robe.

Tenya tensed when Sindril turned to her. "Tenya, you're next."

She drew in a deep breath, trying to still her wildly pounding heart. She knew she had to do as the others had done, but the sight of the swiftly moving water below her filled her with dread.

Sindril sensed her hesitation and smiled gently. "You must do this for your mother, Tenya. I know you have the courage."

She nodded, wrapping her hands tightly around the pommel of the saddle.

She dug her heels into the little mare's sides, urging her forward. Gray earth crumbled beneath the animal's hooves as she slid down the bank to the river's edge. Tenya kept her eyes on the far shore where Felina and Hanifar stood, their faces reflecting encouragement.

As the water lapped at the forelegs of the mare, the animal suddenly balked, nearly throwing Tenya from her back. Tenya managed to stay on, clinging desperately to the animal's mane. She laid a gentling hand on the mare's neck and willed herself into the animal's mind. As she'd done with the murbeest, she soothed away the tendrils of fear, replacing them with a golden glow of calm.

The swirling water rose to the chest of the mare and she started swimming, legs kicking powerfully against the current. As she'd seen Hanifar and Felina do, Tenya slipped out of the saddle and into the frothy water. She felt it pull at her body, trying to drag her down into its mysterious depths. Her long, dark hair, released from its confining hat, swirled around her like black seaweed.

The far shore seemed to recede instead of getting closer. Tenya fought desperately against the current, trying to stay as close as possible to the mare without getting kicked by her powerful hooves. She kept her eyes focused on the figures of Hanifar and Felina standing slightly down river from her.

The effort of keeping the mare calm and reassured kept her own fear at bay. She concentrated on swimming strong and steady, fighting against the insistent pull of the swift current. She dared not stop; afraid the river would snatch her up and swallow her.

The mare's flailing hooves touched bottom and she scrambled up the far bank, dragging Tenya with her. Felina came over to help steady her on her feet and gave her a quick hug, pulling back to smile down at her. Tenya smiled weakly in return, relief at having made the dangerous crossing safely making her knees nearly buckle. She had to cling to her aunt for a moment to allow the sensation to pass.

Sindril, and then Jessen, came next, with Tenya watching fearfully until both men stood safely on the shore, bedraggled and dripping.

"Well, I wouldn't want to do *that* too often," Sindril declared, wringing out his hat before plopping it back on his head. The others agreed, laughing, and the tension of the river crossing was broken.

"Now, if I'm correct, beyond these ridges should lay the fringes of the Plain of Naryn." Sindril pointed to the line of broken hills in front of them.

Tenya followed the direction of his finger and could still see the faint greenish glow in the sky. Sick dread overcame her and she had to force it down with a tremendous effort of will. She wanted nothing more than to turn around and run back to the Ferrish Wood as fast as she could.

"We'll hold a vote," Sindril continued. "All those who wish to spend the night here, and then proceed to the Plain in the morning, raise your hands."

No one moved. For as much as Tenya dreaded the thought of entering the domain of the Demon Master, she wanted the journey over with as quickly as possible. One more night spent here meant one more night for her mother in her icy prison. And, one more night for Zardonne's army to kill and destroy.

Sindril nodded. "Very well, we'll continue on. But, I must warn you, there won't be much opportunity for sleep or rest once we reach the Plain."

The others gazed steadily at him, their decision unaffected. Everyone seemed to have the same idea,

Tenya thought–reach the tower of ice as quickly as possible and free the Mistress.

Again, Jessen rode on ahead, scouting the best way through the jagged ridges while watching for any danger lurking in their crevices and hulking rocks.

The warm air soon dried everyone's clothing and Tenya and Felina again tucked their long hair up under their floppy hats. The way through the broken hills proved slow and treacherous. Nature had been cruel here, or perhaps Zardonne's evil had scarred the land. The black rock thrust up in many places in pointed, sharp spikes, creating a hazard to the horses' hooves and forcing them to pick their way very carefully over the ground. Coarse, brittle grass clung grimly in brown patches amid the fractured rock. No trees grew here, merely low, twisted shrubs with spindly branches and few leaves.

Edgy and restless, Tenya guided her mare through the ugly land. The oppressive, malevolent atmosphere seemed markedly more intense here than it had been on the other side of the river. She could almost feel the evil and corruption oozing from the very pores of the earth itself.

The only sounds came from the sharp ticking of the horses' hooves on the broken ground and the occasional snort from one of the animals. Even they acted restless and nervous, as though sensing the depravity of the land.

Up ahead, Sindril stopped suddenly, his small, wiry body leaning forward in intense concentration. "Something's wrong," he said.

"What is it, Sindril?" Tenya reined her horse beside him. She glanced quickly about, suddenly assailed with apprehension.

"It's too quiet," the little man muttered. "Where is Jessen? Why can't we hear him up ahead anymore?"

"Perhaps he just stopped to rest," Tenya suggested. Despite her words, her sense of disquiet grew.

Hanifar joined them, his green eyes worried. "Do you think something might have happened to him?"

Suddenly, they spied him, bent low over his horse's neck, racing madly toward them. He shouted words they couldn't hear, now and then looking back over his shoulder at something that must pursue him.

"A Death Patrol is coming!" His words finally reached their ears. They glanced at one another, shock evident on all their faces.

The air rent with a crash as though someone pounded on two enormous drums. The dark sky above the broken hills lit up with sharp bolts of lightning that crashed and shattered against each other.

Tenya stared, appalled, as a horde of hideous creatures poured out of the narrow gorge behind Jessen.

CHAPTER 22

Sindril wheeled his horse about, shouting to the others to follow him. Jessen caught up to them and they rode swiftly over the dangerous ground toward a tumble of shattered black rock that would hopefully provide them with some protection from the howling mob bearing down on them.

As they leaped from their horses to the ground behind the boulders, Tenya glanced back over her shoulder and gasped in horror. The army of grotesque creatures, and their equally hideous riders, had almost reached them.

Instinctively, she turned to face the oncoming horde and called on the white fire in her veins, sending it spinning from her fingertips in a sheet of flame. The creatures at the forefront, unable to slow their charge, plunged into the curtain of fire. Howls of pain rose on the already clamorous air.

Beside her, Sindril used the magic of his jeweled staff to send deadly beams of red sparks toward the oncoming enemy. Hanifar's rapidly moving hands rained streamers of his own white fire on the advancing Death Patrol. Tenya could not see Felina and Jessen, but she knew they stood somewhere behind her, using their own magical powers.

Their attack initially slowed the advance of the Demon Master's creatures. For several minutes, they milled about in noisy disorder and panic. Unfortunately, a Death Rider led the patrol and he quickly dispelled the confusion, reorganizing the troops into some semblance of order once more.

Tenya counted twenty creatures in the Death Patrol, not all of them nightmarish figures. Four or five humans also numbered among the enemy, riding horses and wearing strange metallic armor and helmets. She crouched behind the black boulders, the dry, acrid taste of fear filling her mouth. Even with the combined powers of all five of them, could they succeed in escaping the attack alive?

The sky boiled with violent eruptions of lightning and thunder. A strong, choking odor of metal and dust assaulted her nostrils and made her eyes sting.

"Tenya, look out!" Sindril shouted from beside her before pushing her aside. A long lance with a razor-sharp tip thudded into the ground where she'd stood a second earlier, and stuck there, quivering.

She stared at it for a moment, realizing belatedly that she had not erected the protective white shield around her body. She called it forth immediately. The comforting tingle assured her and she turned back to the frenzied battle.

The Death Rider raced about behind his patrol, barking orders, white foam flying from the slavering jaws of his mount. The demon pointed and three of the members of his troop wheeled to the left. The Death Rider swung his targ and charged to the other side, sending three more of his soldiers to the right.

"They're trying to surround us!" Tenya shouted, recognizing the Death Rider's intent.

The five of them stood back-to-back in a circle, watching all sides, as the Death Patrol divided and moved around the tumble of broken rocks in an attempt to hem them in. Jessen pointed at a figure on a horse rushing toward them. An invisible hand lifted the rider from the saddle and flung him screaming through the air. His cries cut off abruptly as he smashed into the ground and lay still.

Another creature, this time a deformed figure with a scaled face and flying ropes of black hair, charged into Hanifar's rain of white fire and ignited like a torch, its hoarse cries splitting the tumultuous air.

Tenya turned her attention back to the Death Rider. Perhaps if she concentrated all her efforts on destroying him, the other members of the Death Patrol would panic and flee at the loss of their leader.

The Death Rider's huge, bulbous head turned sharply toward her, as though sensing the course of her thoughts. Panic fluttered through her, but she quickly suppressed it and took a deep breath. Her skin tingled and her veins sang with the powerful force of the magic in her blood. Glowing white fire spiraled from her fingertips, weaving through the charging creatures on an unerring course for the Death Rider near the back of the troop.

The demon saw it coming and jerked out of the way just in time. Tenya felt a blast of pure rage emanate from the creature. She winced slightly but refused to be cowed by the Death Rider's sudden, furious attention.

The Death Rider raised his hand. She prepared for the green ball of lightning that shot from his pointing finger, sending her own fire to meet it. The two bolts of magic collided midway, ripping the air apart with a thunderous crash that nearly deafened her. The whole area lit up with blinding flashes of light and sparks, hissing and spitting in the air.

Through the brilliant glare, Tenya saw the Death Rider charging toward her. In his mindless rage, he ignored those of his troops unfortunate enough to be in his way. One rider fell from his horse and went down under the targ's clawed hooves, managing only one short scream before being trampled into the rocky ground.

As the Death Rider continued his mad approach, Tenya felt the tingle of the white shield on her sensitive skin. The white fire dominated her body, spreading through her with a powerful vitality that was heady and exciting.

The world receded to the black creature on his grotesque mount. She knew the battle still raged about her. She could sense Sindril and the others at her sides and back, using their magic to overcome the charging enemy. Yet, the frenzied conflict seemed to be carried out in total silence on the periphery of her vision. All of her senses focused on the oncoming

Death Rider, for she knew that his destruction would be the only thing that would save them.

The Death Rider pulled his mount to a stop almost directly in front of her. His black, slit eyes blazed at her, but she stood her ground, calmly watching him.

"YOU SHALL ADVANCE NO FARTHER!" the Death Rider's deep, sepulchral voice boomed. "THE DEMON MASTER FORBIDS IT."

Tenya raised her chin. "We have come to free the Mistress." Her voice rang out clearly. "Neither you nor Zardonne will stop us."

"YOU ARE A FOOL, GIRL! THE DEMON MASTER IS ALL POWERFUL. HE CAN CRUSH YOU LIKE AN INSECT."

"He hasn't crushed me so far," Tenya pointed out, dryly. "Perhaps he's not as strong or infallible as he thinks."

The Death Rider jerked in rage, his mount gnashing its wicked teeth and foaming at the mouth. "ZARDONNE WILL BE MASTER OF ALL! BUT, YOU SHALL NOT LIVE TO SEE IT."

The creature's sudden blast of green light struck her white shield like a burst of thunder, knocking Tenya off her feet. The thin glowing shield protected her from the rocky ground, and she sprang back up. She shook her head slightly, her ears ringing from the deafening clang of the demon's magic against her own.

The Death Rider raised his arm again, prepared to send another blast of deadly green energy. She dropped to her right knee and rolled to the side. The streak of light hit the ground where she had been standing and dug a deep, smoking furrow in the earth.

She came up out of the roll into a low crouch and sent spirals of brilliant white fire toward the Death Rider. He swiftly pulled his mount out of the way and the spirals of fire swept past him, engulfing another member of the Death Patrol in their deadly embrace instead.

Ah, so the Death Riders have learned to respect my powers, Tenya thought, wryly. *They no longer consider them puny.*

Even as she thought this on one level of her mind, another level sent signals to the powers in her body, commanding a steady stream of white fire toward the dodging monster in front of her. The Death Rider howled in rage and pain, the flames igniting patches of his spiked, bulbous skin. Feebly, he tried to raise his arms to unleash his power once again, but her magic proved to be stronger than his. Like the Guardian had done, the Death Rider suddenly flared, engulfed in flame, and then winked out–disappearing into the ashy air without a sound.

Tenya straightened, staring at the spot where the Death Rider had been. Howls of panic and terror filled the air and she looked up to see the remaining soldiers of the Death Patrol wheeling their mounts about to flee back into the shattered hills. The broken bodies of their comrades lay where they had fallen, strewn across the rocky ground in grim reminder of the bloody battle that had just been fought.

The violence of the sky subsided, leaving only restless black clouds moving across it. The suffocating wind scented with metal and ashes ceased, and a silence descended, blanketing the land and leaving only faint echoes of war and death.

"Is everyone all right?" Tenya asked finally, looking about at the others. Though dirty and disheveled, the rest of the little group assured her they were unharmed.

Sindril gazed upon her with new respect. "There can be no mistaking your strength now, Tenya. Even this close to Zardonne's domain, your powers are extraordinary. You are truly the Daughter of the Wind. But, more importantly, you have become Mistress of the White Fire."

Mistress of the White Fire…

An odd thrill tingled through her body. She had grown from a child of strange dreams into a woman of remarkable powers. She and her mother commanded the infinite powers of two of nature's most extraordinary forces. That revelation gave her the confidence to believe that, together, they would have the strength and ability to drive the Demon Master back into the Dark Rift, there to remain forever more.

"If everyone is unharmed, then we must continue on," Sindril said. "News of our victory will soon reach the ears of Zardonne. We have no time to lose if we wish to free the Mistress."

They gathered up their horses from where they had sought shelter in a rough defile several yards away while the battle had raged. Within minutes, they were mounted and on their way through the narrow gorge. They could see no sign of the remaining members of the Death Patrol.

The ravine soon widened, opening out into a vast, desolate plain. Foul odors permeated the air and hundreds of small pools of green, bubbling water dotted the plain. A sickly glow rising from the pools of viscous liquid illuminated the whole area.

For a moment, Tenya tensed at the sight of numerous hulking figures on the plain, fearing that more of Zardonne's monstrous creations waited to attack. She let out a breath of relief when she realized the figures were weirdly shaped pinnacles of reddish rock crouched in silent but menacing immobility. Her nose wrinkled at the stench of corruption and foulness that seemed to ooze from the very pores of the black soil. She wondered how she would ever get up the courage to cross the evil land. Almost immediately an image of her mother locked in her icy prison bolstered her determination.

Sindril rode his horse close and wrinkled his nose. "It's not very appealing, I know, but, unfortunately, we must enter the Plain if we wish to accomplish our mission."

"I know," Tenya said. She laid a gentling hand on her prancing mount's neck.

"Do you know which way we must go, Sindril?" Felina asked.

The little man looked thoughtful. "Unfortunately, I have only a vague idea of the direction in which the tower lies. Elea could not be very specific when she told me of her prison. Zardonne had only mentioned that it was in the remotest part of the northern section of his domain, no doubt trying to instill in her the apparent hopelessness of her situation."

"Do you think we should separate and search for it?" Hanifar suggested.

Sindril shook his head vigorously. "No, we shouldn't. If we separate, we'll be more vulnerable to Zardonne's monstrosities and, what's worse, some of us may become lost on the Plain. That's not a fate I would wish on anyone, not even my worst enemy. Together, we at least stand a chance of battling the creatures the Demon Master is certain to send our way. You'll probably find that your powers are not as strong here as they normally would be, a result of the negative influence of Zardonne's magic. But, our powers combined should be sufficient to allow us to reach the tower."

Despite the fact that night approached, the group decided to push on. The glow from the reeking pools would be enough to illuminate the way, and the shadows would provide concealment for them in their trek across the Plain.

Sindril decided on a northeast direction. Since the Plain remained relatively flat over most of its vast expanse, it seemed likely they would spy the tower from a considerable distance, and be able to correct their course if they happened to misjudge.

The horses balked when they first set foot on the foul, black soil of the Plain, but patience and firm urging from their riders soon had them moving again. They shied away from the pools of green, bubbling liquid and stepped gingerly around the odd pinnacles of reddish rock that loomed up in their path.

Occasionally, the simmering bubbles on the surface of the pools would burst with a sharp pop, or a cloud of hissing steam would suddenly erupt from the foul surface. Aside from that, silence reigned on the Plain.

Foul and putrid, like the stink of a thousand corpses rotting in the hot sun, the smell of the Plain of Naryn seemed to seep insidiously into the very pores of Tenya's skin until she felt as though she would never be clean again. She couldn't escape it, even when she covered her nose and mouth.

The journey was beginning to wear on her nerves, and she noted the power in her veins noticeably weakening as they traversed farther across the Plain. It still sang deep within her body and responded when she reached for it, yet its intensity had decreased. She could only hope it wouldn't fail her when she needed it.

The little group stayed close together. No one wanted to risk losing the others in the black shadows of the encroaching night. The hours wound out, long and unnerving; the nightmarish journey seeming to go on forever. At any moment, Tenya expected to see another Death Patrol charging toward them across the Plain, or the huge, terrifying silhouette of a Guardian against the dark sky. She searched the surroundings and she knew the others did the same, but the dark seemed only to strain her tired eyes.

Up ahead, she could see the pale, blond figure of Jessen on his horse. The pair moved steadily, unconcerned. She blinked her weary eyes, and then blinked again. Was that...? Was that movement?

Just to the left of him. She blinked again. *There on the ground...*

Before the notion could register fully in her mind, something long and snakelike whipped up into the air with amazing speed, wrapped around Jessen and pulled him from his horse.

CHAPTER 23

Tenya's horrified cry split the night, "Jessen!"

Without thought, she dug her heels into her mount's ribs and the little mare sprang forward. The others heard her shout and looked quickly to see what was wrong. They saw her dashing toward Jessen's horse and swiftly followed.

Tenya could just make out his figure thrashing about on the ground. Something as thick as a man's arm and several feet long wrapped about his waist and shoulders, squeezing him in a deathly grip. Even in the darkness, Tenya could see the white, strained look on his face.

"Help me!" Tenya cried, leaping from the little mare's back. "Something is attacking Jessen." She grabbed at the snakelike object and her fingers sank into a slimy mass that felt and smelled like rotten vegetation. She recoiled in revulsion.

By then, the others had also reached Jessen and slid from their horses to help her. Felina made a soft sound of disgust when she touched the smelly mass wrapped around Jessen's struggling body.

"What is it?" Tenya gasped, trying to grip the repulsive, flaccid object.

"This must be one of the strangling vines Zardonne has strewn over the Plain." Sindril grunted, as he too pulled at the thick, oozing object. "We must get it off him or it will strangle him to death."

Jessen beat futilely at the vine with his left hand. His struggles were weakening, his face turning an alarming dark shade. The thick mass pinned his right arm tightly against his side.

The others renewed their efforts, peeling the vine away inch by inch–only to have it slither out of their grasp and encircle the boy's body once more.

Tenya moaned softly in frustration. If they didn't remove the vine soon, Jessen would most certainly die, but use of their hands was proving to be ineffectual.

She gripped the repulsive vine tightly and closed her eyes. White fire coursed through her veins and she felt the repulsive object in her hands writhe convulsively, nearly pulling itself out of her grasp. She held on tightly and sent more of her power into the mass, careful not to injure Jessen in the process.

When she opened her eyes, the vine was enveloped in the vivid white glow of her fire. It fell away from Jessen and, the next moment, disappeared in a flash of green light.

Tenya's power receded, slipping back to its secret place deep within her body. Unlike those other times when she used the white fire and experienced a heady exhilaration and vitality, this time she felt drained and strangely weak. *The debilitating influence of Zardonne's evil, no doubt,* she thought, uneasily.

Jessen still laid on the ground, breathing shakily, his face white and strained. He struggled to get to his feet.

"Take it easy, Jessen," Sindril advised, pushing the youth gently back to the ground. "Lie still for a moment and catch your breath."

Tenya dropped to her knees beside him. "Are you all right?"

Still unable to speak, the young man nodded weakly. Clearly, the strangling vine had come very close to crushing the life out of him.

"We will stop here for the night," Sindril said, rising to his feet. "Jessen will need to rest."

"No, no," the youth protested, struggling up to one elbow. "Don't let me delay our journey. I'm all right now. We must continue on."

Sindril looked down at him doubtfully. "Are you certain? You need time to recover from your ordeal."

Jessen pulled himself up further, wincing slightly. He probed gently at his chest. "I'm fine. My ribs are only slightly bruised. Once I'm on my horse, I'll be able to continue."

Sindril and Hanifar exchanged glances. Hanifar's firm mouth twitched in a faint smile. "The people of the Shetii Clan are very resilient," he said. "If Jessen says he is able to go on, then rest assured, he speaks the truth."

Sindril nodded. "All right, then. We continue on. Everyone keep a sharp eye out for more of those deadly little vines."

Sindril and Hanifar helped Jessen up on to his horse. The youth sat in his saddle a little gingerly, but otherwise seemed fit enough to continue travel.

Tenya calmed her skittish mare and then remounted, glancing with a small shudder of revulsion at the spot on the ground where the vine had been. No sign of it remained now. It had vanished without a trace, thanks to her burst of magical power. But, how many more of them lay strewn across this forsaken plain, just waiting to slip with unbelievable speed around another of them and crush them to death?

The group moved forward cautiously, keeping an eye out for the thick, snakelike vines on the ground. Against the blackness of the soil, they found it difficult to discern objects despite the sickly green glow that illuminated the Plain, and stopped twice to rest, overriding Jessen's protests.

Tenya wondered tiredly how much farther they had to travel to reach the tower. She searched the distant dark horizon, but could see nothing rising in icy splendor above the flat expanse of the Plain.

She straightened in her saddle, trying to ease the cramped muscles of her shoulders and back. Fatigue made her lethargic and she knew she had to stay alert. Too many deadly traps on the Plain could spring on them at any moment.

She glanced over at Jessen riding beside her, his pale face pinched and strained. He held himself rigidly. Obviously, the strangling vine had caused him a great deal of pain, but he withstood it stoically. Tenya admired him for his strength and resilience and wondered if she would be as brave if she were in his place.

The Plain stretched on into infinity, the distance to the far horizon immeasurable. Only the startling pinnacles of rock that loomed up out of the dark shadows gave definition to the flat desolation.

The farther they traveled, the more listless and apathetic Tenya became. She felt as though a sluggish stream flowing through banks of quicksand carried her along. Her mind clouded until she could no longer think straight. Half-formed thoughts evaporated into thin air, disappearing into thick mists that seeped slowly into her body.

Exhaustion gripped her. She wanted only to slide from the back of the little mare and lie on the soft ground, losing herself forever in the dark folds of sleep...

"Tenya!"

Vaguely, she became aware of someone shaking her arm, jolting her out of the pleasant dullness that enfolded her like a soft blanket. She protested weakly, wanting to be left alone in her lethargic state.

"Tenya, Zardonne is clouding your mind! Fight it. He is trying to drag you down into death." Sindril shook her again.

She blinked, trying to focus her eyes. Through a haze, she saw Sindril's small, worried face floating in front of her, and she tried to shake off the fuzziness.

"Tenya, snap out of it! Don't let Zardonne win. If you give in, you will die."

She made small, annoyed sounds, wishing he would go away and leave her alone. She desperately needed to be left in peace to sleep. Why did he persist in shaking her arm and shouting at her? She tried to knock his hand away.

Her eyelids were so heavy…she could hardly keep them open. She began to slip from the little mare's back, unable to keep her seat in the saddle.

"Tenya! Fight the spell. Don't give in. Fight it."

Something seemed to nudge her mind, a little voice of warning that managed to penetrate the cloudy haze that had settled over her. *Something's wrong...terribly wrong...* She tried to think, to concentrate on what the little man was shouting in her ear. Something about Zardonne and a spell...

Zardonne! A cold wind suddenly blew through her mind, scattering the heavy mists into tatters. She emerged from the enchanted fog like a drowning person lunging up out of a sea of icy water, gasping and fighting for breath, her heart hammering in her chest.

Sindril's wizened face came into focus, hovering nearby, his dark eyes distressed. "Sindril...? Wh-what...?"

His features relaxed into relieved lines. "Tenya, thank goodness. I thought I'd lost you for a moment."

She pressed fingertips to her forehead, trying to rub away the last vestiges of haziness from her mind. "Wh-What happened?"

His face became grim once more. "Zardonne must have placed a spell on us, a spell, which, if successful, would have put us all to sleep forever, never to return to the land of the living. I nearly succumbed to it myself before I realized what was happening. Hurry, we must bring the others back to us and quickly."

Tenya looked behind her. Felina swayed in her saddle, her eyes closed and a blank expression on her lovely features. Beside her, Jessen slumped over his horse's neck, his body starting to slide from it to the foul ground below. Beyond Sindril, Hanifar, also still mounted, sat stoop-shouldered and swaying. Before Tenya's worried gaze, the sleeping spell slackened his strong features and he slumped forward even further.

Mind clear and focused now, Tenya spurred her horse over to Felina and Jessen, while Sindril moved quickly to Hanifar.

Tenya decided to awaken Jessen first. He was weak from his injuries, and she dared not let him slide deeper under the spell. She caught him before he slipped from the saddle and pushed him upright, then shook him hard. His head snapped back and forth on his neck and his eyes briefly opened.

"Jessen!" She yelled. "You're in Zardonne's grasp! Wake up. Wake up!"

"Go...'way..." he mumbled.

"Jessen, you have to fight it!" She shook him again, nearly jerking him off his horse. "Wake up or you will die, and Zardonne will have won."

She couldn't be sure if it was her words that finally reached him, but with a jerk, he came back, sputtering and gasping much as she'd done. "What happened?" he cried.

"Zardonne placed a spell on us. Help me with Felina."

Together they rode to her aunt, Tenya's heart thrumming with fear. Felina appeared to have slipped deeper under the spell. Her shoulders slumped, her head drooped and her reins lay slack upon her mount's neck.

Jessen called to Felina on one side, while Tenya shook her from the other, yet their efforts made little headway. They were still trying to rouse her when Sindril and Hanifar joined them. Together they called to Felina, each taking a turn at shaking her.

Tears in her eyes, Tenya watched Jessen give her aunt another shake.

The next minute, Felina sat up straight, blinking her eyes. "Elea...?"

"Are you all right, daughter?" Hanifar asked.

She turned to meet his gaze. "Yes, I...I thought I heard Elea speak to me. She said, 'Wake up, Felina. This is no time to sleep. And stop slouching in the saddle.'"

Humor mingled with their relief and they shared a brief bout of laughter before sobering.

"That was touch and go," Sindril murmured to Tenya. "Another few minutes and we might not have been able to overcome the spell."

She shuddered. How close they had all come to eternal sleep! Thankfully, Sindril had had the presence of mind to fight off the effects of the spell and save the rest of them from certain death. From now on, they would have to increase their guard to avoid any more such surprises from Zardonne.

Before long, Tenya noticed dawn approaching. In one respect, the daylight relieved her. They would be able to see their surroundings more clearly. On the other hand, the deep shadows of night had provided them concealment.

No matter, she thought, grimacing inwardly. *Zardonne obviously knows of our presence in his domain. No amount of shadow will afford us protection now. Perhaps, the only thing that will aid us is speed.*

"We must hurry," Sindril stated, echoing her thoughts. "It's imperative we find the tower as quickly as possible."

Felina distributed hunks of bread and cheese, which they ate in the saddle, and then the five of them spurred their horses to greater speed, taking care to avoid the edges of the pools and the gray flats of quicksand that dotted the Plain.

The eastern horizon continued to lighten, bringing the weirdly shaped outcroppings of rock into sharper focus. As the day grew brighter, the group could discern the thick, repulsive shapes of strangling vines on the black soil and were able to give them a wide berth. The vines infested one area so thickly that they lost more precious time in detouring around them.

Tenya began to wonder if they were traveling in the right direction. It seemed as though they'd been riding for days over the forbidding Plain and still the tower could not be seen.

Suddenly, something stung her cheek and, startled, she looked up. A snowflake drifted on the still air, landing on the tip of her nose with a tiny cool touch. The temperature suddenly cooled, as well, as though an icy wind gathered strength, and two more snowflakes landed on her right hand. She went still, scarcely daring to breath, hoping against hope that, this time, the vision would become a reality.

Moments later, the sky filled with cold, stinging snowflakes.

"It's snowing," Jessen cried.

And she knew with absolute certainty...they'd found the tower of ice.

CHAPTER 24

The tower loomed before them, rising in incandescent beauty against a sky filled with snow. Surrounded by the oppressive, foul heat of the Plain, the structure sat in the middle of its own icy winter. The trees at the base dripped with heavy icicles and snow whipped in stinging whirlwinds around the gleaming walls.

The tower itself had a strange, terrible beauty. Shards of iridescent light played within the walls of ice and it rose at least a hundred feet into the sky, a solid, cylindrical block of ice. No openings marred the smooth, featureless walls, but the whirlwinds of snow made it difficult to tell.

Tenya stared at it. Up until now, it had seemed an elusive, imaginary thing, made real only by the visions she'd had of it. And the long, dangerous journey to reach it had made it seem almost unattainable at times. Now, the quest had ended.

Even in all of its icy beauty, the tower still seemed imaginary. But the gusts of cold wind that reached her where she sat her horse convinced her otherwise. Her mother's prison stood before them in cold reality.

She wanted to charge forward at once, driven by her desire to free Elea. Levelheaded as ever, Sindril held her back. "Take it easy, Tenya. We must first make certain there are no guards around the tower."

She nodded reluctantly, recognizing the wisdom of his words. They had gone through a great deal to reach this place, and it would be foolish to let their guard down now and plunge thoughtlessly ahead without first assessing the dangers.

They approached the tower slowly, searching the stark grounds surrounding it. Icy blasts of snow buffeted them, driving glacial fingers through their clothing. The cold proved to be as uncomfortable as the heavy, stinking heat of the Plain.

Tenya's eyes watered from the wind and the stinging snowflakes. She hunched her shoulders against the cold, bending low over the pommel of the saddle to present a smaller target for the insidious wind.

The grounds around the tower appeared deserted. She didn't see any hulking forms of the terrible Guardians, nor could she see any other figures in the whirlwinds of white. Could it be that Zardonne didn't know they'd not succumbed to his powerful sleeping spell, and so he'd not deemed it necessary to place a guard around the tower?

Sindril seemed to have the same thought, for he cautiously said, "It appears all is clear. Zardonne probably didn't think we would get this far and so has not prepared a welcoming committee to greet us."

Hanifar nodded. "We can always hope."

"Do you think it's warmer inside?" Jessen asked, his teeth chattering slightly.

"We'd at least be out of the wind," Hanifar said.

Felina wrapped her arms around herself to still her shivering. "I've seen no way in. Not even a window."

Recalling her earlier vision, Tenya searched the gleaming walls at the base.

"There! A door!" she exclaimed, pointing to a narrow, dark rectangle in the wall. She remembered in her vision how she'd tried to open the door and it had refused to budge under her desperate attempts. She prayed this time she'd have better luck.

The group reached the door at the base of the tower and dismounted.

"We'll need someone to stay out here with the horses while the rest of us enter to find the Mistress," Sindril said.

Immediately, Jessen spoke up. "I will do it."

Sindril gave him a look of concern. "Do you feel up to it?"

The blond youth nodded. He appeared mostly recovered from his encounter with the strangling vine, but Tenya observed that he still moved stiffly. She shivered at the thought of how close to death he had come.

She handed him her reins and smiled reassuringly. "We'll be as quick as we can."

He returned her smile with a chuckle. "Then, it's back to the Plain so we can roast again."

The others handed him their reins and Jessen led the horses to a thicket of ice-encrusted trees a short distance away.

Sindril and Tenya paused at the heavy wooden door set deeply into the iridescent wall and exchanged a quick glance. A tremor of excitement rushed through her. Beyond this narrow door, her mother awaited release from her prison.

There appeared to be no latch, nor any other means of opening it. Pushing against it did no good. It refused to budge.

Tenya glared at the door in frustration. After all she'd been through to reach this place–to be thwarted by a simple, wooden door.

"Wait," Sindril said. "I have an idea." He stepped back and pointed his jeweled staff at the door.

A soft red glow shot from the tip and spread over the wooden surface. In seconds, an object began to take shape. It gained solidity about halfway down the right side of the door. Soon, it became identifiable as a door latch that glowed with its own faint, red radiance.

Sindril looked up with a smile. "Magic against magic. I knew Zardonne would not make it easy for us to enter his prison."

The glow from the tip of the staff receded but the latch continued to shimmer with a ghostly luminance.

"All right, everyone, be on your guard. There's no telling what we may encounter on the other side of this door," Sindril advised.

Her tension mounting, Tenya steeled herself. What *would* they find inside? What nasty little surprises did the Demon Master have in store for them? She couldn't imagine it would be a simple matter of just entering the tower, then calmly walking back out with her mother.

Sindril reached for the glowing latch. Tenya half-expected to see his hand pass right through it, so much of an illusion did it appear. To her relief, he grasped it firmly and pushed down. The door opened soundlessly and Sindril opened it about an inch.

He glanced back over his shoulder at the others, gave a nod, then pushed the door open farther, and quickly slipped through it. He gestured for them to follow and Tenya entered next, her heart thudding uncomfortably in her chest. Felina followed with Hanifar right behind her.

They found themselves standing in a circular room, completely bare except for a winding staircase of wide, shallow steps that led upward. No windows or openings of any kind appeared in the gleaming walls.

Tenya's breath escaped in dense puffs of vapor that immediately froze into crystal clouds. She could see her reflection in the glitter of the ice, shortened and widened by the curvature of the wall. The cold penetrated her woolen cloak and other garments easily, making her feel as though she wore nothing at all.

Without speaking, Sindril pointed up toward the top of the staircase. Since no other doors opened off the circular room in which they stood, it seemed likely that Elea's prison room would be upstairs.

The four of them started slowly up the steps, alert for any sign of traps or guards. The stairs made a ninety-degree turn to the left and the circular room below disappeared from sight. They could see only a few feet ahead, for the steps made another sharp turn, again to the left. Shards of bright, iridescent light played within the wall beside them.

Following closely behind Sindril, Tenya became increasingly troubled by a sensation she couldn't quite put her finger on. She peered ahead as much as she could, not liking the fact they couldn't see beyond the next turn, or back down the stairs behind them.

Sindril reached the corner and paused before slipping around it. He glanced back at her and the others; the same unease she felt reflected in his eyes.

Stepping forward, he turned the corner and let out a startled shout. Tenya moved forward just in time to see him stumble and start to fall. She rushed toward him but hastily stopped, swallowing her own cry of horror. Hanifar and Felina halted just behind her.

Before her, the stone staircase abruptly ended in a yawning precipice that seemed to stretch on forever before the steps continued on the other side. Glittering icicles dripped down the streaked walls of ice, disappearing to a bottomless abyss far below.

Sindril had stumbled over the edge before he could stop himself and now clung to it with white-knuckled fingers, his legs dangling out into cold, empty space. Tenya stared in horror.

His fingers slipped a little on the smooth edge and Sindril said between gritted teeth, "I-I can't hold on much longer!"

"Make a chain," Hanifar ordered.

Tenya dropped to her stomach near the edge and he and Felina each grabbed one of her legs. Tenya firmly grasped Sindril's hands. "Hold on, Sindril! Don't let go. We'll pull you up."

Then, she glanced over the edge, and vertigo snared her. Her vision spun and began to blacken. She had to close her eyes. But, behind her, she felt Hanifar and Felina reassuringly tighten their grips on her legs and she managed to quell her panic.

Sindril's hands closed firmly about her wrists and she pulled. Despite his small, wiry size, she found it a great strain on her shoulders and arms as she tried to drag him up over the smooth edge of the precipice.

She found she couldn't move him at all, even with Hanifar and Felina pulling on her legs. His dead weight swung in the empty air and her shoulder muscles ached as they bunched and strained. Desperately she pulled, yet still made no progress. Fear flooded through her in huge icy waves.

Suddenly, something niggled at the back of her mind, a feeling she had missed a significant point. She looked around, searching for a clue to the nebulous, shadowy feeling. Then, she knew what it was that bothered her.

She looked down at Sindril, her fear swept away like flotsam on a swift current. Despite his efforts to remain calm, she could see the fear lurking within his dark eyes.

"Sindril, listen to me," she said quietly. "You are in no danger. Do you understand? You could take your hands away from mine right now and you would not fall."

A tiny frown appeared between his eyes. "Tenya, what are you saying? There's nothing beneath my feet. I dare not let go."

"Yes, you can," she said calmly, holding his eyes with her steady gaze. "Do you remember the words of Rondilar that you quoted to me when we entered the Ferrish Wood?"

Faint understanding dawned in the little man's eyes. His gaze intent on her calm face above his, he said slowly, "'Open...your mind...to the magic...'"

"'...and you shall walk in the realm of reality.'" Tenya finished.

"You're saying this is an illusion?"

She nodded. "It's a trick from Zardonne. You're not in any danger. Trust me."

Sindril nodded slowly. His gaze still on hers, he drew a deep breath...then let go of her wrists. Instantly, the yawning, bottomless chasm disappeared with an audible crack, and Sindril lay flat on a small, square landing of the stone staircase.

Behind her, Tenya heard gasps from Hanifar and Felina. They removed their tight grips and helped her to stand.

"How did you know?" Felina asked. "It looked so realistic."

"I thought so, too, at first," Tenya said. "But, something about it bothered me. For one thing, the chasm was far too big for the space it could possibly occupy, and for another, we would have seen the pit when we entered the tower, since it would have been in the center of the room. But, what struck me first was the appearance of the far walls–blurry and unfocused, like a mirage in the hot sun. It made me think of the edges of the Ferrish Wood, the way they shimmer and blur. Suddenly, Rondilar's words came to me and I knew this was nothing more than an illusion conjured up by Zardonne."

"But, a very realistic one," Sindril said, rising from the floor and straightening his clothes. "I could have sworn I was dangling over empty space."

Tenya nodded. "That was part of the strength of the spell. As long as you believed you were in danger of falling to a horrible death, I have no doubt you would have done exactly that. But, when we opened our minds to the magic and saw through the illusion, the spell was broken and we were returned to reality."

"Thank goodness for that!" Hanifar exclaimed in relief, expressing everyone's feelings in his heartfelt words.

CHAPTER 25

They continued up the winding staircase, breath exploding in icy clouds, alert for more magical surprises left by Zardonne. Tenya wondered if the Demon Master actually knew of their presence inside the tower or if the illusion of the chasm had been prepared beforehand to prevent anyone from rescuing her mother. And, how many more obstacles would they have to overcome before they found her?

As though conjured by her uneasy thoughts, the next obstacle presented itself with a bone-chilling shriek that clawed icy fingers up and down her spine. The little group had just cautiously slipped around another sharply angled corner when a monstrous apparition appeared in front of them.

The creature towered at least nine feet tall with rust-red scales covering its body from head to foot. The ridges of its face appeared bulbous and deformed. One flaming-red eye blazed high on its forehead and the other dipped low toward its chin. Saliva dripped from a wide-open mouth filled with gnashing teeth.

Tenya and the others shrank back against the wall as the monster in front of them growled and snarled on the steps above, brandishing a long shaft with a wickedly sharp circular blade on its tip. A stench, like the rot of decay, rolled from the creature in choking waves.

Before Tenya could react, Hanifar stepped forward, the folds of his robe falling back as he raised his hands. A streak of white fire raced from one of his pointing fingers and struck the monster's left shoulder. However, either his age or the undermining effect of Zardonne's power weakened the strength of Hanifar's fire. It merely knocked the creature back a step and made it bellow in rage.

It swung its weapon in a vicious sweep and the flat of the blade caught Hanifar in the chest, lifting him from his feet and sending him flying backward with a startled grunt.

Tenya gasped in horror as her grandfather hit the wall and slid to the floor, blood trickling from a gash on the side of his head. Although he lay still, she had no time to rush to his aid. The creature charged down the steps with a guttural cry, swinging its weapon in deadly arcs.

Sindril raised his short staff, but before he could command its power, the creature's weapon knocked it from his hand, sending it skittering down the stone steps behind them. Then, Zardonne's monstrous guard advanced on Sindril.

Tenya looked wildly about. The narrow staircase left little room to maneuver or to use her white fire without possibly injuring the others. If only they could spread out and surround the creature, they might be able to destroy it.

She felt a sudden gust of cold wind and looked up. Felina had conjured a vision of a screeching bird that flew at the monster's head. The thing grunted and struck out at the bird, trying to knock it out of the air. The vision of smoke and air served to distract the creature for a few moments, but Sindril had nowhere to go and could only press against the wall.

Tenya couldn't be certain whether the red-scaled creature was real or another illusion. It certainly seemed to have substance, having sent Hanifar flying through the air and knocking Sindril's staff from his hand.

Now, Felina conjured up a huge, growling beast that circled Zardonne's guard and darted toward it in swift rushes. The creature roared in impotent rage, unable to touch the hallucinatory animal.

Even as she willed her mind to a calm place, Tenya wondered if her powers would be strong enough to destroy the creature. Or would she, like Hanifar, only be able to give it a light tap that would serve merely to enrage it further and cause it to become even more dangerous?

She had to try. She would not surrender meekly to Zardonne's powers, not when she had come so close to freeing her mother.

Almost as if reading her thoughts, the creature turned to face her, ignoring the slathering beast circling it. Its flame-red eyes held a savage kind of glee.

Tenya stared back, pushing her fear deep down inside and reaching for the tingling vitality of her power to give her courage. "Sindril, you and Felina take Hanifar back down the stairs," she said quietly, not taking her eyes off the ugly creature only a few steps away.

"Tenya, we're not leaving you here alone," the little man hissed.

"Don't argue with me, Sindril. Go! I need to be able to concentrate fully on our fine friend here, and I can't do that if I have to worry about you three."

"Tenya–"

She risked a quick glance at him and smiled encouragingly, "Please, Sindril, do as I say. Grandfather needs help, and I think I can distract this repulsive creature long enough for you and Felina to get him to safety. Please, Sindril, hurry! Our friend grows impatient. I don't think he'll remain still for much longer."

Frowning worriedly, Sindril edged his way toward Hanifar, who still lay unmoving on the stone steps, blood trickling down the side of his face. Felina, after a worried glance at Tenya, moved to the other side of her father.

Tenya continued to stare at the growling creature on the steps above her, holding its hot, red glare with her own, and trying to keep its attention on her long enough for Sindril and Felina to take Hanifar back down the stairs. Without turning, she became aware that they had disappeared around the corner and she felt a quick flash of relief.

"All right, my friend. Now, it's only you and me."

The creature snarled, pulling slack lips back over wicked teeth. The grip on its weapon tightened and it advanced slowly, swinging the long staff in menacing arcs before it.

Tenya stood her ground. The soft white glow of her shield tickled her skin and the power sang smoothly in her veins. Her mind remained crystal clear, as sharp and glittering as the ice wall against which her back rested.

As the grotesque monster drew closer, she tightened the muscles in her legs and crouched slightly. In the next instant, she sprang to one side, past the startled guard and up the steps behind it. Spinning nimbly, she sent spirals of white fire leaping from her fingertips.

Unlike Hanifar's magic, hers burned bright and pure white, dazzling the eye in its brilliance. The streaks of fire struck the guard in the back and sent it flying forward into the wall. It hit with a loud thud and bounced back, arms flailing frantically for balance.

Tenya scrambled backward up several more steps as the long shaft with its deadly blade swung dangerously close to her head. Before the creature could fully recover its footing, she hit it again with several blasts of white fire, lifting it clear off its feet and flinging it once more at the unyielding wall. The monster's weapon slammed into the ice and broke in two with a loud crack. The portion with the circular blade clattered across the stone landing and disappeared around the corner.

Tenya lifted her hand to fire another salvo and stopped, shocked at what she saw.

A startling transformation began to take place in the creature–its rust-red body darkened past the shade of blood to glistening ebony, and it seemed to *stretch*, to grow, becoming taller and wider until it filled the small, square landing. A hooded cloak appeared to exude from its body, like a shed skin, membranous, thick and black.

The terrifying creature began to turn slowly to face her.

Tenya's heart pounded harder and the crystal sharpness of her mind shattered, splintering into spears of panic that pierced her calm and control.

She scrambled backward up the steps, slipping on the smooth stone. Her eyes locked on the gigantic black figure that loomed above her and on the black hood that hid the creature's face.

A whimper started low in her throat as black, skeletal hands reached up toward the hood. She knew with bone-chilling certainty that if she looked upon the face hidden within, she would succumb to madness or death. Despite her resolve, she stared in frozen horror, unable to tear her gaze away.

The skeletal hands rose inexorably toward the hood. A faint glow appeared inside the folds, mesmerizing her. She tried to reach deep within for her power but only a sluggish ripple in her veins answered her call. It did not want to respond to her command.

"LOOK UPON MY FACE!" a sepulchral voice suddenly echoed around her.

The bony hands slowly pushed back the folds of the hood. The glow beneath brightened and a reek of unspeakable corruption filled the cold air.

"LOOK UPON MY FACE!" the voice ordered again.

She felt the overwhelming pull of its power enter her, pushing aside her strength and her will, forcing her eyes to fix on the flaming countenance about to be revealed in all its horror.

Yet, deep inside her mind, a thin thread of sanity remained, a sliver of rationality that warned her to resist. If she gave in to the creature's hypnotic powers, she would be lost forever.

But, the thin thread stretched, growing weaker, nearing the breaking point...

Don't be fooled! The rational part of her brain screamed at her. *It's a trick. You mustn't give in to it. Remember Sindril and the chasm.*

The crystal sharpness returned to her mind. She slowly straightened. Above her, the towering figure seemed to waver. A howl split the air, a wail of frustrated rage, and the creature shrank rapidly down once more to its former shape and size.

This time when she reached for the power in her veins, it responded instantly, singing through her body in exhilarating waves. The guard disappeared in a curtain of white fire. Rivulets of water streamed down the wall behind it, melted by the powerful force of her magic. The intolerable stench of corruption disappeared with the guard, leaving no trace on the frigid air.

Tenya remained where she was for a moment, allowing the last of the terror to drain from her body.

She shuddered slightly, reliving those moments of dread when she'd thought she'd be forced to gaze upon the Demon Master's face.

Illusion it may have been, but it had still been very deadly.

She hurried down the stairs, concern for the others paramount in her mind. She would not allow herself to think of the possibility that Hanifar might be dead.

Sindril and the others waited on a landing several feet below where she had battled the guard. Hanifar sat against the wall, his face deathly pale. Felina crouched beside him, wiping blood from his ghastly head wound. Tenya noticed with great relief the faint rise and fall of her grandfather's chest.

Sindril was keeping lookout by the corner. When he saw Tenya, his small, wizened face brightened. "Tenya!"

She gave him a quick hug. "I'm fine. How is Hanifar?"

"Alive. But, he's in no shape to continue on."

She nodded. "That's what I feared. You and Felina must return with him to Jessen and take him back to the Ferrish Wood as soon as possible. I'll free my mother."

Sindril shook his head. "No, I won't let you continue on your own. Felina and Jessen can accompany Hanifar back to the Wood, but I'm staying with you."

"Sindril–"

He held up his hand. "This time *you* will not argue with *me*. I'm staying and that's final. I will not leave you alone. And, you know how stubborn I can be."

She smiled ruefully. "Yes, I know. Very well, I'll be grateful for your help."

Although Felina protested at leaving them on their own, she agreed that Hanifar needed help that could only be administered if he returned to the Ferrish Wood. He could not continue on and he could not be left alone while the others searched for Elea.

"Tenya, be careful." Felina rested her hands on Tenya's shoulders. Her eyes gleamed with unshed tears. "Tell my sister I love her and bring her safely back to us."

"I will," Tenya promised. "Be careful, too. Don't get caught by one of Zardonne's patrols."

Felina nodded and turned quickly away. Hanifar's eyes fluttered open as she bent down to shoulder him to his feet. Once upright, he shuffled slowly along with Felina's help, his strong, handsome face pained and white.

"You'll be fine, Grandfather," Tenya told him, giving his cold hand a tight squeeze. "I'll see you soon and I'll have Mother with me."

He managed to smile faintly. "I know, my child. Be careful."

Tenya and Sindril watched anxiously as the two slowly made their way down the winding steps, Hanifar leaning against the wall for additional support. When they disappeared around a corner, Tenya released her breath in a soft sigh.

"They'll be all right," Sindril assured her. "As Hanifar said, the people of the Shetii Clan are amazingly resilient and strong."

She nodded silently, biting her lower lip to keep her tears in check. "We must hurry and find my mother. There's no more time to lose."

CHAPTER 26

Your mother told me there were at least two guards that she knew of," Sindril whispered, as they passed the landing where Tenya had battled the creature. "That must have been one of them, which means there is still at least one more lurking about, maybe even several. We'll have to keep our eyes open."

Tenya nodded silently. Now that the terror of Zardonne's illusion had passed, she felt strong and vital again, senses thrumming with a fine, sharp edge. She knew that soon she would come face to face with her mother and free her from her prison. Then, they could concentrate their efforts on destroying the Demon Master and his diabolical mastery over the world.

The staircase wound up and up. Tenya and Sindril moved slowly, cautiously peering around each corner before turning it. Their reflections, distorted and cracked, shimmered in the walls beside them, startling them more than once into thinking some grotesque creature stalked them.

Just as it seemed the climb would last forever, Tenya peered around a corner and saw a short, narrow corridor stretching out before them. It ended in a solid, blank wall of glimmering ice. Another creature stood in front of the wall, looking both apprehensive and nervous. It might have been a twin to the creature she had battled earlier, so similar were they in appearance, from the rust-red scales covering their bodies to their bulbous, deformed heads.

This time, Tenya did not hesitate. She stepped around the corner and grimly loosed the white fire in her fingertips. The creature barely had time to register her presence before the sparkling sheet of white light enveloped it. Only a faint, echoing cry issued from the monster before it disappeared in a brilliant flash. Water running from the melted ice wall behind it pooled on the stone floor.

Tenya and Sindril ran swiftly down the corridor. They drew up in front of the gleaming wall and began running their hands over its smooth, cold surface, searching with their fingertips.

"She's behind the wall, Sindril!" Tenya said excitedly. "I can feel her."

"There must be a door somewhere, or some other means of opening this wall."

"Here!" Tenya's fingers encountered a knob that blended in perfectly with the glassy surface of the wall. She tried turning it, but it resisted. Of course, Zardonne would not have left it unlocked.

She glanced at Sindril and he nodded, stepping back. She aimed her finger and a thin beam of white fire struck the knob, shattering it into a million crystal pieces that tinkled in the air like wind chimes. A roughly circular hole, its edges melted into smooth curves, appeared where the knob had been.

Tenya's heart started to hammer. Her hands shook with mingled dread and excitement. She forgot the freezing cold, the dangers of the journey just undertaken, the battle with the guards, her own fears and uncertainties. Beyond this wall of solid ice, her mother waited expectantly and Tenya trembled weakly with anticipation and impatience.

She and Sindril exchanged glances. Again, he nodded slightly and together they put their shoulders against the cold wall and pushed. It began to move smoothly inward, making no sound. A chill from the ice probed deep into her shoulder and spread through the sinews of her body, but Tenya ignored it. When the opening appeared big enough, they stopped pushing and slipped through the narrow crack.

Inside the round, sparsely furnished room, gleaming pinnacles of ice shot through with brilliant streaks of color rose from the floor and hung from a high ceiling. Three stone seats sat back against the curve of one wall and a round, stone table with a top at least two feet thick appeared to be the only other furnishings. The cold, bare room, devoid of any traces of personality or warmth, also appeared totally empty of life.

Tenya stared about in dismay. Her mother had to be here! She had sensed her presence behind the wall of ice. "Mother?" she called, uncertainly.

The sound of her voice seemed to lift up in a soaring echo to the high ceiling above and bounce back at her from the gleaming walls. The chill of the room penetrated her woolen cloak and burned her skin with icy fingers beneath her tunic and trousers. She shivered, crossing her arms over her chest and hugging herself tightly.

"Mother?" she called a second time, and the echo reverberated throughout the cold room.

Mother...Mother...Mother...

"Tenya!"

She whirled swiftly.

Her mother stood a few feet away, a tall, slender figure with black clouds of hair falling softly about her shoulders down to her waist. Large, green eyes dominated the features of her exquisite face. A long robe of dark forest green clung in folds about her slender body.

She held her arms out to Tenya, the sleeves of the robe falling back to her elbows with soft whispers of sound. "My child."

"Mother?" Tenya whispered uncertainly, taking a small step forward. She stared at the woman in front of her, afraid to believe, afraid it was only another trick, another illusion that would start to shimmer and change into the monstrous figure of Zardonne. Yet, a part of her yearned desperately to run to the woman who claimed to be her mother, to be enveloped in those pale arms, her face buried in the soft black tresses. Tenya felt torn and strangely afloat, like a tiny boat set adrift on a vast and menacing sea.

The woman smiled gently and moved forward, still holding out her arms.

"It's really me, Tenya," she said, in her musical voice. "I am not an illusion. Zardonne's powers cannot operate within these rooms, only outside them."

The soft words broke through the paralysis that had seized her and, with a small cry Tenya ran into the arms of the woman whose image she had treasured all those lonely years. Gentle arms closed about her and drew her close. Strands of soft hair, smelling of summer breezes, tickled her nose.

The years seemed to melt away and Tenya felt like a small child again, desperate for a kind word or a loving touch that would erase the crushing loneliness and despair that filled her life. Tears welled and spilled down her cheeks, like a dam suddenly bursting, breached by the rising waters behind it.

Slim fingers tilted her chin up and brushed away strands of hair that clung to the tears on her cheeks, and Tenya found herself looking into green eyes so like her own; eyes that glittered brightly with unshed tears.

"My child, my child," her mother murmured over and over again, as though she, too, could not believe they were really together. She stroked Tenya's face and hair with trembling fingers.

"Mother..." Tenya choked, unable to say more. Her emotions burned raw and chaotic. She could not think clearly. She knew only that she wanted to stay within the circle of her mother's arms forever, and gaze up into her beautiful, haunted face for all eternity.

"My child, I was so frightened for you," her mother said. "I didn't know if you would reach this place safely."

"Zardonne tried to stop us. But, we managed to overcome his illusions and spells." Tenya bit her lip. "Mother, Hanifar was…was seriously injured. One of the guards threw him against a wall and he suffered a blow to the head. Felina and Jessen are returning with him to the Wood as we speak."

Her mother nodded slowly, her face stricken with sadness. "Once he reaches the sanctity of Phantasm, he will heal."

"It's my fault. If I'd acted sooner in attacking the guard, instead of hesitating…"

Elea placed a gentle finger on her lips, cutting off her desperate words. "Hanifar knew the dangers when he volunteered to come with you, Tenya. He knew his powers were not as strong as they once were and he might not survive the journey. He knew all that and still he came, out of love for me and for you. You mustn't blame yourself for anything. You did everything you could possibly have done and both Hanifar and I know it."

"But–"

Her mother shook her head, a gently admonishing smile on her lips. "Tenya, do not persist in blaming yourself. You could not have prevented what happened."

"She gets her stubbornness from you, my Mistress."

Sindril chuckled behind her and Tenya started. She'd completely forgotten him in her joy and wonder at finally seeing her mother in person.

"Sindril!" Her mother took one arm from around Tenya and firmly grasped the little man's hand.

"You've done well, my loyal friend. You've given me back my daughter and I thank you for that."

Sindril shrugged, his dark eyes glinting with his usual, mischievous humor. "I don't believe you had ever lost her. I had to use very little influence to bring her here to you. In fact, I had to hold her back several times to keep her from running headlong into danger in her eagerness to reach you."

Tenya smiled at him, brushing tears from her cheeks. "He's right, and I'm extremely grateful to him for his good judgment when mine failed me. I can see why you sent him for me, Mother. He's a very loyal and wise friend."

"It's easy to be loyal to two such beautiful ladies." He swept them a teasing gallant bow.

Her mother laughed, and then said briskly, "We must hurry. The sands of time are running against us." She brushed a strand of dark hair from Tenya's damp cheek. "I'm sorry we can't take more time for our reunion, my child, but Zardonne must be stopped soon or it will be too late."

"I understand," Tenya said quietly.

Her mother gave her a quick hug. "Then, we will be on our way." She looked around the cold, bare room and gave a small shiver. "There is nothing here that I wish to take with me. The red stone has served its purpose. If Zardonne discovers it now, it doesn't matter."

Sindril led the way out of the room. "Both guards have been destroyed. I don't think there are any more. At least, we didn't encounter anyone else around the tower or inside it."

Elea smiled faintly. "Perhaps Zardonne was so certain of his ability to keep me a prisoner he didn't think any more than two guards would be needed."

Their cautious descent down the narrow winding stone staircase was undisturbed by deadly illusions or demonic creatures. Tenya wondered out loud if perhaps the Demon Master was actually unaware of their presence in the tower and the tricks they had encountered upon their entrance had been safeguards placed there long ago to discourage any attempt at rescuing the Mistress.

"That could very well be," her mother agreed. "But, Zardonne is crafty and clever. It could be that he wishes us to think that, hoping to catch us off-guard. We must remain alert at all costs."

They passed the landing where Hanifar had been attacked by the guard. Frozen drops of her grandfather's blood gleamed in dark spatters on the ice wall, creating their own patterns amid the streaks of iridescent color.

Elea slowed and touched her fingertips lightly to the dark spots. She closed her eyes briefly and a calm serenity passed over her face. "They will be nearing the borders of the Plain soon. Hanifar's wound will improve as the dark influence of Zardonne's power weakens. Once outside the borders, their progress will quicken and so will the healing process."

She opened her eyes and smiled at Tenya. "Soon we will join them, my daughter, and there will be much celebration. But first, there is the matter of Zardonne to be dealt with."

At last, they stood at the narrow wooden door at the base of the tower.

Sindril opened it cautiously, and stumbled backward as a blast of freezing wind and snow came through the opening, nearly knocking him off his feet.

The three of them slipped outside, struggling against the fierce wind that spiraled around the tower and bent the limbs of the ice-encrusted trees in creaking moans. Through tears that blurred her eyes, Tenya could just make out the three horses standing among the trees, heads lowered against the onslaught of wind. She recognized the third horse as Hanifar's. Since he would have been unable to ride by himself, Felina and Jessen had left the horse for her mother.

Elea stopped and straightened slowly, closing her eyes and lifting her face into the direct force of the cold gale. Tenya saw a soft glow surround her mother's body.

The wind hesitated for a moment. Tenya felt the lull and then a vehement blast, that seemed to come from out of nowhere, nearly knocked her off her feet. She thought she could hear a howl of rage in the wind, a shriek that had nothing to do with the elements of nature.

Through it all, her mother stood absolutely still, eyes closed in a face of serenity. The glow around her body deepened. Standing beside her, Tenya could feel power radiating from her, an intense, tingling sensation that filled her with wonder and awe.

The wail of the wind rose and it flung itself in wild circles as though trying to escape the invincible force of her mother's power. But, the Demon Master's tenuous hold over the wind could not withstand Elea's mastery of its myriad powers. A thin shriek rose on the air, climbing higher and higher as the blasts spiraled into a narrow cyclone that spun itself into nothingness.

Suddenly, all was silence. One moment, there had been the fury and might of Zardonne's winter storm, and the next, there reigned a quiet so profound and deep that Tenya wondered if she had only imagined the fierce, chill wind that had whipped about the tower of ice.

The glow around Elea's body faded and she opened her eyes. A smile tilted the corners of her lips. "I didn't know if I was strong enough to break Zardonne's spell over the wind, but my powers did not fail me. How good it feels to exercise them again! I've missed the sensation of them coursing through my body, of being in control once more. I was afraid my imprisonment might have weakened me so badly that I would not be able to call upon my powers when I needed them. But, they didn't disappoint me."

Without the numbing cold of Zardonne's spell-induced winter, the oppressive, suffocating heat of the Plain rushed in to surround them, bringing with it the nauseating stench of its corruption. The drooping icicles on the stark trees melted in the heat and dripped with a monotonous patter.

They heard a faint cracking sound behind them and whirled to stare at the tower of ice rising up to the sky in gleaming splendor. As they watched, long narrow cracks appeared in the glittering surface, widening into deep fissures that spiraled around the circular walls of the tower. Loud grinding noises accompanied the cracks, swiftly rising in volume until the sound hurt their ears.

"The tower is falling to pieces!" Sindril shouted over the deafening noise. "We have to get out of here!"

CHAPTER 27

They ran for the horses under the dripping trees. The animals pranced nervously, disturbed by the rending and shaking of the tower nearby. Elea mounted Hanifar's horse, while Tenya scrambled up on to the back of the little gray mare. Sindril, in one running bound, leaped up on to the back of his horse. They dug their heels into their mounts' sides, sending them into a mad dash away from the disintegrating tower.

Tenya glanced back over her shoulder and was struck by the sight of the tower of ice swaying from side to side, its smooth walls marred by long, spiraling cracks. She wondered dazedly if the sudden cessation of the winter spell had caused such a cataclysmic effect on the tower. Or, perhaps her mother's escape had triggered the disintegration process.

Whatever the cause, the tower literally was shaking itself to pieces.

A tremendous resounding crack split the air. They wheeled their horses around and watched in amazement as the zigzagging cracks racing around the walls suddenly met. The entire top of the tower tilted sharply to one side. There was a gathering roar and the sheared ice broke off completely, exploding into thousands of jagged pieces against the earth far below.

A safe distance from the collapsing tower, the three of them stared at the unbelievable sight. More deafening cracks sounded and the foul air shook with the tinkle and chime of shattering ice crashing to the ground, burying the naked trees at the base of the tower and sending gleaming splinters flying in all directions.

Within scant minutes, the tower that had risen a hundred feet in cold, terrible beauty had been reduced to a jumble of broken ice. Silence descended on a land still trembling from the crushing weight of the falling ice.

Tenya, her mother and Sindril exchanged awestruck glances.

"Well, I wonder if that means Zardonne is not pleased with us," Sindril said a little shakily, despite his grin.

Elea gazed at the glistening pile of broken ice that had once held her prisoner, a still, enigmatic expression on her face. "I have dreamed for sixteen long years of escaping that cold, terrible place. Now, it's gone and a suffocating weight has been lifted from my body." She smiled at Tenya and brushed her fingertips over her cheek. "I am truly free."

Tenya smiled back, the sting of tears behind her eyelids. Her mother positively *glowed*, her beauty heightened by her newfound joy; joy of her escape, but more so, joy of their reunion.

Turning their horses, they rode away from the destroyed tower.

Despite having had very little sleep in the past several hours, Tenya felt strangely alert, mind and body buoyed by the heady adrenaline stirred up by her adventures in the tower. She only wished they were riding toward the safety and tranquility of the Ferrish Wood instead of into battle with the Demon Master. But, she knew her mother would never run and hide in the Wood, content with her safety and that of her daughter, leaving the world at the mercy of Zardonne...and neither would Tenya.

They reached the border of the Plain by early evening without incident. The sickly glow from the green pools brightened as the skies overhead darkened, and a lonely, keening wind rose on the fetid air.

Tenya saw her mother's body stiffen slightly and her eyes close. The same tranquil expression she had adopted outside the tower before banishing Zardonne's fierce wind brushed her delicate features now; and the keening wind gave one last soft sigh before it stilled.

Her mother opened her eyes, a pleased smile on her face. "It feels good to communicate with the wind once more. Zardonne has tried to control it, but he doesn't have the power to bend it completely to his will. It's like a temperamental child. But, also like a child, it can be very loyal and loving if treated right."

They entered the narrow ravine where the Death Patrol had set upon Tenya and the others. The bloated corpses of the creatures killed in the attack still lay where they had fallen and Sindril recounted the battle to Elea. A pleased smile lit her face when he described Tenya's destruction of the Death Rider.

"I had hoped the time was right," she said, smiling at Tenya. "I was close to your age when my powers became strong and manageable, and I'd hoped the same would be true of you. Even though your father, Bentar, is not of the Shetii Clan and possesses no magical powers, it is still the mystic qualities of the Clan that will be dominant in you. Your ability to destroy Zardonne's Death Riders gives me great hope."

Tenya glowed at her mother's words. Even if the Demon Master or one of his servants might end her life shortly, she treasured these precious moments with her mother...who felt more real to her than the bitter, acid-tongued woman and the sad, melancholy man in the far off Ardis Valley. That life seemed an eternity away, an existence that had been merely a waiting period, a pause until her powers had matured enough for her to fulfill her destiny...a destiny that lay with this woman before her now.

As though reading her thoughts, her mother smiled and reached out to stroke her hair. "Yes, we are together at last, my child. We shall never be parted again, not even in death."

"Mistress, I hate to intrude," Sindril's quiet voice broke in, "but time is passing and we must soon be on our way."

Elea smiled at him. "You are wise and practical as always, my friend. You're right. We must move quickly."

They sped as swiftly as they reasonably could through the broken hills toward the Belisar River. Their progress seemed frustratingly slow, but it would have been foolhardy to push the horses too quickly over the dangerous ground.

As they rode along, Tenya kept throwing surreptitious glances at the figure of her mother riding by her side. She had to keep reassuring herself that she was real and would not disappear right before her eyes.

The more distance they put between themselves and the tower of ice, the more her mother seemed to change. The paleness of her face disappeared, replaced by radiance that seemed to come from within, as though the soft luminance of a candle glowed just beneath the surface of her skin. A natural grace and elegance flowed from her, and Tenya remembered Felina saying that where her mother walked the sun smiled and the streams laughed. She could understand how that could be true. Even the ugly, broken land through which they now traveled seemed less harsh and forbidding than before, as though a benevolent sun had come out from behind a dark cloud and spread its rays upon the poor, defiled earth. Tenya had no doubt that her mother's presence had caused the profound, benign effect upon the land.

They approached the coarse-grassed meadows leading down to the churning waters of the Belisar River. Within minutes, they emerged, dripping but safe, on the opposite bank of the river.

As they started to remount their horses, Sindril suddenly stopped, throwing his head up into the air. Tenya, alert now to every nuance and change in the little man's demeanor, asked quickly, "Sindril, what is it?"

He remained still, the expression on his face one of intense concentration. "Someone's coming," he said.

Tenya held her breath, straining to hear whatever had caught Sindril's attention. She thought she heard the faint, distant thundering of many hooves or marching feet coming their way, but it could have been the booming of her own heartbeat. She glanced at her mother. She remained calm and unperturbed, sitting still and straight on the back of her horse, her head turned slightly in the direction from which Tenya thought she'd heard the thunder approaching.

"Friend or enemy, Sindril?" her mother asked quietly.

The little man listened intently, his foot still resting in the stirrup where he had placed it before pausing in the act of mounting his horse. "It's difficult to tell." He cocked his head slightly. "But I would say they are fairly close and it's quite a large party."

"Perhaps, it would be best if we conceal ourselves until we can determine the politics of our unknown visitors," her mother said.

"That is a wise idea."

Tenya and Sindril mounted quickly and the three rode away from the river bank and the open meadow where they were far too exposed. The scarred, broken ridges of black rock flanking the meadow provided many hiding places. They found a cave cut into the hillside like a dark, yawning wound. It was fairly deep and high-ceilinged, allowing them to lead the horses inside, while still providing enough room for them to arrange themselves near the entrance to keep watch without being seen.

Tenya spent a few moments calming the nervous animals, and then joined her mother and Sindril at the mouth of the cave.

The distant thunder grew louder. She could distinguish individual hoof beats, now, and knew that Sindril had been correct in his assumption of the large size of the party.

Pressed against the cold, damp rock of the cave wall, her heartbeat quickened. The faint singing of the white fire in her veins responded swiftly to the surge of adrenaline in her body. She knew if she required it in the next few moments, it would answer her call quick as lightning.

She peered around the edge of the cave entrance. Black dust clouds announced the arrival of the foremost riders. In the next moment, she saw the riders themselves–huge, hulking figures in silver and gold armor on the backs of powerful horses. She drew back slightly as they thundered past the cave and rode on to the coarse grass of the meadow near the river, pulling their huge mounts to a swift stop.

There must have been at least a hundred of them crowding into the meadow, lances and spears bristling in the air. They made an impressive, yet terrifying, sight. There appeared to be no hideous monsters among them, but their huge size and obvious formidable strength would be enough to give even the bravest man pause.

Tenya heard her mother give a small laugh before stepping from the cave, out in plain sight.

"Mother!" Tenya whispered urgently, grabbing her mother's sleeve and trying to draw her back into the safety of the dark cave.

Her mother looked back at her and smiled. "It's all right, my child. I know what I'm doing." She walked slowly forward, her long, dark green robe flowing behind her.

"Sindril!" Tenya hissed, but the little man made no move to stop her.

The men on the horses didn't see her mother at first for they had their backs to the cave. Then, one near the front turned toward the man behind him and spotted her walking toward them. Obviously startled, he grabbed the other man's sleeve. "Rigas, look!"

The other man turned and, from her place near the mouth of the cave, Tenya could see a bushy red beard poking out from the faceplate of his gold helmet. He carried a long, slender lance with a gold-and-silver pennant flying from its tip. The man's mouth dropped open when he saw Tenya's mother.

By now, the other men had caught on that something was happening and they all turned to look. Tenya drew in her breath and tensed, ready to fling deadly spears of white fire into their midst the moment they tried to attack her mother.

"Sindril, we must do something," she whispered, urgently. "They'll kill her."

To her utter surprise, the little man grinned widely. "I think not, Tenya."

She stared at him and then back at the muttering, milling army of horsemen outside the cave. Her mother had stopped, now, and stood only a few feet away, her attitude one of total composure.

"Why not?" Tenya asked, bewilderedly. "Aren't they Zardonne's men?"

Sindril shook his head, still grinning. "Hardly, my dear. These are the famous horsemen of the Coros Region. They would no more do the Demon Master's bidding than you or I would."

Her mother spoke, her voice tinkling like music on the wind, "Greetings, friends. I am Elea, Mistress of the Wind. May I ask who your leader is?"

The man with the bushy red beard closed his mouth abruptly and cleared his throat. He bowed slightly. "Mistress, we know who you are," he said in a gruff, respectful voice. "I am Rigas, leader of the Coros horsemen. We are at your service."

Her mother smiled. "Then, if you know who I am, you must have encountered my father, Hanifar, with his two companions, my sister Felina and Jessen."

"Yes. Only a few hours ago we came across them. They were attempting to cross the river here, but it was much too dangerous for your injured father. We directed them farther downstream and aided them in their crossing. They told us of their attempted rescue of you and said that two more of their party were in the tower of ice trying to free you. They asked if we would come to their assistance. We came as quickly as we could."

"I'm extremely grateful for that, my friend. As you can see, my rescue was successful, but I will still require your help in battling Zardonne."

"We have pledged our allegiance to your cause. We will gladly fight by your side."

The other men shouted their agreement, brandishing their lances and spears in enthusiastic fervor.

Inside the cave, Sindril grinned impishly. "You see, Tenya? There is nothing to fear from these men."

Once again, she had to admit the truth of his words. There seemed to be no danger whatsoever from these imposing, awe-inspiring men on their powerful mounts. Indeed, intense waves of loyalty and zeal seemed to pour from them and envelope her mother.

Sindril took the reins of their three horses and led them outside the cave. Tenya followed, still a little nervous in the presence of such strong, forceful men.

Her mother turned slightly with a quick smile and drew Tenya close to her side. "This is my daughter, Tenya, and my loyal friend, Sindril. They are the ones who rescued me from the tower."

The men touched their fingers respectfully to their helmets, bowing slightly and staring curiously at Tenya. She shifted uncomfortably under their candid gazes.

"I think we can safely camp here for the night," Her mother said to Sindril and Tenya. "You both must be exhausted and our friends here will make certain no one bothers us. Do you agree, Rigas?"

"There should be no problem, Mistress," the big man said. "My men have ridden long and hard this day. They, too, need a rest. Tomorrow will be another long day of battle. We will recoup our strength tonight. I have some of the best lookouts in the Coros army. They will make certain that Zardonne's creatures do not come near us."

Her mother nodded. "Very good."

That night, Tenya did not dream. Curled up against her mother's side, she slept deeply and peacefully for the first time in countless days.

CHAPTER 28

Tenya awoke to a camp bustling with activity. Bridles jangled and horses snorted as the Coros horsemen prepared to leave. Milon, Rigas's second-in-command, strode briskly among them, shouting orders. She spotted the robed figure of her mother standing off to one side with the Coros leader, Rigas, his bushy red head already encased in the gold helmet. The two appeared deep in conversation.

Tenya stretched, more relaxed and refreshed than she'd been since this strange, dangerous adventure had begun. Her limbs felt light and strong, untroubled by the weary lethargy that had plagued her on the Plain of Naryn. Even her mood had brightened at the sight of a weak, pale sun shining cautiously from behind the clouds.

"Perhaps that is a good omen," Sindril spoke from behind her.

She turned to see his familiar, impish grin. "What is?"

"The sun." He indicated the slivered edge of luminance beneath the shelf of clouds.

Tenya smiled, amazed once more by the little man's ability to sense her thoughts. "I hope so."

"How did you sleep?"

"Quite well, thank you. I think having the Coros horsemen here helped me to feel a little less vulnerable."

Sindril pretended to look hurt. "What? Have you no faith in me to protect you, after all we've been through?"

"You're the best protector a girl ever had, Sindril, but a *hundred* protectors are even better," she parried.

He chuckled and handed her a chunk of bread and a piece of dried meat. "Here's breakfast. Eat quickly. We'll be leaving shortly."

She accepted the food gratefully, not realizing until the sight of it how hungry she was. There had not been much time for eating the day before when the priority had been to rescue her mother from the tower as quickly as possible.

The men broke camp swiftly and efficiently. Tenya found that her mare had already been saddled and she mounted, joining her mother and Sindril.

Elea flashed a smile and lightly touched Tenya's fingers where they rested on the pommel of the saddle. "Are you ready, my child?"

Tenya took a deep breath, swallowing past a sudden lump of panic in her throat. She nodded, not quite able to trust her voice.

They rode near the front of the column, with Rigas and Milon flanking them. The men's mood seemed exuberant, as though they looked forward to the upcoming confrontation. Tenya realized they probably did, for they were fighting men, trained and hardened in battle and charged with the excitement and stimulation of the promised conflict.

She soon found herself affected by their fervor. Her pulse quickened and a singing thrummed in her veins as though the white fire vibrated with anticipation. She realized, with some surprise, that the panic and fear had receded far back in her mind.

She glanced over at her mother. A shining radiance that dazzled the eyes danced about her. The sun's pale rays seemed to seek her out, spotlighting her tall, straight figure on the horse's back. Her black hair floated behind her like a soft silky cloud, stirred by a breeze that seemed to touch only her and no one else.

The men broke into a loud, rowdy fighting song, their deep voices ringing out into the heavy air. To Tenya's amazement, Sindril joined in, his lighter voice mingling with the rest. He sang heartily, waving his arm in the air and clapping the shoulder of the man to the right of him, who in turn pounded him on the back and nearly knocked him out of his saddle. Undaunted, Sindril righted himself and sang on without missing a single note.

They reached the high canyon that overlooked the foaming Belisar River by early afternoon. The roar of the water far below drowned out the loud, ringing voices of the men. Tenya could taste the faintly acidic spray of the water on her lips.

Within a few minutes, however, they left the roaring river behind and rode into the charred, damaged land that had been utterly destroyed by Zardonne's wanton army. Rigas led them around the devastated villages, and Tenya silently thanked him for the detour. She had no wish to view those lifeless, blackened ruins once again.

As they came across ever-increasing evidence of Zardonne's unpardonable destruction, the men's voices slowly eased away into silence. A taut anger replaced their earlier exuberance and they became grim-eyed and forbidding.

By mid-afternoon, Tenya's nerves had stretched to the breaking point. At any moment she expected Zardonne's army to erupt from behind the broken ridges and swoop down upon them. Her muscles ached with the tension that kept her rigid in the saddle and the little mare picked up on the nervousness, fidgeting restlessly and tossing her head.

If her mother experienced the same agitation, she gave no sign of it. Her serene composure helped to calm Tenya, but her pulse continued to flutter, every now and then. Sindril's presence also comforted her, for the little man had grown in her affections and respect. She knew he would do his best to see that no harm came to her.

In the distance, she could just glimpse the top of the strange square plateau outlined against the gray sky, when Rigas called a halt. Dusk had fallen and faint tendrils of stagnant mist rose from the huge, stinking bog that lay before them. If she squinted hard enough, she could just make out the eerie shape of the single twisted tree on top of the plateau.

A second later, a greenish flash in the sky above the plateau dazzled her eyes. Distant, muffled thunder came to her on the heavy air and streamers of black smoke rose like ominous clouds on the far horizon. Tenya's skin prickled with an uneasy sensation.

"Our friend, Zardonne, is obviously playing his games just beyond that plateau," Rigas said grimly, his face fierce beneath the visor of his gold helmet. He turned to Elea. "Mistress?"

Tenya's mother watched the unsettling display of light and smoke in the distant sky, her expression unreadable. But, Tenya noticed the knuckles of her hands whiten on the pommel of her saddle.

"Yes, he is there," Elea said, at last, her voice totally devoid of expression. "And he knows we are here, too. He awaits us."

Tenya couldn't help the shiver of dread that coursed down her spine. Up until now, Zardonne had been a forbidding, yet shadowy, figure in the background, exhibiting his terrible powers through other forces while remaining hidden from sight. The prospect of now confronting him face-to-face terrified her. She recalled her frightening dreams, and the unspeakable dread she'd experienced when it seemed the Demon Master was about to reveal himself to her. She steadied her legs against the sides of the little mare to stop the trembling of her knees.

"Then, we must not keep the Master waiting," Rigas declared. He turned to face his men. "The time has come," he said, raising his voice to be heard.

The murmur of voices died down until not a sound could be heard on the still air.

"We ride into battle against Zardonne and his army of monsters. Some of us will not survive, but our deaths will be for a good cause. Zardonne's tyranny and destruction must be stopped. Hold in mind, most of his army is fallible. They can be killed with ordinary weapons. And those that cannot, those that have magical powers, can be destroyed by the Mistress and the others like her." He raised the staff with the narrow pennant high into the air. "Prepare to attack!"

The men erupted into a loud, ringing cheer, their faces darkened with excitement. Brandishing their weapons, they repeated Rigas's battle cry.

Tenya felt as though she burned with a fever. Her senses swam with panic and fear and anticipation. The men's contagious battle fever could not be denied. And though she did not relish the thought of the upcoming confrontation, a sense of impatience and impassioned ardor still drove her.

With a loud roar, Rigas urged his powerful horse forward, holding the staff with the pennant out in front of him like a lance. A hundred voices echoed his cry and the Coros horsemen thundered in his wake. Tenya found herself caught up in the rush, the sturdy little mare jumping forward in a startled leap. She struggled to keep up with her mother and Sindril.

They pounded over the uneven ground, black dust flying up into the air and choking them. They skirted the boggy edges of the swamp as close as they dared to save time going around.

The thunder of the horses' hooves deafened Tenya. She concentrated on her mother's figure in front of her. Dust clogged her nostrils and stung her eyes. Her ears rang with the pounding of the horses' hooves and the wild shouts of the men. She strained to keep her mother in focus, terrified she would lose sight of her. Vaguely, she knew Sindril's wiry figure flew along beside her on his horse.

Suddenly, she heard a piercing shriek from somewhere above her and her throat clogged with terror. Above them, a Guardian streaked across the sky, its gigantic human head angled toward the ground, its eyes lit with a phosphorescent yellow glow.

She cringed, expecting the creature to plunge down toward her at any moment. Instead, it gave one last screech and flew on, its huge, powerful wings beating the air in thunderous strokes as it disappeared in the direction of the black plateau.

Tenya sagged in relief. Obviously, the Guardian was merely acting as a scout for Zardonne, no doubt returning to him now to report the position of the advancing army.

The square plateau grew larger as they rapidly approached. Tenya risked taking her eyes off her mother for a moment to watch the eerie display of green lightning in the dark sky above the rock formation. She noticed several black dots circling above the plateau, and the realization struck her that there must be dozens more Guardians wheeling high above the battleground.

The presence of the formidable creatures above them did not affect the advance of the Coros horsemen. Their battle frenzy at fever pitch, they charged ahead, eager to join the struggle going on behind the plateau.

Tenya wondered dimly what horrors awaited them on the other side of the looming black rock. The thunder grew louder, splitting the roiling sky like gigantic drums filled with boulders. A strong odor of metal and ashes whirled through the clamorous air, making it difficult to breathe.

Guardians screeched above them now, their cries and the roar of their powerful wings constant and nerve-wracking. Tenya dared not look up, fearing she would lose her nerve completely if she did. She concentrated on her mother in front of her. The soft golden glow she had noticed earlier now pulsed like a brilliant halo around Elea's body.

Almost unconsciously, Tenya called forth her own protective white shield and it sprang into being around her. She took immediate comfort in the familiar tingle of it against her sensitive skin.

Above the din in the sky and the shouts of the Coros horsemen, she could now hear other sounds–sharp, crackling noises and muffled screams, the clash and jangle of weapons meeting weapons, the roar of hundreds of voices raised in battle cries.

Her senses screamed with the power of her fear and panic. Perspiration broke out all over her body and ran in rivers down her spine.

Death drew near. It came for her in the terrifying form of Zardonne, the Demon Master. He would be merciless and unbelievably cruel, and she could expect no quarter from him. Somehow, she would have to rob Death of his prize.

CHAPTER 29

The Coros army skirted the eastern flank of the black plateau and charged into a scene of unbelievable turmoil and madness. For as far as the eye could see, thousands of human and inhuman creatures were locked in battle with each other on ground already littered with blood and corpses. Smoke and flame scorched the green skies and ash as black as coal dust fell like rain on the conflict below.

Although, at first glance, it appeared to be utter chaos, Tenya could now see several organized pockets of fighting men on horseback and on foot. Here and there, poking defiantly up into the tumultuous air, varied-colored pennants–like the one carried by Rigas–represented different factions of the resistance.

More Death Riders than Tenya cared to think about led savage attacks against the resistance fighters, and the dull green flash of their magic bombarded the air with a deafening cacophony. Overhead, Guardians wheeled and dove, unearthly screams adding to the din.

Interspersed among the Death Riders' green magic flew the brilliant, colorful streaks of light that told Tenya members of the Shetii Clan battled out there among the others.

Rigas hesitated for a moment and then guided his men toward a low, scrubby hill where several men in resplendent green and silver armor sat on horses watching the fighting below them. One of the men held a long lance with a green pennant flying from its tip.

When he came within earshot, Rigas shouted loudly to the men on the hill. "Men of the Delmas Valley! Who is your leader?"

One of the men came forward warily, holding a huge broad sword out in front of him. "Who wishes to know?" he demanded.

"I am Rigas, leader of the Coros horsemen. We come to offer our assistance. And we bring the Mistress and her daughter."

The small battalion of men on the hill started and a loud murmur rumbled among them. They crowded forward until the man who had spoken to Rigas raised a hand, commanding them to halt. "You may approach," he said to Rigas.

Tenya and her mother rode forward with Rigas while the rest of the horsemen stayed behind, one eye on the battle below and one on the group on the hill.

The man, who appeared to be the leader of the battalion, respectfully touched a finger to his helmet when the three came to a halt in front of him.

"Mistress, it is good see you free once more. We had almost given up hope. The battle has not been going well against Zardonne. We fear he will win again this time." His weary face turned to regard Tenya with undisguised curiosity. "We had heard rumors that your daughter was soon to join the resistance and this news has bolstered our spirits. Now that you are both here, perhaps all is not lost."

Tenya's mother smiled at him. Her face, although pale and drawn, still radiated a serenity that seemed to brighten the surroundings and push back the terrible sounds of battle going on around them. "My friend, I am very grateful to you and your people for your continued loyalty and support. Without your bravery and resistance, Zardonne would have overpowered Tellaron long ago and we would all have been killed or bent to his will. My heart is heavy with the gratitude I feel for all your sacrifices and courage."

The man's grim, tired features brightened at her words. He tried to hide his feelings behind gruffness as he swept an arm out to indicate the bloody, tumultuous battle going on below. "There's been no sign of Zardonne," he said. "He has not shown his cowardly face yet. Instead, he has let his Death Riders do his evil for him."

"He is here," Elea said, quietly.

The man looked sharply at her. "Are you certain?"

Her face remained expressionless. "He is here," she repeated, leaving no doubt in anyone's mind.

Again, a shiver of cold dread crawled up Tenya's spine and she found herself glancing furtively about, seeking out the terrible, black figure of the Demon

Master. All she could see was a milling, churning mass of indistinguishable figures spread out over the rocky, body-strewn ground. Above the clash of weapons and the grunts of men on horseback colliding violently with each other, the cries and screams of the wounded rose.

Tenya's skin prickled as she imagined that flaming countenance turned in her direction, seeking her out and her mother, as well, on the top of this exposed, vulnerable hill.

"He will not show himself yet," she heard her mother saying. "He wishes to play games with us first, to show us how much power he has gained. He wants to taunt and tease me and then to destroy me once and for all in front of my people."

"He won't be able to do that, will he?" the leader of the Delmas soldiers asked anxiously.

Her mother didn't answer for a moment, her eyes staring out at the scene of bloodshed and confusion. At last, she said quietly, "I have been a prisoner for sixteen years, and during that time, Zardonne has grown progressively stronger. This will not be an easy battle to win."

"But, we *will* win it!" Rigas declared, defiantly.

Elea smiled quickly at him. "Keep that faith with you at all times, my friend. It will be needed in the hours to come."

Her light, musical voice rose slightly so that all the men surrounding her could hear. "The darkest time is about to arrive, my friends. It will seem as though the whole world is shattering around you, as though the skies themselves are about to split apart and fall down upon you. You will reel from the horrors that Zardonne will throw at you. But, you will be strong! You will resist his evil and fling it back at him. You will laugh in the face of his powers and show him you do not fear him. He thrives on fear and terror, his powers gain strength from them. Resist his influence and don't give in to the fear. Show him there is no place in this world for him, for we do not abide *monsters*!"

Her words proved to be a rallying cry; the men responded to them like dry grass to a flame. Leaving behind a small patrol for protection, the rest of the soldiers plunged down the hillside into the midst of the fury below, fired with battle zeal. Rigas and his army of Coros horsemen followed on their heels, their wild cries splitting the air as they joined in the conflict.

"Where do you think Zardonne is?" Tenya asked her mother, trying to keep her voice from shaking.

Her mother's gaze traveled slowly about the perimeters of the battlefield. From the slight advantage of the hill upon which they stood, they could see for quite a distance in three directions. Directly behind them loomed the black, forbidding plateau with its lonely tree on top.

"I can feel his presence," she said. "He is somewhere nearby, but a black mist descends every time I try to see him. He doesn't want me to know where he is just yet."

"Mistress, I think we have trouble coming our way." Sindril's quiet voice came from behind Tenya.

A rush of creatures, clawed, hoofed and human, scrabbled up through the jagged rock and spindly shrubs of the low hill upon which they stood, coming straight for them. Their howls rent the air, mingling with the pandemonium below.

The patrol of men quickly surrounded Elea, Tenya and Sindril, enclosing them in a protective circle. Tenya caught a glimpse of a small group of mounted men breaking away from the whirling mass beyond Zardonne's minions, riding furiously toward the hill, coming to their rescue.

The white shield pulsed against her skin as she raised her hands and sent white fire blazing down the slope to the creatures clawing their way up. At the same time, she felt a rush of wind by her ear as her mother loosed her own power on the creatures. Several of them disappeared in a blaze of white light, while Elea's wind lifted others and catapulted them, screaming, into the ominous green sky.

More of the hideous creatures poured out of the churning battle and swarmed up the hillside, scrambling over bodies or trampling those unfortunate enough to stumble in the rush. The horsemen who had seen the danger to those on top of the hill now clashed with the creatures and tried to drive them off.

Tenya's ears rang with the noise and fury of the battle. She felt as though a burning fever had invaded her body, her veins alive with the power of the white fire. The little gray mare, freed from the pressure of Tenya's hands on the reins, spun and whirled at the command of her knees. The horse's breath whistled in and out of her flared nostrils.

"Tenya!"

At the same instant she heard Sindril's warning, something dragged her from the little mare's back.

The white shield protected her from the rocky ground, but the impact momentarily knocked the wind out of her. Before she had time to recover, something huge and scaly pounced on her, pinning her heavily.

She looked up into a face straight out of a nightmare. Blazing orange eyes glared hatefully down at her above a protruding, split snout. Her mother's words flickered across the backdrop of her mind.

You will resist his evil and fling it back at him! You will laugh in the face of his powers and show him you do not fear him.

Instantly, her fear was gone...as if it had never been. She stared up at the creature above her and the power surged through her body, almost stunning her with its force and pressing her back into the ground. The scaly creature's orange eyes widened in sudden realization, and then it vanished in a dazzling flash of white.

Tenya sprang lightly to her feet, whirling to face another attacker from the rear. She dispatched that one, too, with another surge of magic.

Miniature cyclones danced about the top of the hill, spun from the outstretched fingertips of her mother. The cyclones sought out and lifted the attacking creatures, flinging them high into the sky. Tenya's hair whipped about her head from the force of her mother's power.

"This way!" Rigas suddenly appeared at their side, his helmet slightly askew on his head and his bushy red beard poking out in wild disarray.

Tenya vaulted on to the back of the skittish mare and wheeled to follow her mother and Sindril as they charged after Rigas, down the opposite slope of the hill toward the plateau. Above them on the hilltop, Zardonne's creatures howled in impotent rage as they saw their quarry escape. The soldiers of the resistance held them back and prevented them from following.

Rigas led them to a shallow defile bordered on one side by the towering wall of the plateau and on the others by shrunken, spindly trees with scraggly branches and no leaves. Here, they stopped to catch their breaths.

Behind them, they could hear the battle raging on. The darkening skies reverberated with the thunder of the green lightning and, overhead, a Guardian streaked by, its phosphorescent yellow eyes stabbing down at them. A powerful gust of wind from her mother sent the creature screaming in a wild cartwheel across the sky.

"I think we are slowly but surely pushing them back," Rigas said, his gruff voice holding a note of cautious triumph. "The men's spirits have been heightened by the knowledge that you are now here among them. They are fighting with renewed determination."

"That's good," Elea said. "Evil is strong, but good is even stronger and will prevail eventually. We must not give up."

"No, Mistress."

"You must return now to your men," she told him.

"But, I can't leave you alone," he protested. "You've already had a narrow escape. It won't take long for those creatures to discover where you are and attack again. You are far too exposed here."

She laid a hand on his burly arm. "My friend, you are needed in the battle against Zardonne's mortal creatures. I must find Zardonne and confront him. Your own mortality will be of no assistance to me in that battle. It is one that we three alone must wage."

He hesitated still, uncertainty and battle fever waging a war across his heavy features.

"Go," Elea urged, gently. "See that you and your men destroy the Demon Master's army. Without it, he will be helpless to overpower the world."

Rigas seemed to abruptly make up his mind. "Be safe!" he cried, and wheeled his huge horse about to dash back toward the battle going on behind the low hill.

"What now?" Sindril asked, as they watched the burly man dwindle in the distance.

"Zardonne's presence is stronger," Elea said. "He is somewhere nearby. The time is coming closer and we must be prepared for him."

As her mother said the words, Tenya knew the truth of them, for she too began to sense the black aura of a strong power close by. It grated against her skin and nerves, jangling the very sinews of her body. She felt as though something pushed insistently at her mind, trying to insinuate itself in her brain.

The same feeling had occurred a few times before when Zardonne had tried to bend her will to his. She resisted, erecting a mental barrier against the insidious touch in her mind. It finally disappeared, leaving behind just the faintest trace of corruption. She experienced a small thrill of triumph.

"Will he show himself soon?" she asked.

Her mother searched the countryside. "Yes, I think he will. I feel him closer now."

She had no sooner finished speaking when suddenly the air around them disappeared, sucked into a hollow vacuum.

CHAPTER 30

Tenya gasped, her lungs straining for precious oxygen. Dazedly, she wondered if she had also gone deaf and blind, for the whole countryside had disappeared into a white, featureless mist. The battle that, only moments ago, had raged in undiminished furor had also vanished, leaving a heavy silence.

Illusion, she thought, desperately, clawing at her throat. *I'm still alive! This is not death.*

Just as suddenly, she could breathe again, feeling the cool rush of air into her tortured lungs. Sensation returned to her body; the touch of air on her skin burned with exquisite pain.

The white mist, however, remained, blinding her to everything around her. She could sense the presence of someone close by and recoiled for a moment, thinking Zardonne had found her. Instead, cool fingers closed around her own and her mother drew her close against her body, lending her precious stability and security in the blankness of the mist.

"Zardonne!" Tenya heard her mother's voice lift through the heavy layers of fog. "The time has come when we meet again in battle. I am no longer your prisoner. Once again, I am your equal."

Tenya jumped as a pillar of flame suddenly erupted right in front of her and disappeared in a curtain of sparks. Demonic laughter accompanied the fire, seeming to come from everywhere at once, so that Tenya had no idea of the real direction of the source.

"YOU WILL NEVER BE MY EQUAL!" a hollow voice boomed. It reminded Tenya of the Death Rider's voice in the village of Tundel, only ten times louder and far more terrifying.

"YOU AND YOUR PRECIOUS DAUGHTER WILL BE DESTROYED THIS TIME! I AM STRONGER THAN BOTH OF YOU. YOU CANNOT DEFEAT ME."

"You are wrong, Zardonne. That is why you tried to destroy Tenya. You knew her powers, young and new and unrestrained, would be enough to vanquish you forever. But you failed, Zardonne. You could not destroy her, for she is much stronger than you are."

"YOU LIE!" the sepulchral voice shouted. "I AM THE DEMON MASTER, THE HOLDER OF ALL THE DARK POWERS THAT BE. NO ONE IS STRONGER THAN ME. I AM ZARDONNE, THE ALL POWERFUL."

"Zardonne, the Vanquished!" her mother shouted back. "You will never win, my old enemy, for in your quest for mastery, you will destroy the world, and then you will be master of nothing."

"THE WORLD WILL NOT BE DESTROYED. THE PEOPLE WILL ALL FEAR ME AND FALL DOWN BEFORE ME IN TERROR. THEY WILL SUBMIT MEEKLY, FOR THEY ARE COWARDS AND WEAKLINGS."

"Look around you, Zardonne. Why do you think battle rages? It's because these men and women are *not* cowards. They are willing to risk their lives to stop you. They seek an end to your dominance. Do you see them falling to their knees in cringing submission? They are fighting *against* you, Zardonne."

"ENOUGH!" the voice boomed, shaking the earth beneath Tenya's feet.

"Yes, enough!" her mother echoed.

Wind rushed past Tenya, gathering the heavy white mist into a narrow funnel that billowed up into the sky. She could see her mother now, her arms raised above her head, and the world around them reappeared. They faced the dull black wall of the square plateau. Behind them, the battle raged on, but the sounds seemed distant and muted.

Zardonne's demoniacal laughter boomed out once more, this time coming from somewhere above them.

Tenya craned her neck and, there on the very top of the plateau, towering above the strange twisted tree, stood a gigantic black figure silhouetted against the lightning-streaked sky.

Her heart constricted.

Death.

He cannot touch you, an inner voice whispered. *You are stronger than he. Remember that and he cannot harm you.*

She felt Sindril's light touch on her arm. "Have faith, Tenya," he said quietly. "Yours is a pure and noble power that Zardonne cannot touch."

On the other side of her, her mother's hand still gripped hers, and Tenya felt a sudden tingle run through her body, as though a thread of incredible power and strength connected them together, a silken thread that made her feel whole and complete.

Above them, the terrible misshapen figure raised its arms to the sky.

"I AM ZARDONNE, MASTER OF ALL THE DARK POWERS. I HAVE DEFEATED YOU ONCE, MISTRESS OF THE WIND. AND I SHALL DEFEAT YOU AGAIN."

Tenya started involuntarily as pillars of roaring flames sprang up all around them, enclosing them in a deadly circle. She tightened her grip on her mother's hand, afraid of losing that contact, that thread of connection that bound them inexplicably together.

The searing, crackling flames blazed only feet away and she tried not to cringe from them, telling herself they could not harm her. She only wished she shared Sindril's absolute faith in that conviction.

Her mother's magic collided with that of Zardonne, her cyclones of wind spinning his pillars of flame into nothingness. Yet, as quickly as she destroyed his fire, he conjured up more. Now Tenya added her own white fire to her mother's magic. The dark jewel on the tip of Sindril's short staff glowed with dazzling brilliance as he, too, joined the combat.

Energy and vitality flowed through Tenya's veins like quicksilver. Every time the white fire devoured the deadly flames of Zardonne's making, she felt her body expand and vibrate with the force. Her power had strengthened so much it could be controlled through thought alone, pouring out through the whole of her body and not just her fingertips.

Green lightning flashed around them. The distant screams of the Guardians overhead added to the din in the background.

Suddenly, Tenya felt her feet leave the ground. For a moment, her concentration broke with the unusual and rather exhilarating sensation of hovering weightless above the black soil. A light wind touched her body and she realized her mother's power bore all three of them upward on a gentle cushion of air.

Tenya tightened the muscles in her legs, trying to brace herself. Her pulse accelerated as she watched the featureless wall of the plateau fall away at an increasing pace.

Trust.

She glanced over at her mother, but Elea's lovely face was lifted upward, her green eyes concentrating on the black figure above on the plateau. It had not been her who had spoken that faint word in Tenya's mind.

The air around her stirred slightly and she realized the wind itself had spoken to her. She relaxed, suddenly knowing she was safe in the embrace of her mother's powers.

Then suddenly, they arrived, and hovered level with the top of the plateau. A howl of rage split the air. Zardonne had retreated to the far side, his towering figure looming impossibly tall above the twisted tree in the middle of the smooth ground.

"FOOLS, YOU CANNOT HOPE TO OVERPOWER ME. I AM THE DEMON MASTER."

To Tenya's heightened senses, Zardonne's hollow words seemed less terrifying and more like those of a petulant child on the verge of a temper tantrum. And in fact, she suspected his bluster and boasting was meant as much to reassure himself of his power, as to inspire terror in others.

Something invisible slammed into the cocoon of wind that surrounded them. Tenya rocked backward, gasping in shock. She heard her mother take in a sharp breath as she staggered under the force of Zardonne's magic. Sindril fell forward, but the cushion of air yet held him aloft. Tenya quickly grasped the little man's arm and help pull him upright.

Her mother tightened the cocoon of wind around them, quickly regaining her poise after Zardonne's sudden attack. Tenya saw a ball of fire race toward them, thrown by the black figure. But it shattered into a million flying sparks before it reached them, unable to penetrate the wind barrier.

Her mother set them gently down on the ground near the edge of the plateau. The top of the rock formation looked entirely flat and smooth, as though a giant hand had neatly sliced it off with a sharp knife. The only feature seemed to be the gaunt, twisted tree in the middle, gnarled roots visible at its base.

After setting them down, her mother turned her full concentration on the towering figure on the far side of the flat expanse of rock. A great wind rose in a shrill lament and swept across the plateau. Zardonne roared with rage and then suddenly vanished. An instant later, he reappeared farther along the edge of the plateau.

Tenya, startled for a moment by his sudden disappearance, turned to face him and the white fire poured out of her body to join the mighty wind of her mother. The wind embraced the fire and spun it toward Zardonne. He counteracted with a blast of searing, intense fire that billowed toward them like a curtain of death.

Tenya lost her balance as the powers collided and the very earth shook with the thunderous force of their meeting. She lost her grip on her mother and fell to the hard ground, her body rolling from side-to-side as the plateau rocked. The thread that had connected her to her mother snapped, leaving her spinning in an empty void.

She pressed her hands to the shaking ground, trying to push back to her feet. Her ears rang with the din of the warring powers above her and she tried to shake off the dizzying nausea that gripped her body and threatened to drag her down into a black, bottomless pit.

"Mother!" she cried weakly. She tried to steady herself, to look around in search of her mother, but the plateau shook continuously, its very foundations creaking and groaning. She could not keep her balance.

"Mother!" she cried again, desperation strengthening her voice. She had to find Elea and Sindril. She needed the physical connection with her mother and the quiet, indomitable strength of Sindril. She had never felt so alone in her life. Not even the miserable nights in her tiny alcove in the hut in the Ardis Valley could compare with this feeling of utter, devastating loneliness.

"Tenya!"

Her mother's voice!

Tenya started to crawl toward the sound, the white shield protecting her body against the ground, but the continuous shaking of the plateau made it extremely difficult to keep her balance.

"Tenya, here! That's right. Keep coming. You're almost there."

Encouraged by her mother's voice, she pushed on, trying to peer ahead. The air thickened with flying ashes and dust, and she could not see more than a few feet ahead of her.

"GIVE UP, SORCERESS!" Zardonne's thundering voice rent the air. "I WILL DRAG YOU DOWN INTO THE PITS OF HELL FROM WHICH YOU WILL NEVER RETURN. YOU ARE AT MY MERCY. THERE IS NO WAY FOR YOU TO WIN."

A hand suddenly grabbed Tenya's leg and she kicked out violently, trying to dislodge it. "Wait, Tenya! It's me, Sindril." She collapsed in relief, hugging the rocking ground as the little man crawled up beside her. "Don't listen to him, Tenya," he advised, staring directly into her eyes. She nodded mutely.

"Come." Sindril took her hand and pulled her along beside him. She felt a great relief and comfort in his presence. The white fire in her veins sang with renewed vigor.

Moments later, she knelt beside her mother who hugged her close, her face strained with anxiety. "My child, you're safe."

Tenya nodded, too overcome with emotion to say anything.

Giving each other support, the three of them rose to their feet and, instantly, the shaking of the plateau ceased. Zardonne screamed with rage, shaking his black skeletal fists at the trio. He had moved again and now stood several hundred yards farther along the edge of the plateau from where Tenya had seen him last.

He seemed smaller, somehow. She thought it might be her imagination or perhaps wishful thinking, but the towering figure seemed to have lost some of his gigantic proportions. Could it be that their combined powers had a weakening effect on him, depriving him of some of the strength of his own powers?

"He's weakening." Sindril echoed her thoughts, his voice quiet.

Her mother studied the menacing figure intently, eyes expressionless. "We must be careful. It could be a trick."

They advanced slowly. Zardonne backed away, holding one bony hand out toward them as though to ward them off.

"Be careful," Elea said, quietly. "Zardonne cowers before no one. He's up to no good."

They continued forward cautiously. The black figure continued to retreat. No longer did he fling deadly fire at them and Tenya briefly wondered if perhaps he realized he'd underestimated their power; and now desperately sought some way out of his dilemma. He no longer shouted in defiance and triumph.

Yet, just as her mother doubted his intentions, Tenya, too, sensed Zardonne's cringing merely represented an act. He would not be one to give up or ever to admit defeat. Even if he knew he could not possibly win against them, he would not make victory easy for them.

Her head snapped up as an unearthly shriek sounded close by and one of the circling Guardians streaked past, only a few feet above their heads. Tenya felt the fetid rush of wind from the beating of its huge, outstretched wings and instinctively ducked.

The creature flew toward its master standing near the edge of the plateau. While it still hovered several feet above the ground, Zardonne gathered himself and leapt onto the creature's back. His hollow, funereal laughter rumbled in the air.

"YOU HAVE NOT WON YET!" he shouted, and dug his heels into the sides of the Guardian. With a piercing shriek, the creature's wings gathered momentum as it rose ponderously into the sky.

CHAPTER 31

The Guardian rapidly shrank to a black dot in the sky, bearing Zardonne away to the east and the Plain of Naryn. Tenya stared after it, feeling acute disappointment. Would Zardonne elude them after all? She'd been so certain the three of them could destroy him and now he flew out of their reach.

"He's returning to his fortress and wants us to follow," her mother said, her voice tense. "He thinks to entrap us there where his powers will be stronger."

Tenya's pulse fluttered. She recalled Mordis' gloating words about Zardonne's fortress and all its many horrors. Would they be strong enough to overcome the Demon Master's superiority in his own domain?

Her mother moved quickly back to the edge of the flat plateau; Tenya and Sindril followed. Without the cool touch of her mother's fingers on her own, Tenya felt strangely bereft, and yet that invisible silken thread still connected them. Deep inside, she knew she would never be completely alone again, even without her mother's physical presence. There would always be that wondrous affinity binding them together as mother and daughter, and as kindred spirits of power.

Her mother once again wrapped them in a gentle cocoon of air and transported them quickly back down to the ground below the plateau. It looked as though Rigas had been right. The battle appeared to be going in favor of the resistance. The lines of humans and Shetii Clan that had been scattered haphazardly over the battlefield no longer appeared isolated and overwhelmed by the sheer numbers of the enemy. They now extended in an unbroken front that stretched for hundreds of yards across the bloody ground, determinedly pushing back the less-organized pockets of Zardonne's army.

Now with Zardonne out of the picture, the din and fervor and smells of the battle once more overwhelmed Tenya, instead of being a background commotion to her confrontation with the Demon Master. The detachment of Coros horsemen led by Rigas stood out conspicuously among the grim and milling combatants.

Tenya's mother led her and Sindril to where Rigas and Milon sat astride their enormous mounts, behind a small contingent of men battling a group of fanged and scaled monsters.

"Rigas!" Elea's voice rang out.

The man jerked in the saddle. "Mistress, are you all right?" he asked.

She nodded. "Quickly, my friend, we need two of your swiftest horses. There is no time to lose. Zardonne has escaped back to his fortress and we must go after him."

Rigas nodded and gestured for two of his men to give up their mounts.

Tenya stared up at the great black stallion that was brought to her, feeling dwarfed and awed by the animal with his flaring nostrils and glittering eyes. For a moment, she panicked at the thought of riding such a beast, for he was totally unlike the gentle little gray mare.

Tentatively, she reached out her hand and touched the tossing mane of the animal, trying to project her thoughts into his mind as she had done with the murbeest. Instantly, she found herself in a place of swirling colors and shadows, of niches and corridors filled with darkness and light. The animal's mind churned in incredibly active and intelligent thoughts, unlike those of the placid murbeest. Gentleness also resided there, surprising in such an awe-inspiring, regal beast. She knew instantly that she could trust her life to the animal and had no reason to fear him.

All of this took place in a space of seconds and, without hesitation, Tenya put her foot in the clasped hands of the man who had brought the horse forward and allowed him to boost her up into the saddle. Sindril quickly followed, settling himself in front of her and taking up the reins. The second man helped her mother into the saddle of the other powerful beast, whose red coat shone like burnished copper.

"Can we help?" Rigas asked. "I can send some of my men with you."

Elea smiled quickly, shaking her head. "Your men are needed here, my friend. I can see already that the resistance is slowly winning this battle. You must continue to push Zardonne's army back. I have great confidence in you and trust that your courage and valor will win this day."

Rigas's weary face flushed with pleasure at her words. "Our thoughts go with you. Be safe."

She nodded and swung the great red beast about with apparent ease, galloping away from the small group of men who returned to the battle with renewed vigor. Sindril urged his mount to follow in Elea's wake.

The power and strength of the animal beneath her knees astounded Tenya. She clung tightly to Sindril as the landscape rushed by in a rapid blur. The wind brought tears to her eyes, but, also, an incredible sense of exhilaration and pleasure.

They rode eastward, the square black plateau and the noise and commotion of the battle falling far behind them. No one followed, for the resistance focused their efforts on defeating Zardonne's army, their morale and determination greatly strengthened by the knowledge that the Mistress of the Wind walked freely among them once more.

The Plain of Naryn loomed up before the two racing horses. Without hesitation, her mother led them across the stagnant, foul ground, swiftly skirting the bubbling pools of green liquid and pale gray flats of quicksand. The weird formations of reddish rock seemed to rush at them and then fall behind with whistling speed.

Guardians attacked, plunging down at them from the black, rolling sky, their piercing shrieks battering at their eardrums. The creatures could not withstand her mother's cyclones of wind or Tenya's streaks of white fire, succumbing to destruction as quickly as they attacked. Unhindered, the three rushed on toward Zardonne's fortress.

Far up ahead, Tenya saw a huge gray structure looming above the Plain. It looked like a gigantic arch with numerous unidentifiable objects hanging from it. Nothing could be seen beyond the thick, towering legs of the structure, for a pale translucence, shot through with moving streaks of light and dark bands of shadow, hid from view whatever lay on the other side.

"What is it?" Tenya shouted to Sindril.

"The Gate of Death," came back his terse reply.

She stared at the approaching structure, recalling Mordis' description of it. "Do we have to go through it?" she asked.

In front of her, Sindril nodded, grimly hanging on to the reins of the powerful, charging horse. "There's no way around it. We must enter if we hope to reach Zardonne's fortress."

The Gate loomed closer, seeming to throw its gigantic, menacing shadow into their path. The objects hanging from the towering arch appeared to be human bodies, grotesquely twisted and mangled, swinging slightly in the air currents. Tenya turned her eyes away and tightened her grip on the little man in front of her.

The ever-changing and constantly moving light and shadow between the arching legs of the structure seemed to brighten and swirl more rapidly as the horses approached. Tenya could feel violent, malicious waves of power emanating from the Gate now, rushing out to meet them and stop their dash toward it. The hanging corpses lining the arch spun swiftly in the rising wind. A low keening wail started up and rose to a shrill crescendo, startling Tenya, who, for one horrified moment, thought the mangled corpses had come back to life and were screaming in pain and anguish. But, the terrible shrieks came from behind the now violently swaying legs of the Gate, as though something there screeched in demonic rage.

Tenya's mother nudged her mount over to Tenya and Sindril. The golden glow around her body flared with dazzling brilliance, outlining the flying nimbus of her black hair. An incredible radiance shone from her features. Her green eyes blazed with a light almost too brilliant to gaze at directly.

Tenya stared at her mother, stunned by the transformation. She looked like some kind of unearthly goddess who had been born in the sun and now carried its blazing power within her.

"Call upon the full might of your powers, Tenya!" her mother's voice rang out. "The Gate will try to repel us, but it will be no match for our combined magic."

The indecision, the dread, the nauseous feeling of horror evaporated like smoke in a high wind, and Tenya's thoughts converged into a single, bright nucleus that focused entirely on the thrilling power in her veins. She concentrated on the gray, swirling translucence of the area between the rocking legs of the Gate, vaguely aware of the stiffening of Sindril's body before her and the glowing presence of her mother beside her.

Her skin prickled and the hair on the back of her neck rose as a faint hum filled the air, growing and overriding the high-pitched wail that continued from behind the Gate. The bones in her body vibrated as the white fire's singing joined the rising hum and built to an almost unbearable pressure in her veins.

A light as brilliant as the sun itself suddenly flared in front of her eyes and a gigantic rush of wind, faintly redolent of summer flowers, filled the air like the thunder of ten waterfalls.

The Gate of Death imploded! The shattered pieces sucked in upon themselves in a whirling vortex, taking with them Zardonne's grisly and obscene trophies, and the gray, streaked translucence that had hidden from view what lay beyond the Gate.

A gigantic fortress as black as death itself loomed before Tenya's dazzled eyes, sprawling like a blight upon the land as far as the eye could see. Its upper turrets and spires were lost in the rushing masses of dark clouds scudding across the sky. High above, on ledges that thrust out from the walls, Tenya could see the distinctive shapes of several Guardians. The ground around the base of the fortress cracked and steamed, heavy with the stink of sulfur and fire. Flames leaped and died in the cracks, their hiss like the foul breath of a giant creature. Not a tree, nor a bush, nor a single blade of grass lived within view of the fortress; only masses and masses of thick, repulsive strangling vines.

Without hesitation, the glowing figure of Elea charged forward on the great beast beneath her knees, passing the spot where the Gate of Death had stood only moments before. Tenya and Sindril followed.

The strangling vines leaped up from the ground to attack them, but the slimy ropes fell back, scorched and hissing, the instant they encountered the shields around the bodies of the three on horseback. The powerful flying hooves of the Coros horses trampled the vines into obscene ooze.

Far above, Tenya heard the piercing shrieks of the Guardians, but they did not attack.

Zardonne has realized that his creatures no longer have any effect on us, she thought, feeling grim satisfaction and triumph. Then another thought occurred. What other surprises did he have in store for them? How much more powerful would he be in his own domain?

Within a few feet of the black fortress, her mother leaped from the saddle, landing lightly on her feet on the cracked ground. Sindril brought his mount to a halt beside her and followed suit. Tenya swung a leg over the saddle and dismounted, feeling as though she slid down the heaving side of a massive mountain.

"Send them back to Rigas," Tenya's mother told her. "We have no further need of the gallant beasts."

Tenya nodded and placed a hand on the flared nostrils of the great black animal standing beside her. She stared into the flashing, intelligent eyes and projected an image of Rigas, and the square plateau, into the horse's mind, then slapped him briskly on the rump. The huge beast snorted and whinnied, tossing his great head as though nodding, then wheeled about on his powerful hooves, heading back in the direction they had come. The stallion that her mother had ridden rose for a moment on his hind legs and then thudded back to earth, swiftly giving chase to the black stallion.

Flames suddenly leapt from a wide fissure directly in front of Tenya, reaching out to her with fiery arms. She almost fell backward in surprise, but quickly recovered and stood her ground. The white shield around her body hissed. The flames made contact and instantly disappeared in a sharp crackle of sparks with a sound like a great, disappointed sigh. She didn't feel the slightest touch from the fire and glanced at her mother.

Elea stood in a golden halo of light as bright as the sun, green eyes blazing with brilliant power. Wind tugged at her black hair and robe like a teasing, capricious child urging her to play. Such an aura of mighty power surrounded the figure that Tenya almost staggered back from its vibrations.

"Zardonne awaits us," her mother whispered.

She regarded the black fortress with luminous eyes, and then turned to Tenya, taking her hands in her own fingers. Tenya's skin tingled with the touch of quivering power beneath the hands of her mother.

"Be brave, my daughter," her mother said softly, gazing down into her eyes. "You are the Mistress of the White Fire. Your power is greater than that of Zardonne. Remember that in the dark hours to come, for he will try to trick you and destroy you with your own fears. You must push aside the fear and uncertainty, for he will play upon it to strengthen himself. Have faith and know that no matter what happens, I will always be by your side." Her voice caught for a moment as she lifted a hand to stroke Tenya's tangled hair. "You will never be alone again, my child. I promise you that with all my heart."

Tenya stared up at her, too full of emotion to speak. She could only nod wordlessly, the rich sting of tears clogging her throat.

Her mother's grip tightened gently for a moment and then she turned to Sindril, who waited quietly in the background. She clasped his hands and smiled down at him. "My dear and loyal friend, you have been with me for so many years and have always been there when I needed you. I cannot express all the gratitude and affection I hold in my heart for your continued loyalty. It's perhaps selfish of me to ask more of you, but I can't imagine you not being by my side. I pray that you will survive this encounter and will live to tell your great, great grandchildren of your courage this day."

For the first time since she had met him, Tenya saw Sindril blush and look flustered. "Mistress, I would gladly lay my life down for you," he said, somewhat gruffly. "I have sworn to serve you and that I will do for as long as I have breath in my body."

Her mother nodded, her brilliant eyes dimmed somewhat by sadness. "I wish that I didn't have to ask this of you and Tenya. But, Zardonne has left me no choice."

"Nor us," Sindril reminded. "There will be no peace in Tellaron if the Demon Master is allowed to reign supreme. We have the means to stop him and that must be our primary concern. Our lives will be worthless otherwise."

The moment of culmination had come, Tenya knew, when the paths of her short life converged in a single, cataclysmic point and determined the rest of her destiny. Would it be death or victory--annihilation or triumph? Had she been fated to become Mistress of the White Fire for this brief period of time, her life ending here and now? Or, would she continue down the path into a future that stretched into unknown infinity?

CHAPTER 32

A great, resounding boom suddenly split the skies wide open, releasing a barrage of green lightning and hailstones the size of boulders. The three reacted swiftly, prepared for some such attack from Zardonne. The wind from Elea's glowing fingertips flung the deadly hailstones harmlessly away and Tenya's fire and Sindril's magic shattered them into tiny pieces. The flames in the cracks flared higher, reaching out to them with greedy tongues of death, only to fall back in disappointment when they could not touch them.

Tenya felt a great calmness in the core of her being as she fought Zardonne's evil magic by her mother's side. It spread through her body, through her blood, to her bones and muscles and sinew, blending them into a tranquil whole.

The white fire roared through her veins, singing its exhilarating song of power, pure and simple. Its unleashing came easily now, not like the first hesitant attempts when she'd just discovered her powers, and set about exploring their strength and capability. Now, she could master the potent vitality of the white fire and command it to her will.

The white shield around her body sparked with energy. She felt her skin prickle with the electricity of it. Without realizing she had done it, she saw that she had caused the white glow to include Sindril, as well.

The hailstones and lightning stopped abruptly and a new menace presented itself in the form of several Death Riders. Ten or more of them suddenly appeared on their hideous mounts and charged the trio.

The three stood in a tight circle, shoulder-to-shoulder, as they faced the attacking demons. Tenya felt her mother's golden power flow into her own body along the invisible silken thread and mingle with the surging white fire in her veins.

A Death Rider leaped toward them, the huge, slavering jaws of his targ gaping. Simultaneously, Tenya and her mother lifted their hands and a streak of pure-white fire borne on a rushing current of wind lifted the Death Rider from the back of his mount straight up into the air. With a blinding flash, the demon suddenly exploded and disappeared, his ashes sucked upward into the black, rolling clouds high in the sky.

The other Death Riders came at them relentlessly, their charge accompanied by a deafening boom of thunder and the acrid taste of metal and ashes. Balls of green lightning streaked from their hands toward Tenya and her companions.

The ground heaved and buckled as though something monstrous and alive tried to escape from beneath it. Tenya struggled to keep her footing while concentrating on the Death Riders at the same time. The air vibrated with the static crackle of the two opposing powers.

Zardonne's minions screamed and howled in impotent rage, their deadly magic unable to penetrate the glowing shields of the three. One by one, the Death Riders exploded, disappearing into the fiery air like flaming ghosts.

"Into the fortress!" Elea cried, whirling, as the last demon vanished in a crackling stream of sparks.

The whole wall of the black fortress in front of them suddenly erupted into a sheet of flame, the heat of it so intense that it threw them backward like leaves on a strong wind.

"YOU WILL NOT ENTER!" Zardonne's disembodied voice thundered.

Tenya picked herself up, instinctively throwing her arm in front of her face to shield her eyes from the blazing wall in front of her.

The Portal of Fire...

According to Mordis, the Portal of Fire was the only way into the Demon Master's fortress. Not an easy feat as the Portal was capable of igniting unwelcome intruders like a torch.

Tenya threw a swift glance at her mother. Her face glowed brightly, the crackling flames of the Portal reflected in the brilliance of her eyes. Yet, she seemed unperturbed by the hot, raging fire that prevented them from entering the fortress.

"You cannot keep us out, Zardonne!" Elea cried, regaining her feet. "You have failed. There is no hope of victory."

"NO! VICTORY WILL BE MINE!" the hollow voice boomed, insane with rage. "YOU CANNOT STOP ME."

The Portal flared brighter, the heat intensifying. Tenya felt the brush of it even through her protective shield and wanted to back away from the blazing conflagration. But she didn't. A glance at her mother showed she remained still, her body straight and tall as she faced the roaring fire.

Overhead, the Guardians shrieked, ponderously lifting from the ledges and taking to the air. But they did not attack, keeping well out of reach of the magic of the three far below on the ground.

Tenya tuned them out, knowing somehow that she had nothing to fear from them. Instead, she concentrated her attention on the formidable Portal of Fire.

"Look at me, Tenya." She heard her mother say.

She quickly turned to face her, startled by the unusual firmness of her mother's musical voice. She found herself caught up in the dazzling luminance of her mother's eyes, everything receding swiftly until nothing remained but that shining brilliance.

"Listen well to me, Tenya. There must be no fear in your heart. Only by the complete absence of terror can you hope to enter the Portal of Fire and survive. Zardonne will feed on any scrap of fear he detects within you, and by doing so, will destroy you. Remember that the white fire will protect you. No

314

matter what happens, know that your powers are greater than those of evil. Trust me, my child."

Tenya nodded, held by her mother's compelling gaze and the quiet, forceful words washing over her like a balmy sea.

"Stay by my side," her mother went on. "Remember my words. There is no doubt they will be tested." She turned to face the Portal once more and Tenya turned with her.

The flames of the fiery door appeared to diminish, suddenly becoming less intense. Through a strange mist of detachment, Tenya wondered if she only imagined their weakening because of Elea's words, or if indeed the flames were dying.

She seemed to be filled with a bright white light. Her body and mind felt ethereal, as though she floated on a plane other than a physical one; as though she was no longer bound to the heaving earth but drifting in a dimension of spiritual purity. No darkness or shadow lurked anywhere. There was no place for fear or cowardice to hide.

When she followed her mother into the Portal of Fire, it seemed as though she did so in a dream. The roaring flames parted with great hissing sighs and she passed through untouched by their deadly heat. True, her body burned, but with the heady singing of her own fire, not with the dark power of Zardonne's magic.

There came a great rumbling howl from a distance, its echoes ringing in her head like the muffled tones of a gigantic bell. The flames of the Portal licked hungrily on either side of her, unable to reach her.

LOOK UPON THE POWER OF MY FACE, DAUGHTER OF THE WIND!

Zardonne's voice hissed in her mind, trying to break through the barrier of her will, but she ignored it. The clear purity of her inner light rejected the Demon Master's presence, thrusting it aside easily.

YOU WILL DIE! The hollow, disembodied voice screeched madly. LOOK AT HOW I TREAT THOSE WHO FAIL ME AND WORK AGAINST ME.

The fiery door suddenly vanished. In its place, row upon row of black pillars reached to an invisible ceiling far above. Mangled corpses that only remotely resembled the humans they once had been hung from each pillar, their grotesquely battered faces twisted in grimaces of terror and agony, reflecting the unbelievable horror of their deaths.

Two of the contorted bodies directly in front of Tenya seemed vaguely familiar to her, although the brutality of their wounds made it difficult to recognize them.

Sindril put into words her suspicions when he said quietly, "Mordis and Falgar. I see they've paid for their failure to do the Demon Master's bidding."

Tenya stared at the two bodies high up on the black pillars. They had indeed paid dearly for letting her escape them, not once but twice. The old hag would no longer find prizes for her master, nor would the simple-minded giant Falgar do the old woman's bidding without question. Mordis' quick tongue had not been able to save her this time.

"YOU WILL SUFFER THE SAME FATE!" Zardonne's voice no longer screeched in Tenya's head but echoed around the vast room with its black pillars of death.

"We are not helpless humans like these!" Tenya found herself shouting. "The great Zardonne may be able to exert his will on those unable to fight back, but he will find that it is not so simple to defeat those whose powers are even greater than his."

"I AM THE DEMON MASTER! I WILL DESTROY YOU AND CLAIM VICTORY OVER THE WORLD."

Black smoke interspersed with radiant tongues of flames suddenly billowed in front of the pillars, and a face, gigantic and wavering, glared out at them from the curtain of smoke. For the first time, Zardonne, the Demon Master, revealed himself to Tenya in all his terrible depravity.

Stark white bones thrust out from tatters of skin on a face that dripped and oozed with dark slime. Two orbs of green light, blinding in their ghastly brilliance, blazed where eyes should have been. On the bare skull grew not hair but thousands of tiny white worms that wriggled obscenely.

Tenya felt herself staggering backward. Revulsion and horror cracked the crystal shield in her mind as she felt herself drowning in the blazing orbs glaring down at her. She fell under the sudden weight of Zardonne's triumphant voice, unable to stop the intrusion of it into her mind.

YES, LOOK AT ME, DAUGHTER OF THE WIND! LOOK UPON MY FACE. THERE IS NO ESCAPE. I AM YOUR MASTER AND YOU SHALL OBEY ME.

Pain stabbed into her mind and she whimpered softly. She raised her hands in front of her face, trying to scramble away from the terrible visage that hung in the smoky air only feet away from her. Zardonne's hollow, gloating laughter filled her ears.

Suddenly, strong fingers gripped her shoulders, shaking her. She moaned, trying to pull away, her eyes shut tightly. Still, Zardonne's ghastly face imprinted itself boldly upon her mind.

"Tenya, look at me!"

She jerked, feeling the invasion of another voice, but this time it whispered light and musical, cutting through the pain and terror.

"My daughter, look at ME! You must look at me now."

She opened her eyes and her mother's luminous gaze shone from a white, strained face.

"Thrust the fear away, my child," her mother ordered quietly, her eyes staring intently into Tenya's. "He cannot harm you if you don't let him. Remember, the way to triumph is through light, not the darkness of fear."

Tenya clung to her mother, feeling the thread that bound them thrum with vibrant power. It poured into her, rekindling the white light that had filled her before, and Zardonne's triumphant voice suddenly vanished from her mind, cut off as abruptly as though a door had slammed shut.

The black smoke swirled madly. Zardonne's image howled; the black hole of his mouth opening wide to release a torrent of wriggling snakes. This time, Tenya did not succumb to the Demon Master's horrors. She realized that Zardonne had chosen her because she was the most vulnerable of the three. But with her mother's help, she had succeeded in regaining the crystal shield in her mind and she now stared unmoved at Zardonne's image.

"Do what you will, Demon Master," she said, grimly. "I no longer fear you."

In an instant, the black smoke and the tall pillars with their mangled corpses disappeared. The three found themselves standing on the edge of a sheer rock cliff. Hundreds of feet below them, a seething cauldron of molten lava and fire churned and belched, sending streamers of sulfuric flame up into the air. Ghastly howls and screams could be heard rising from the burning pit.

"The Dark Rift," Sindril whispered beside Tenya. "That hellhole below is where Zardonne originally came from."

The Demon Master stood several hundred yards away, arms raised high to a sky that glared with a vibrant red glow. His hideous face burned with alternating patterns of red and black. Suddenly, the black, misshapen figure lowered his arms and glowered at them, the green phosphorescent orbs in his face blazing with unholy light.

"THE TIME FOR GAMES HAS PAST. YOU AND YOUR SPAWN HAVE MADE A GRAVE MISTAKE IN FOLLOWING ME HERE TO MY DOMAIN, FOR HERE MY POWERS ARE FAR GREATER THAN YOURS. YOU ARE FOOLISH TO THINK YOU CAN DEFEAT ME."

Tenya's mother returned his fiery gaze, her features bathed in an unearthly glow that reminded Tenya of a sun shining through pale mist. "I defeated you once, Zardonne, and almost a second time. *You* made a grave mistake by ignoring me in my prison all these years. It gave me the opportunity to strengthen my own powers. Without your interference, I had sixteen years to concentrate on them. And, my daughter has had time to develop *her* powers without any attention from you. Your reign of terror has ended, Zardonne. You're no longer master of anything."

"I AM THE MASTER OF EVERYTHING!" he roared, and Tenya felt the very earth shake beneath her feet with the force of his anger. Below her, the molten lava and flames flared higher, hissing with mighty sighs.

"YOUR REIGN AS MISTRESS OF THE WIND WILL END THIS DAY!" Zardonne went on, his hideous face burning with triumph. "AND YOUR SPAWN WILL NOT LIVE TO TRY TO TAKE YOUR PLACE. I WILL SHOW NO MERCY TO MY ENEMIES."

"Your words are mighty, Zardonne, but they are empty husks upon the wind. Already, the resistance is defeating your army, and you have seen how your Death Riders and Guardians are ineffectual against our powers. Your own powers are weakening. The world is rebelling against you and soon there will be no place where your evil can reach."

"I SHOULD HAVE DESTROYED YOU SIXTEEN YEARS AGO!" Zardonne roared.

"But, you could not," Elea said calmly. "The best you could do was to imprison me. But, now, even in that you have failed. Your powers were not strong enough to keep me in my prison when another power–in the form of my daughter–presented itself. Even in your own domain, Zardonne. The cycle of your evil has completed itself. It is now ended, here today, in this final confrontation. You will be sent back into the Rift, *never* to return."

"NO!"

The fierce red glow of the sky flared brighter and a sudden clap of deafening thunder startled Tenya. Stinging, acrid smoke and ashes suddenly swirled in mad cyclones around them.

Beside her, Tenya heard Sindril cry out in a single, sharp yelp of pain.

She whirled to see the little man suddenly snatched from his feet by an invisible force and lifted high into the air, arms and legs jerking spasmodically like a puppet on a string.

CHAPTER 33

Sindril dangled in the air above Tenya's head, his small, wizened face contorted in agony as his limbs continued their frenzied movements. Streaks of green light swirled around him, darting in to touch him, and each time they made contact, he jerked in pain. Tenya saw him clench his teeth, refusing to cry out again.

"What are you doing to him?" she cried, whirling to face Zardonne. The black figure threw back his head and roared his hollow laughter, his eyes blazing with their hellish light.

Above her, the light surrounded Sindril's right arm and jerked it straight out from his side. An audible crack sounded as the bone in his shoulder broke and he could no longer prevent a moan from escaping. But he clamped his teeth down on his lower lip, drawing blood, determined not to cry out in agony.

Tenya stared at the little man, anguished by his suffering. She drew a deep breath, feeling it build inside her body, gliding through her veins like a river of molten lava. The center of her being became a place of blinding light.

She turned once more to face Zardonne, who continued with his insane laughter as his hands traced patterns in the bitter, pungent air–patterns that caused Sindril to convulse and jerk above her head. She saw the Demon Master through a haze of white light, unaware that her eyes had taken on the brilliant, luminous glow that shone from her mother's eyes. A quiet coldness settled over her body, not a physical thing but an extension of her mind...an infinite, glittering component of her spirit.

Her body felt light and ethereal, as though at any moment she would leave the ground and float in the air. The white fire in her veins sang excitedly, vibrating her very bones with its stimulating power.

"Zardonne," Her quiet voice cut through the air.

His laughter stopped abruptly, as did the elaborate movements of his hands. Sindril slumped in the air, still held by the invisible bonds that had lifted him, but no longer surrounded by the darting fingers of pain-inflicting green light.

The Demon Master stared at Tenya's glowing figure, the black hole of his mouth twisting into the grotesque parody of a smile.

"SO, SPAWN OF THE MISTRESS, DO YOU WISH TO CHALLENGE ME? DO YOU WISH TO GIVE YOUR LIFE IN EXCHANGE FOR THIS WORTHLESS TOAD'S?"

"I challenge you, Zardonne," Tenya said calmly.

"SO BE IT."

The invisible force that held Sindril in the air suddenly released him and, with a faint cry, he dropped heavily to the ground. He remained there, clutching his right arm, his wizened face strained and white.

Tenya realized, vaguely, that Sindril was free from Zardonne's deathly grip, and that her mother stood somewhere behind her, but the full force of her attention remained on the gigantic, black figure in front of her. She no longer feared that Zardonne would invade her mind as he had earlier. She had learned to shield herself against him and knew he could not touch her that way again. Not even an echo of fear thrummed in her body, only that brilliant, strong light.

Zardonne moved a little closer. The ugly red glow of the sky bathed his ghastly features in alternating shades of light and shadow. Triumph imbued his features as though he relished the coming contest and had no doubt about its outcome.

Tenya heard the soft murmur of her mother's voice behind her and the perfume of scented summer breezes filled her nostrils. "Tenya, my child, know that I am with you always. There can never be a separation of us again, not even in death. The final step of your growth is now at hand, for you have the inner light that is necessary for the mastery of your powers. Use it to the fullest extent of your abilities and you will know victory."

Tenya looked down to behold a sword in her right hand–a sword that glowed with the dazzling white of the shield that surrounded her body. It felt light and insubstantial, like an illusion, but its power ran through her fingertips into the inner core of light suffusing her body.

A sword suddenly appeared in Zardonne's hand, also. He flicked it almost playfully in front of him, a death-like smile on his face.

"YOU DARE TO PIT YOUR PUNY POWERS AGAINST THOSE OF THE MASTER!" he sneered. "WE SHALL SEE WHO WILL BE THE STRONGER."

Tenya said nothing at all as she gazed at the demonic figure. She tested the sword in her hand experimentally, relishing the light, delicate feel of it and the quiver of its power through her fingertips. The clear, pure light in her body hummed softly through her blood.

Without warning, Zardonne sprang forward, sword thrust out before him. Tenya leaped lightly to one side and his sword hissed by her. Green light streaked in the wake of the magical metal.

Her own sword quivered and she felt the hand holding it lift of its own accord. A faint whisper sounded as the sword struck at Zardonne only a few feet away. The demon jerked and grunted, a puff of smoke rising from his flesh where the glowing sword had touched. He jumped backward out of the way.

Tenya pursued him, pressing her advantage, the sword in her hand humming with power. Once more, she struck at him, but he saw the blow coming and twisted to one side before it could reach him. His weapon clashed with hers and vivid sparks showered the air, hissing as they landed on the ground.

Tenya felt the weight of Zardonne's sword pressing on hers and she struggled not to buckle under it. He applied more pressure and her right arm quivered. Then, the white glow around her body flared brighter and strength flowed into her arm. She shoved the sword away and sprang backward. Zardonne grunted at the sudden release of pressure on his weapon.

Tenya crouched slightly, watching every movement of her foe. Zardonne's green, phosphorescent eyes blazed out of his distorted face. He no longer smiled his triumphant sneer. She wondered if he realized that victory over her was not going to be as easy to achieve as he'd first thought.

Before he had a chance to attack her, she again sprang forward and clashed her weapon against his, driving him back a step. He opened his mouth wide, releasing a torrent of hissing, wriggling snakes, but Tenya could no longer be intimidated by his illusions. The sight of the snakes in no way disturbed the clear sharpness of her purpose. She swung her sword in a series of quick flurries, trying to thrust past Zardonne's weapon to his deformed body. The illusion of the snakes instantly disappeared when he realized it had no effect.

He howled in rage. Tenya's swift blows continued to drive him backward. His body began to fade as he tried to vanish like he had before on the plateau. Just as quickly, it took on substantial form again.

Noting the rapid reversal of his transformation, Tenya felt a quick jolt of triumph, realizing what it might mean. "You are weakening, Zardonne! Your powers are diminishing the longer we fight."

"NO!" He tried to disappear again.

This time he succeeded, his body vanishing in a phosphorescent cloud of sparks. Some instinct warned Tenya and she whirled in time for Zardonne's reappearance behind her. He held his sword thrust out to impale her. She leaped backward, but the tip of his sword touched the white shield near her right shoulder, lifting her off her feet and slamming her to the ground. For an instant, she lay stunned. Then she saw Zardonne's face twisted with the strain of reaching past her defenses and the sight heartened her.

She scrambled to her feet before he had a chance to press his advantage. The sword in her hand flared brightly, the white glow tracing vivid patterns in the air before her as she advanced.

Zardonne raised his sword to parry her thrust. The tip of Tenya's sword slid down the blade of his weapon and into his right arm. Instantly, the limb burst into flame and he howled in pain, dancing backward. The flames suddenly disappeared and, with them, Zardonne's arm. His sword dropped to the ground, released by a hand that no longer existed to hold it.

Zardonne threw back his head and shrieked with rage and pain at the glowing red sky. A torrent of deafening thunder and green lightning rent the air, ripping it apart. His black figure began to expand toward the split heavens. Before he could reach the gigantic proportions he had been capable of earlier, he wavered and shrank back to his former size, his bellows growing more frenzied and insane at this further betrayal by his powers.

"He weakens, Tenya!" Elea called out. "Let the power take command. Open your mind completely to it and it will not fail you."

Tenya's veins hummed, the song of the white fire rising to an exquisite crescendo that transcended all previous levels she had experienced. Her whole body felt transformed into a vessel of blinding light and white fire.

Zardonne regained his sword, holding it now in his left hand. His hellish eyes blazed furiously as he glared at Tenya, standing several feet away.

"YOU SHALL PAY DEARLY FOR THIS!" he hissed, stabbing the sword through the empty air where his right arm had been.

"And, you shall pay dearly for the evil and suffering you have forced upon the world!" Tenya's voice rang out.

She wondered for a moment who had spoken, for the voice sounded so unlike her own that she did not recognize it. It seemed almost as though she had spoken through a vast, empty chamber that had lifted her words into clear, ringing reverberations.

Zardonne hissed again and the sword in his left arm swished rapidly through the air. Instantly, a black fog, thick and dense, descended on Tenya, snuffing out the brilliant glow of her radiance.

There followed a tiny instance of suffocation and blindness, of unspeakable foulness penetrating her nostrils, and then the black fog disappeared, lifted into nothingness by cyclones of wind spun from her mother's fingertips. Tenya's body quivered as the lustrous glow of her inner light flared once more into a brilliance that could not be looked upon directly.

Zardonne, realizing that once more his magic had failed to destroy her, leaped away with a maddened shriek. The sword disappeared from his hand, its magical properties useless against Tenya's sorcery. He raced toward the edge of the sheer rock cliff, where the vivid reflections of the seething cauldron hundreds of feet below played rapidly on the black lusterless rock wall.

Tenya could not guess at his intentions, but she knew with a sudden certainty that if she did not stop him immediately he would surely find an escape. Barely feeling the ground beneath her feet, she pursued the fleeing Zardonne. She became aware of her mother keeping pace by her side, the glow from both their bodies intermingling in a crackling combination of power.

"Don't let him escape, Tenya!" her mother cried.

Zardonne stopped at the edge of the sheer drop and looked back at them, eyes blazing in his ravaged face.

"I SHALL BE BACK SOMEDAY! MARK MY WORDS, FOR YOU HAVE NOT SEEN THE LAST OF ME."

He turned and leapt, triumphant laughter ringing out into the heavy, ash-filled air.

Tenya knew with a sudden certainty that if he reached the other side of the chasm he would be gone beyond her reach. He would escape and return someday as he promised, to wreak further havoc and suffering on Tellaron.

Her mother must have sensed it, too, for she cried out in a clear, ringing voice, "Now, my daughter! We must bind our magic together and destroy the monster."

A tremendous rush of power surged through Tenya's body. The white fire leaped from her veins and mingled with a blast of powerful wind from Elea's glowing fingertips. Like a swelling tidal wave, it raced toward the airborne Zardonne, reaching gigantic proportions that encompassed the whole flickering horizon against which the demon's black figure was silhouetted.

The up-swelling wave hit the flying figure. The force of the blow made it seem as though the red sky itself had exploded and split wide open, releasing at once all the thunder and lightning the heavens were capable of producing. Zardonne's body abruptly halted in mid-air and a strangled cry wrenched from him as the white fire and wind engulfed him in a powerful grip.

"NO-O-O-O!"

His struggling body began to fall rapidly, borne swiftly downward on the stream of white fire...down toward the seething, blistering cauldron of molten lava and fire. The flames flared up hungrily toward the plummeting figure, as though eager to be fed. The hot stench of sulfur filled the air.

Tenya watched dispassionately as Zardonne's howling, struggling figure hit the boiling mass of lava and flames. A sudden, violent explosion from the cauldron spewed pillars of molten death high into the air. The howls and screeches of the demons from beyond the Dark Rift intensified as Zardonne, the

Demon Master, disappeared into the churning lava and fire.

Beside her, Tenya heard her mother say, "Quickly! We must seal the Rift!"

Combining their powers once more, they sent tons of black, jagged rock down into the seething cauldron, filling it to the brim. Tenya's white fire melted the boulders into a molten liquid that quickly solidified into a smooth seal that completely covered the yawning chasm, abruptly cutting off the hissing steam and pillars of molten lava and the frenzied screams of the demons far below.

CHAPTER 34

Tenya, we must leave this place at once!"

As though from a great distance, Tenya heard her mother's voice and the note of urgency in it. She drew quickly away from the edge of the sealed-off chasm, realizing for the first time that the ground around her shook and heaved violently.

Her mother's fingers touched her arm. "Zardonne's domain in this world is destroying itself now that the Dark Rift has been sealed," she shouted close to Tenya's ear, for the din around them made normal conversation impossible.

Tenya suddenly became aware of the absence of the bright white light that had filled her body. Its extraordinary power still echoed in her veins, but the heady strength of it had disappeared. Even the white shield around her body faded slightly, although she could still feel the tingle of it against her sensitive skin.

She wondered with a sudden desperation if the powerful magic that had enabled her to destroy Zardonne had vanished forever, taken into the fiery Dark Rift along with the Demon Master himself.

She turned to her mother, clutching her arm, eyes wide with alarm. "Mother, the power...!"

Her mother smiled reassuringly. "It's still within you, child. There's just no need for it now. You have destroyed Zardonne and now the power rests; as does mine."

Indeed, Tenya could see that the bright glow that had surrounded her mother no longer shone, leaving only faint traces on her pale skin.

Another violent upheaval of the ground beneath their feet almost sent them flying backward. Her mother tightened her grip on Tenya.

"We must hurry and leave this place," she urged. "Without Zardonne's evil magic to sustain it, the whole place is breaking apart. If we are not careful, it will take us with it."

The dark red sky split into jagged cracks, releasing shafts of pale gray light that touched the ground and tore it into steaming fissures. One such shaft of light nearly hit Sindril and, if he had not rolled out of the way in time, he would surely have been split in two. The little man suppressed a cry of agony as his quick roll landed him partially on his broken shoulder. Beads of perspiration popped out on his forehead and rolled down his dirt-streaked cheeks.

Tenya and her mother made their way over to him as quickly as they could on the bucking, quaking ground. The black rock around them swayed and broke off into great, crumbling blocks. Sulfur and hot ash swirled in the air, making it difficult to breathe.

Between them, they helped Sindril to his feet. Tenya's mother looked at her over the little man's head.

"Hold him tightly, my child. I'll try to carry us out of danger. But, I can only do so for short distances. I only pray it will be far enough."

Tenya nodded and braced herself. A pure, cool wind stroked them as gently as a mother would a child, lifting them off their feet. The violent currents of poisonous air began buffeting them roughly. Elea's face settled into concentration, her eyes closed, as she commanded her wind to carry them away from the rapidly disintegrating landscape.

Tenya clung tightly to Sindril, trying not to jostle his broken arm as the three of them rode the careening currents of air. Elea had to be alert to avoid the deadly shafts of pale gray light that continued to stab down from the cracked red sky.

Suddenly, they no longer hovered above the Plain of Naryn. Tenya found the transition abrupt and startling, for here the ground looked stable and solid and the sky above shone with the morning sun, instead of being stained blood red and cracked. Her mother set the three of them down gently and they all turned to watch the destruction of Zardonne's domain.

The shafts of pale light streamed steadily down from the red sky above the Plain and a distant rumble like muted thunder started and quickly grew to an ear-splitting crescendo. Tenya could feel its vibrations in the very bones of her body.

There came a flash as brilliant and blinding as though a dozen suns had collided. The trio threw themselves to the ground and covered their eyes, yet the light still seared their closed eyelids.

When the light finally disappeared and the deafening thunder subsided, they cautiously raised their heads and looked out upon a black and utter void. The Plain of Naryn no longer existed.

Absolute nothingness reigned where once the Plain had stood--no red sky, no cracked and heaving ground, no pools of sickly-green liquid, and no black fortress rising in deadly menace to the sky above. Zardonne's domain in Tellaron had disappeared completely, as surely as though a dense black curtain had fallen across its face. Not even the faintest trace of lingering evil and corruption tainted the air around Tenya and her companions.

As the three slowly got to their feet, staring at the empty black void, a great thundering noise sounded in the distance. For just an instant, Tenya thought that Zardonne had come back from the Rift, ready to throw back the black veil over his domain and scream out his diabolical laughter at them.

She breathed a sigh of relief when she realized the noise was caused by the thunder of many hooves, an army of a thousand or more having become visible through thick clouds of dust. Even from this distance, she recognized the huge, powerful steeds of the Coros horsemen out in front. Pennants waved above the awesome and impressive spectacle of the advancing soldiers.

The three stood waiting silently for the army racing toward them. As they near, Tenya spotted Rigas and Milon out in front, leading the large army.

Thick, choking dust swirled around them as the soldiers in front brought their mounts to an abrupt halt before them. Rigas leapt from his saddle and hurried over to them, his face grimy and tense.

"Mistress, are you all right?"

Her mother smiled gently. "Indeed I am, my friend. All is well with us."

"What happened? Where is Zardonne?"

"The Demon Master has gone the way of all things evil, down into the depths of Hell where his kind belongs. He has been banished once more into the Dark Rift."

Rigas's rough face showed bewilderment. "It was the strangest thing! There we were, fighting fiercely against Zardonne's army–and pushing them back, I might add–when, all of a sudden, they vanished! There was a loud noise, like a hundred thunderclaps at once, and a black mist descended, hiding everything from view. When it lifted, Zardonne's army was simply *gone*. There was no trace of it anywhere."

Her mother nodded. "When Zardonne was driven back into the Rift, his mastery over the dark powers in this world was destroyed, as well. His monstrous creations could not sustain themselves without his powers."

"Sindril! Tenya! My friends, are you all right?" A familiar voice rang out, and another man jumped from his horse to push his way to where they stood.

Tenya recognized the broad-shouldered figure with the bushy black beard.

"Hurn, you old goat!" Sindril shouted, clapping his friend on the shoulder.

"Sindril, you old lizard, I'm glad to see you still alive," Hurn said, gruffly. Seeing that the little man held his right arm gingerly against his chest, the tavern keeper curbed his enthusiasm and contented himself with a rough squeeze of Sindril's left shoulder before turning to Tenya.

His black eyebrows rose above his eyes and he seemed almost afraid to look at her, his bearded face filled with awe and respect. She knew he must have realized that no trace of the timid young girl he had met a short time ago in his village remained. She stood tall and straight, her face composed, knowing that the aura of quiet strength and clear, pure luminosity that shone around her mother surrounded her also.

Tenya threw her arms around him in a quick hug. "Hurn, I'm so glad to see you again," she cried, pulling back to look up at him. "How is Sarath? I trust that she's well."

Hurn seemed flustered for a moment, clearly not expecting the young sorceress to greet him with such youthful enthusiasm and obvious sincerity. He became uncharacteristically tongue-tied and Sindril watched him with undisguised amusement.

"Sarath is fine," Hurn finally managed to say, after first clearing his throat loudly. "And-And, you?"

Tenya smiled at him, sensing his discomfort, and touched his arm. "I'm well. Thank you for asking."

Hurn nodded and then turned his attention to her mother, standing a little behind Tenya. He touched his fingers to his heart in a gesture of respect and bowed his head. "Mistress, I'm pleased to see that you are safe and well."

She, too, touched him gently on the arm. "Thank you, my friend. And, thank you also for being so kind to my daughter when she visited your village."

The big man shifted uncomfortably. "She earned the respect and loyalty of all the villagers in Tundel," he said, quietly. "Instead of hiding under our beds in fear, she inspired us to fight against Zardonne's army. It is we who must thank her for giving us back our spirit and courage."

"Nonsense, Hurn," Tenya said briskly. "You always had your spirit and courage. Look how your people were willing to attack Sindril and me when they first thought we were Zardonne's minions come to bring more harm to their village. It took a great deal of bravery to confront us like that." Then, seeing him redden, she changed the subject. "Did you see combat?"

He nodded grimly. "Unfortunately, yes. Part of Zardonne's army came through the mountain passes as we feared. We met them with our army of five hundred. We had managed to gather together as many of the far-reaching villagers as we could in the time before the enemy came. I'm proud to say we fought well and our losses were minimal. Zardonne's soldiers didn't know the mountains as we did and we were able to set upon them in ambush. I think they were not prepared for the attack we launched, expecting instead to find us easy prey, hiding in our villages and meekly waiting to be slaughtered."

Tenya smiled at him. "You and your people did well, Hurn, as did all of the resistance against Zardonne. The Demon Master's evil and destruction would have been far more widespread and difficult to control if the resistance had not repulsed his advance."

The full implications of the past few hours suddenly struck her. The Demon Master no longer existed in Tellaron. His wicked reign had ended and his domain had become a black empty void upon the earth. The mother she had longed for and missed these last sixteen years had been freed from her icy prison and she, Tenya, had discovered a power within herself she could never have imagined in that far off world of the Ardis Valley.

The time of chaos and madness had passed. Now, came the time for rebuilding and replenishing, for cleansing the lands of the abominable taint of Zardonne and his vileness.

She smiled softly; a time for beginning a new life as part of the Shetii Clan, of getting to know Hanifar and Felina and Jessen and the others.

Most of all, the time had come for strengthening the silken threads that intricately bound her to her mother, Elea, the Mistress of the Wind.

THE END

ABOUT THE AUTHOR

Cheryl Landmark lives in a quiet, picturesque hamlet called Gros Cap in Northern Ontario, Canada, with her husband, Mike, and faithful canine companion. She loves dogs, reading, jigsaw puzzles, and, of course, writing novels in her spare time.

This is the second edition of WIND AND FIRE. It was originally published by Asylett Press in 2009. Cheryl is also the author of a fantasy novel called POOL OF SOULS and a young adult adventure called SHADOWS IN THE BROOK.

Visit her website at:
www3.sympatico.ca/cheryl.landmark